LIBRARY

TEN DROLL
TALES

TEN DROLL TALES

BEING THE STORY OF THE FAIR IMPERIA, THE
VENIAL SIN, THE MERRIE DIVERSIONS OF HIS
MOST CHRISTIAN MAJESTY KING LOUIS THE
ELEVENTH, TOGETHER WITH CERTAIN OTHER
QUAINT AND PIQUANT HISTORIES MAKING UP
THE FIRST DECADE OF THE DROLL TALES OF
MASTER HONORÉ DE BALZAC
RENDERED FAITHFULLY INTO ENGLISH BY
J. LEWIS MAY, WITH AN INTRODUCTION BY
ANDRÉ MAUROIS AND ILLUSTRATIONS BY
JEAN DE BOSSCHÈRE ❦ ❦ ❦

THE ABBEY LIBRARY

Published in Great Britain by
MURRAYS BOOK SALES (Kings Cross) LTD.
157-167 Pentonville Road, London, N.1

Made and printed in Great Britain by
Taylor Garnett Evans & Co Ltd.,
Watford, Herts.

INTRODUCTION

By ANDRÉ MAUROIS

In July 1832, the "Edinburgh Review," under the heading, "French Literature—Recent Novelists," delivered itself of the following remarks:

"Only amongst the confusion caused by such a state of things as this, would an instance be found of one of the most popular writers of the day—Balzac—deliberately composing and publishing, with his name, a work ("The Contes Drolatiques") in which the licentiousness of Boccaccio is imitated in the language of Rabelais; nay, holding out to the public the agreeable assurance that the first volume, if successful, is to be followed by nine more! . . ."

The apprehensions of this chaste periodical were amply justified, for it was a fact that Balzac did intend to publish ten volumes of "Droll Tales," each to contain ten stories. He was an architect fit for a world of giants, and only designs on a superhuman scale had any attraction for him. A hundred tales! This generous figure was suggested to him by the "Cent Nouvelles Nouvelles" by Antoine de la Salle, which he loved and admired. Of the hundred tales he had in mind to write, he published only thirty (in three sets of ten), the first of which appeared in 1832, the second in 1833, and the third in 1837. Of the remaining seventy, we have but fragments of varying importance, the whole of which would scarce suffice to fill a volume.

How came it that a weaver of romances like Balzac, who had already laid the plans of the "Human Comedy"—

though that title had not yet occurred to him—and whom the life of his own times furnished with a greater number of subjects than he could find time to deal with—how came it, I say, that he should undertake so out-of-the-way and exacting a task and condemn himself to sustain, through the length of ten successive volumes, the burden of producing a *pastiche* of the style and vocabulary of a bygone age?

It must first be borne in mind that Balzac looked upon the composition of these stories as anything but a vain and irksome task. On the 19th August, 1833, we find him writing to Mme. Hanska as follows : " The Droll Tales will constitute my principal title to fame in days to come "; and on the 26th October, 1834, after giving the same correspondent a description of his plans for the complete edifice of his novels, he added, " And round about the groundwork of this palace, shall I, like a laughing child, have woven the arabesque of the ' Contes Drolatiques.' " So we see that, in his estimation, these Tales are an integral portion of his work as a whole. They are an expression of a part of human nature which it would be scarcely permissible to include in a novel of his own day. Balzac was a robust fellow with powerful appetites who, according to Champfleury, gave you the impression of a sportive wild boar. The body was as vigorous as the mind and would by no means be denied its quota. Howbeit, of the body the literary conventions of the day suffered little or no mention to be made.

To indite a history of literary squeamishness would be a work of piquant interest. Just as the vicissitudes of fashion require of women that they should sometimes clothe themselves in light clinging stuffs that display every curve of the body, and sometimes encase their limbs in enormous hoops designed to conceal the fact that they have any body at all. So also it is with literary fashions. At one time they permit every human function to be specified by name, as in the days of Juvenal

and, later on, in those of Rabelais; at another, they veer
to the contrary extreme, and oblige the writer to dissemble
the very same acts and thoughts beneath the haze of the
vaguest abstractions.

Any writer who addressed himself to the composition
of such a book would have to ask what causes lay at the
root of such remarkable variations. To begin with he
would, I fancy, find them in the widespread law of oscil-
lation. No human phenomenon remains stationary.
It is necessary for the pendulum to swing in one direction
till reaching the point of ultra-freedom it engenders
satiety and disgust. Then a return towards equilibrium
inevitably sets in and, the central point overpast, literature
again swings towards ultra-reticence and unincarnate
loves which, in their turn, once more tend to cloy and
dissatisfy the mind. Nor must we run away with the
idea that the era of the crinoline was any purer than that
of the flimsy tunic. Mystery is far more likely to stimulate
than to lull the passions. The outspoken directness of
Rabelais is, I think, often less dangerous (if danger may
indeed be predicated of fleshly promptings) than the
melancholy austerity of Sainte-Beuve or Fromentin.

It would also be interesting to study the masks to
which poets and novelists have had recourse in order to
express, in times of rigid austerity, those feelings and
desires to which flesh is unceasingly the heir. In our
own times, Freud and his school have furnished an admirable veil for indecency masquerading in the guise of
Science. Archaism (and this brings us back to the
" Contes Drolatiques ") is also a convenient cloak.
Prudery is a grim, but not very intelligent, sentry, who
insists on having the exact password when dealing with
contemporary writers; yet suffers all manner of shades,
spectres and phantoms to pass by without so much as
asking them for a certificate of good conduct. An Eng-
lishman who would be greatly scandalised by some com-
paratively harmless modern novel, will read through

" Troilus and Cressida " or the Nurse scene in " Romeo and Juliet " without a qualm, because Shakespeare is Shakespeare.

So potent is the association of ideas set up in our minds between a given mode of speech, a given fashion of dress, and a certain freedom in the matter of morals and manners, that we freely extend to the authors of our own day the same indulgence that we accord to those of laxer times, if only they take care to imitate the archaic language of the latter. It therefore suited Balzac, who felt an urgent need to give expression to the mighty, overflowing zest for life by which he was possessed, to have recourse to the *pastiche*. This did not prevent the prudes (Georges Sand, for example) from pronouncing the work to be indecent, but it salved the consciences of a whole multitude of readers.

Moreover, these Contes gave him the opportunity to shine as a virtuoso deeply versed in medieval French. In reality, his book is a patchwork of old words and old-fashioned turns of phrase, gleaned at random from all the successive periods which constitute the Middle Ages, the sixteenth century, and especially Rabelais, furnishing the predominant proportion. There is extant a note of Balzac's announcing a *Dizain des Imitations* which was to be, as it were, a collection of *pastiches* in historic sequence. It was his aim " to recapture and to imitate the different styles adopted in the telling of their tales by the authors of the ' fabliaux ' of the twelfth and thirteenth centuries, Louis XI and the Court of Charles the Bold, the Queen of Navarre and the Court of Francis the First, Boccaccio and the Italian School, Rabelais, Verville and the Arabs." He designed, by this means, to prove that the style of the Hundred Droll Tales, though doubtless inspired by their glorious predecessors, belonged, for good or ill, to their author.

Although they were for Balzac a sort of recreation, the

Tales were written by him with all the scrupulous atten-
tion which he brought to the composition of his novels.
" This Tale has cost me a whole month of torture," he
wrote to Mme. Hanska à propos of " The Succubus."
His historic documentation was elaborate and exact.
Take, for example, the heroine of the first Tale—the
Fair Imperia—M. Bouteron, that most erudite of " Bal-
zaciens," has proved beyond question that she is no
fictitious personage. " As a matter of fact, the Fair
Imperia did not live at the time of the Council of
Constance, as Balzac would have us believe ; she was one
of those illustrious courtesans who flourished in Rome in
the sixteenth century. She is not to be confounded with
any of those inferior drabs that ply their trade in the back
parlour of some chandler's shop ; she is a genuine courtesan, one of those refined women who, like the Muses,
lent elegance and charm to the Italian Renaissance.
The Fair Imperia enjoyed special favour at the hands
of the Roman Cardinals. We know that Cardinal
Sadolet found her greatly to his taste. Aretino, in his
youth, saw her in Rome, this same glorious Imperia,
who died in her palace rich, happy and full of honours."

Solid as is the historical basis of these Tales, their
psychological equipment is no less sound. Disraeli,
in a letter to Queen Victoria, describing the Chancellor
of the Exchequer—Ward Hunt—says, " He is very tall,
but after the manner of Saint Peter's, Rome," that is to
say so well proportioned that one does not at once realise
how tall he is. It is the same with all great men. Every
time we come near to them, we are amazed at the size
of the details. To many, even of those who know their
Balzac well, these Tales, viewed from afar, appear a work
of minor importance, a trifle superfluous. But as soon
as we bring a little care to the reading of them, we see
how rich they are in excellent pieces of psychology,
and how great is the advance which their masterly construction shows to have been made in the art of story-

telling since Boccaccio and the Queen of Navarre. An
example of Balzac's remarkable gift of depicting a whole
state of society in a few pages is to be found in his description of the region that came under the jurisdiction of the
worthy seneschal in " The Venial Sin." As for the
language in which these tales are written, the study of
it has afforded a lively pleasure to many a learned phi-
lologist.

Edinburgh itself has made the " amende honorable "
to Balzac, since in 1921 a translation of Nine Droll
Stories " rendered into English of the fourteenth and
fifteenth centuries by Robert Crawford " was issued
under the imprint of the Dunedin Press.

The present translation has been very skilfully done.
It is couched in language sufficiently archaic to retain the
savour of the original and sufficiently modern to be easily
intelligible. Doubtless Balzac would have rejoiced in the
healthy vigour of M. Jean de Bosschère's illustrations.
The edifice of the " Comédie Humaine " already enjoys
as much admiration in England as in France ; henceforth
" the arabesque of the Droll Tales will twine about the
groundwork of the Palace," and thus the aspirations of
their author will meet with due fulfilment.

ANDRÉ MAUROIS.

Monsieur Maurois' Essay, of which the foregoing
is a translation, is an exquisite piece of work. It is
simplex munditiis, clear and fine like a cameo.

Because I was selfish enough to wish to read Monsieur
Maurois' original French in this beautiful type, I asked
my friends the Publishers to include it in the present
volume. They readily and generously acceded to my
request ; and everyone who is sensible of the charm of a
piece of faultless prose will, with me, have reason to be
grateful to them.

J. L. M.

LES CONTES DROLATIQUES

En Juillet 1832, the "Edinburgh Review," sous la rubrique "French literature—Recent novelists" écrivit:

"Only amongst the confusion caused by such a state of things as this, would an instance be found of one of the most popular writers of the day, Balzac, deliberately composing and publishing, with his name, a work (" The Contes Drolatiques ") in which the licentiousness of Boccaccio is imitated in the language of Rabelais;— nay, holding out to the public the agreeable assurance that the first volume, if successful, is to be followed by nine more! . . . ."

La terreur de la pudique revue était justifiée, car il était exact que Balzac avait l'intention de publier dix volumes de Contes Drolatiques, contenant chacun dix récits. Cet architecte, né pour un monde de géants, n'était tenté que par des constructions aux proportions surhumaines, et le chiffre de cent lui était suggéré par l'exemple des Cent Nouvelles Nouvelles d'Antoine de la Salle, qu'il aimait et admirait. Des cent contes projetés il n'en publia que trente (trois dizains), le premier en 1832, le second en 1833, le troisième en 1837. Des soixante-dix autres, nous n'avons que des fragments plus ou moins importants qui ne rempliraient pas même un volume.

Pourquoi un romancier comme Balzac, qui avait à ce moment déjà formé le plan de la Comédie Humaine, bien qu'il en ignorât encore le titre, et qui trouvait dans la vie de son temps plus de sujets qu'il n'en pouvait

traiter, entreprenait-il cette œuvre étrange et difficile et
se condamnait-il à pasticher tout au long de dix volumes
la forme et la langue des vieux auteurs ?

Il faut d'abord noter que Balzac ne considérait pas du
tout les Contes Drolatiques comme une tâche pénible ni
vaine. Le 19 août 1833, il écrivait à Mme. Hanska : "Les
Contes Drolatiques seront ma plus belle part de gloire
dans l'avenir " et, le 26 octobre 1834, après avoir décrit
à la même correspondante ce que sera l'édifice complet
de ses romans, il ajoute : "Et sur les bases de ce palais,
moi, enfant et rieur, j'aurai tracé l'arabesque des Contes
Drolatiques." Donc pour lui les Contes sont un com-
plément nécessaire de l'œuvre ; ils sont l'expression d'une
partie de la nature humaine qu'il ne peut décrire dans ses
romans modernes. Balzac était un homme robuste,
sensuel, qui avait l'air, dit Champfleury, d'un sanglier
joyeux. Le corps était aussi vigoureux que l'esprit et
réclamait sa part avec force. Or les conventions litté-
raires du temps ne permettaient guère de parler du corps.

Ce serait un livre bien curieux à écrire qu'une histoire
de la pudeur littéraire. De même que la mode exige des
femmes, tantôt qu'elles portent des étoffes légères qui
révèlent toutes les courbes de leur corps, tantôt au contraire qu'elles s'enferment au centre de cerceaux énormes
qui suppriment toute idée de la forme de ce corps,
ainsi la mode littéraire tantôt permet d'appeler toutes
fonctions humaines par leurs noms, comme il arriva au
temps de Juvénal et, de nouveau, au temps de Rabelais,
tantôt au contraire interdit de le faire et contraint
l'écrivain à transposer en termes abstraits des actions
et des pensées qui demeurent d'ailleurs les mêmes.

L'auteur d'un tel livre aurait à se demander quelles
sont les causes profondes de ces changements. Je
crois qu'il y trouverait d'abord la loi très générale des
oscillations. Aucun phénomène humain n'est immobile.
Il est nécessaire que le pendule aille jusqu'à la liberté
excessive, que celle-ci engendre l'ennui et le dégoût,

qu'un retour vers l'équilibre commence alors et que, le point central dépassé, la littérature remonte de nouveau vers un langage chaste et des amours abstraites qui, à leur tour, ennuieront bientôt. Il faut d'ailleurs se garder de croire que le temps des crinolines est plus pur que celui des tuniques légères. Le mystère irrite les passions beaucoup plus qu'il ne les endort. Le ton cru et naïf de Rabelais me semble souvent moins dangereux (si la volupté est un danger) que la forme sévère et mélancolique de Sainte-Beuve ou de Fromentin.

Il serait intéressant aussi d'étudier les masques auxquels ont recours poètes et romanciers, pour exprimer en des temps austères des sentiments et des désirs constants. A notre époque le Freudisme a été un merveilleux prétexte d'indécence à forme scientifique. L'Archaïsme (et ici nous revenons aux Contes Drolatiques) est, lui aussi, un manteau commode. La Pudeur est une sentinelle sévère mais peu intelligente, qui applique strictement ses consignes quand elle se trouve en présence de contemporains et qui, au contraire, laisse passer les ombres, spectres et fantômes, sans jamais leur demander leurs certificats de moralité. Tel Anglais sera scandalisé par un roman moderne bien inoffensif et lira sans scrupules "Troïlus et Cressida" ou la scène de la nourrice de Juliette, parce que Shakespeare est Shakespeare.

L'association d'idées qui s'établit dans notre esprit entre un certain langage, un certain costume et certaines libertés de mœurs est si forte que nous étendons aux auteurs de notre temps l'indulgence réservée aux époques de licence s'ils pastichent le langage de celles-ci. Il était donc commode pour Balzac, puisqu'il éprouvait le besoin d'exprimer cette sensualité puissante, débordante, qui était la sienne, d'avoir recours à un pastiche. Cela n'empêchait pas les prudes (Georges Sand par exemple) de juger l'ouvrage indécent, mais cela rassurait beaucoup de lecteurs.

D'autre part les Contes étaient pour lui un exercice

de virtuose qui prétend connaître à fond la vieille langue. En réalité, c'est une mosaïque de vieux mots et de vieilles tournures glanés à travers tout le moyen âge, avec prédominance de la langue du seizième siècle, en particulier de Rabelais. Il existe une note de Balzac où il annonce un *Dizain des Imitations*, qui devait être en quelque sorte une suite historique de pastiches. Il voulait " retrouver et imiter les différentes manières dont ont conté les auteurs de fabliaux des douzième et treizième siècles, Louis XI et la cour de Charles le Téméraire, la Reine de Navarre et la cour de François Ier, Boccace et les auteurs italiens, Rabelais, Verville, les Arabes ; il voulait prouver ainsi que la manière des Cent Contes Drolatiques, engendrée sans doute par celle de leurs glorieux devanciers, bonne ou mauvaise, est à l'auteur."

Bien qu'ils fussent pour lui un délassement, les Contes ont été écrits par Balzac avec autant de scrupule que ses romans. " Ce Conte m'a coûté un mois de tortures," écrit-il à Mme. Hanska, à propos du Succube. Ses documents historiques étaient nombreux et exacts. Prenons par exemple l'héroïne du premier conte, la Belle Impéria. M. Bouteron, admirable érudit balzacien, a montré qu'il ne s'agit nullement d'un personnage fictif. " A vrai dire, la belle Impéria ne vécut pas au temps du concile de Constance, ainsi que Balzac nous le raconte, mais elle fut une de ces illustres courtisanes qui fleurirent à Rome au seizième siècle, non pas une de ces débauchées de bas étage (di minor sorte) opérant dans l'arrière-boutique de quelque marchand de chandelles, mais véritable courtisane et l'une de ces femmes raffinées qui furent les muses de la Renaissance italienne. La belle Impéria jouissait auprès des cardinaux romains d'une faveur particulière. Nous savons que le Cardinal Sadolet la trouvait fort à son goût. L'Arétin adolescent vit, à Rome, cette glorieuse Impéria qui mourut dans son palais, riche, heureuse et très honorée."

Et de même que la documentation historique est solide, l'armature psychologique des Contes est forte. Disraëli décrivant, dans une lettre à la Reine Victoria, le Chancelier de l'Échiquier, Ward Hunt, dit de lui qu'il est très grand, mais à la manière de Saint-Pierre de Rome, c'est-à-dire si bien proportionné qu'on n'aperçoit d'abord pas sa grandeur. Cela est vrai de tous les grands hommes. Chaque fois que l'on s'approche de l'un d'eux, on est étonné par le grandeur des détails. A beaucoup des familiers de Balzac, ces Contes apparaissent de loin comme une œuvre mineure, un peu superflue. Dès qu'on prend la peine de les lire avec un peu de soin, on voit qu'ils sont pleins de traits psychologiques excellents et que leur belle construction montre les progrès faits dans l'art de conter depuis Boccace et la Reine de Navarre. Le remarquable don qu'avait Balzac de peindre toute une société en quelques pages s'y retrouve, par exemple dans la peinture du pays administré par le bon sénéchal dans *Le Péché Véniel.* Quand à la langue, de grands philologues ont trouvé un plaisir vif à l'étudier.

Édinbourg même a fait amende honorable à Balzac, puisqu'en 1921 une traduction de neuf Contes Drolatiques "rendered into English of the fourteenth and fifteenth century by Robert Crawford" y a été imprimée "by the Dunedin Press."

La présente traduction est très adroitement faite, dans une langue assez archaïque pour garder la saveur du texte original et assez moderne pour être facilement intelligible. Sans doute Balzac eût-il aimé la saine vigueur des illustrations de M. Jean de Bosschère. L'édifice de la Comédie Humaine était déjà aussi admiré en Angleterre qu'en France; désormais l'arabesque des Contes s'y déroulera sur les bases du palais, comme l'avait souhaité l'auteur.

ANDRÉ MAUROIS.

CONTENTS

PAGE

INTRODUCTION BY ANDRÉ MAUROIS (TRANSLATION) . v

INTRODUCTION BY ANDRÉ MAUROIS (ORIGINAL FRENCH) xi

PROLOGUE 1

THE FAIR IMPERIA 7

THE VENIAL SIN 27

    HOW THE WORTHY BRUYN TOOK TO HIMSELF A WIFE 29

    HOW THE SENESCHAL DID BATTLE WITH HIS WIFE'S
    VIRGINITY 42

    WHEREIN A VENIAL SIN CONSISTS 51

    HOW AND BY WHOM THE CHILD WAS MADE . . 58

    HOW FOR THESE SINS OF THE FLESH GRIEVOUS
    PENANCE WAS EXACTED AND HOW GREAT SORROW
    DID BEFALL 65

THE KING'S MISTRESS 73

THE DEVIL'S HEIR 93

THE MERRIE DIVERSIONS OF KING LOUIS THE ELEVENTH 117

THE HIGH CONSTABLE'S WIFE 139

THE VIRGIN OF THILHOUSE 161

THE BROTHERS-IN-ARMS 171

THE CURÉ OF AZAY-LE-RIDEAU 191

THE REBUKE 205

EPILOGUE 219

B   xvii

LIST OF ILLUSTRATIONS

Facing page

ALL THE WOMEN RUSHED AFTER IT . . 12

THE DEVIL CAME AND WHISPERED IN HIS EAR . . 28

THE SWEET VICES OF THE GODDESS VENUS . , 36

HE WAS A DASHING BLADE IN HIS YOUNG DAYS . 36

SITTING BOLT UPRIGHT . . . SHE BEGAN TO SMILE . 44

THE LOVES OF BIRDS AND WILD THINGS . . . 60

SHE BEHELD A MONK WHO SEEMED TO BE OUTRAGEOUSLY
MALTREATING A MAIDEN 68

A VIRGINAL FOOT THAT DESERVED A KISS . . 68

RENÉ DE JALLANGES LOWERED THOSE BEAUTIFUL EYES
OF HIS 76

THE LAWYER, IN NO MOOD FOR AMOROUS DALLIANCE
WITH THIS DAGGER 92

CONSUMMATING THE UNION OF A HUSBAND AND WIFE 100

ONLY ONE MAN WHO COULD THOROUGHLY WHITEN THE
SOUL OF A LADY OF STANDING 100

COMES TO PUT HERSELF TO RIGHTS IN THE ROOM WHERE
THE CHEST IS 108

"YOU ARE ALREADY HERE SITTING IN YOUR CHAIR AT
THE CHIMNEY CORNER" 124

HE WAS DELICATELY STRANGLED BETWEEN THE HEAD
AND THE SHOULDERS 132

"TWO BIG DOLLS IN THE LIKENESS OF THIS LADY AND
MYSELF" 132

xix

Facing page

STRAIGHTWAY HE TOOK HIS LANCET AND BLED THE
  YOUNG MAN   140

THAT PLEASANT DUEL IN WHICH SHE ALWAYS PROVED
  HERSELF THE STRONGER   156

WHOM THEY RAN TO EARTH JUST UNDERNEATH THE
  COUNTESS'S WINDOW   164

THE VIRGIN OF THILHOUSE   164

THE ONE ALWAYS SECONDED THE OTHER .   .   .   172

THERE IN THAT BED THEY EXCHANGED ALL MANNER OF
  TIDINGS   188

PICKING HER UP IN A RAGE, HE THREW HER ON THE BED   196

SHE THRUSTS THE HUNCHBACK INTO THE PRESS .   .   196

PROLOGUE

PROLOGUE

HERE behold a book of high savour, full of delectable morsels, well spiced and flavoured for those illustrious trenchermen and discerning wine-bibbers to whom our honoured compatriot, the everlasting glory of Touraine, Master François Rabelais, did of yore address himself. Natheless, let it not be thought that the author is so puffed up with arrogance as to aspire to be aught but a good son of Touraine and to provide merry entertainment for the hungry mouths of the notabilities of that smiling and fertile region, as rich in cuckolds, cockbirds and pocky blades as any land there be, the which hath furnished a brave contingent of famous men to France, among whom the late-lamented Courier of piquant memory, Verville, author of "How to hit the Mark" and many another of right good report; albeit we subtract, rip out and deduct therefrom the Sieur Descartes, a melancholy gib-cat who hath written more eloquently of empty dreams and vain elucubrations than of wine and good cheer; a man whom all the cate-makers and cookshop-keepers hold in abhorrence, ignore and utterly refuse to mention saying, when anyone speaketh of him, "Where doth the fellow dwell?"

Know then that this work is the product of the merry leisure hours of those good old monks of whom there lingered many traces scattered up and down our country, as at Grenadière-lez-Sainct-Cyr, in the burgh of Sacché-lez-Azay-le-Ridel, at Marmoustiers, Veretz, la Roche-Corbon and, eke, in certain repositories of merry stories, to wit the canons of old days and worthy dames who

3

lived in the good old times when a man might jest and
laugh his bellyful without looking to see whether he had
burst his gut, as do the young women of our day who
would fain comport themselves with gravity, the which
befitteth this joyous France of ours as well as a tin can
would become the head of a Queen. Wherefore, sith
laughter is a privilege vouchsafed to man alone, and sith,
God wot, there be occasions enough for tears in the world
without adding to them in books, I have deemed it a
right patriotic thing to publish a groatsworth of merriment for these sad times when weariness falls upon the
spirit like a fine clinging rain, a rain that in time doth
soak us to the marrow, melting away and quite dissolving
our ancient customs which made the commonweal the
weal of the greatest number. Thus as touching those
old Pantagruelists, who whilom left to God and to their
lord the King, the business that concerned them, without
putting a finger in the pie more often than became them,
being themselves content to laugh, they, I say, do grow
fewer and fewer as the days go on, so that I am sore afeard
lest I shall see the notable fragments of their ancient
breviaries, spat upon, beshitten, mangled, scorned,
denounced, whereat I should laugh on the wrong side
of my mouth, seeing that I greatly treasure and make
much of the relics of our Gaulish antiquities.

But remember, also, ye savage critics, ye pedantic
dryasdusts, ye harpies who distort the intentions of every
single one of us, that we do but laugh as children laugh,
and that the farther we fare on life's journey, the more
doth laughter dwindle and wane, even as the oil dieth
down in the lamp. The which doth signify that to laugh
one must needs be innocent and pure in heart; for if
you be not, you purse your lips and knit your brows and
pull a wry face like folk that would hypocritically cloak
their vices and impurities. Look then upon this work
as upon a naked group or statue, certain details of which
no artist could dissemble, and would prove himself a

ninny of the first water did he but add so much conceal-
ment as a fig-leaf, seeing that neither such works, nor this
present book, are designed for nunneries. Howbeit,
though sore against the grain, I have been at pains to
weed out from the manuscripts certain words which,
though old, were yet something over lusty and would
have rent the ears, be-crimsoned the cheeks and distorted
the lips of our mettlesome maids, and of virtue with three
strings to her bow. For we must humour the vices of
the age, and indeed a paraphrase is often naughtier than
the word itself. For look you, we are grown old, and long-
drawn dalliance is more to our taste than the short and
swift encounters of our youth ; for so our enjoyment is
of the longer duration. So then be not too swift to
condemn me, and read me by night rather than by day,
and give me not into the hands of maidens, if there be
any still existing, for the very book would catch fire from
the communication of their heat. But enough of me
and my affairs. Howbeit, for the book I have no fears,
since it is drawn from high and gentle sources ; and all
that hath issued therefrom hath met with great success
as is well proven by the royal orders of The Golden
Fleece, the Holy Ghost, the Garter and the Bath and
many others of renown under whose patronage I do enroll
myself.

" *Now, rest ye merry, my bawcocks, and read the whole
with lightsome hearts, body at ease and loins ungirt, and may
the pox be your portion if ever you disown me when you shall
have read me.*" Thus spake our good and worthy Master
Rabelays to whom we should all doff our bonnets in token
of the reverence and honour in which we hold him as
prince of wisdom and lord of comedy.

THE FAIR IMPERIA

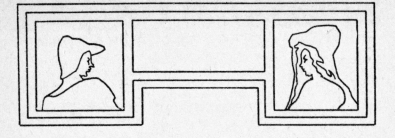

THE FAIR IMPERIA

THE Archbishop of Bordeaux had included among the members of the train that were to accompany him to the Council of Constance, a right comely little priest of Touraine whose manners and address were mightily engaging; so much so that he was taken for the son of la Soldée and the Governor. The Archbishop of Tours had freely handed him over to his brother in Christ when the latter was passing through the said city, for it is a custom of arch- bishops to exchange such presents, sith they know full well how sharply theological cravings do prick and sting one. So it fell out that this young priest came to the Council and was lodged in the house of his prelate, a right moral man and deeply learned withal.

Philippe de Mala (for so the priest was named) resolved to live a godly life and worthily to serve his protector; but he saw in this most mystical Council that there were many folk who lived dissolute lives and yet gained not fewer but rather more indulgences and golden crowns than others who lived righteously and soberly. So it befell one night, when his virtue had been sorely tried, that the Devil came and whispered in his ear, telling him that it were befitting he should see to his own welfare, for that everyone sucked at the dugs of our Holy Mother Church without ever causing them to run dry; a miracle which proved beyond all doubt that God was with her. And the priest of Touraine gave good heed to the Devil's

advice. He promised himself that he would fare sump-
tuously of the succulent joints and cunning condiments
of Germany whenever he could do so at another's expense,
for he was as poor as a church mouse this priest of ours.
As he lived a life of continence (wherein he modelled himself on his poor old archbishop, who sinned no more
because he could not, and so was accounted a saint), he
was often visited with intolerable longings followed by
fits of moodiness, seeing the number of fair courtesans
who tossed their heads at the poor folk and dwelt in
Constance expressly to illumine the understanding of the
Fathers of the Council. He was terribly angered with
himself that he knew not how to address these beautiful
love-birds who treated Cardinals, Abbots, Legates,
Bishops, Princes, Dukes and Margraves with as much
saucy arrogance as they might have treated little penniless
clerks. Of an evening, when he had said his prayers,
he tried to teach himself how to talk to them and to
learn some useful lessons out of Cupid's Breviary. He
invented speeches and rejoinders to suit every imagin-
able case. And yet if, next day towards the hour of
Compline, he chanced to encounter one of these princesses, bedecked in all her finery, lolling at ease in her
litter, attended by pages well armed and accoutred, and
as proud as could be, there he would stand gaping like a
dog catching flies, at the sight of one of these blithe young
women for whom, withal, he was burning with so intolerable a flame.

His Grace's secretary, a gentleman of Perigord, having
clearly proven to him that the reverend fathers in God,
together with the proctors and justiciaries, did purchase
by manifold gifts, not indeed of relics or indulgences,
but of gold and precious stones, the right to conduct
themselves familiarly with these pampered kittens who
lived under the protection of the Lords of the Council,
our poor little Tourainian, precious little ninny that he
was, did set about hoarding up in his mattress all the

golden angels given him by the good archbishop for copy-
ing and scrivener's work, hoping that by this means he
would one day have enough to win him admission to the
courtesan of a cardinal, trusting in God for what should
follow.   He was threadbare from top to toe and looked
about as much like a man as a she-goat dressed up in the
dark resembles a woman ; but urged on by the fire that
was in his heart, he went wandering by night about the
streets of Constance, recking nought of his life.   And
at the risk of getting run through by hired men, he kept
a watchful eye on the cardinals when they went in to the
houses of their lady-loves.   Then he would see the waxen
candles lit up within and, on a sudden, the windows and
doorways would be a blaze of light.   And he would hear
the very saintly *abbés*, or whoever they might be, jesting
and making merry, eating and drinking of the best,
singing their secret Alleluias, and condescending to
bestow a crumb of praise on the music provided for their
entertainment.   The cooks wrought wonders, and the
company began their offices with good helpings of rich
flowing soup, Mattins of tender hams, Vespers of dainty
entrées, and Lauds of sweetmeats.   And when they had
drunk their fill, these worthy priests held their peace.
Their pages would play dice on the steps and their horses
would paw the ground impatiently in the street.

     And all would go well.   But matters of faith and
religion came into it too ; for remember how that worthy
wight Hus died at the stake.   Wherefore ? Why because
he put his finger in the pie without being asked.   And
then how came he to be a Huguenot before the rest of
them ?

     But to return to that nice little boy Philippe.   He got
many a whacking and not a few real shrewd knocks.
But the Devil kept his heart up by making him hope that
he'd one day play the cardinal with one of the cardinal's
women.   His lust made him as bold as a stag in autumn,
so much so indeed that one night he secretly slipped into

the finest house in Constance, on the steps of which he had often seen officers, seneschals, varlets and pages, carrying torches and waiting for their masters, dukes, kings, cardinals and archbishops.

"Ah!" said he to himself, "she must be a fair and gallant damsel who dwells herein."

An armed man, who was guarding the door, suffered him to pass, believing that he belonged to the household of the Elector of Bavaria who was then coming forth from the said abode, and that he was about to deliver a message on behalf of that same Lord.   Philippe de Mala mounted the stairs with all the swiftness of a greyhound with the fury of love upon him and was led by a delectable odour of perfumes to the chamber in which the mistress of the house was divesting herself of her apparel, surrounded by her women.   He stood quite dumbfounded like a thief caught red-handed by the watch.   There sate the lady without wimple or bodice.   Her tirewomen and hand-maidens, busily removing her shoes and her raiment, were baring her body so freely and so dexterously that the bedazzled priest could not repress a gasp of amazement that spoke full eloquently of love.

"And what would you, my little one?" said the lady.

"Give you my soul," he answered, feasting his eyes upon her.

"You can come again to-morrow," she replied, in order to be quit of him.

Whereto Philippe, red as a peony, made answer:

"I will not fail."

Thereupon she fell to laughing consumedly.   Philippe stood looking at her in amazement, panting but delighted, gazing gloatingly upon her with eyes full of tenderness and passionate longing for the tempting love-baits which she displayed, such, for example, as her lovely hair hanging loose down a back as smooth as polished ivory and revealing through countless little frizzy curls the white and gleaming surface of her skin.   On her snowy brow

ALL THE WOMEN
RUSHED AFTER IT

she wore a balas ruby, less rich in billows of fire than her dark eyes glistening with the tears with which her laughter had filled them. She even cast off her Polish shoe, all gold embroidered, as she twisted and writhed with laughter, displaying a naked foot smaller than a swan's beak. That night she was in a good humour; had she not been, she would have had the little priestling pitched head first out of window without more ado than she would have made of her first bishop.

"He hath lovely eyes, Madame," said one of her tirewomen.

"But where does he come from?" asked another.

"Poor child!" exclaimed Madame, "his mother must be looking for him. We must put him on the right track for home."

The little Tourainian, losing not his senses, gazed with a gesture of delight at the bed of rich brocade wherein her pretty body was going to repose. It was a look full of juicy and amorous intelligence, and it titillated the lady's fancy. Half-laughingly, half-lovingly, she answered him again, "To-morrow," and dismissed him with a gesture that Pope John himself would not have disobeyed, especially as he was like a snail without a shell and had just been un-poped by the Council.

"Ah, Madame, there's another vow of chastity turned into lecherous longing," said one of the women.

And the laughter trilled forth anew like the patter of hail. Philippe took his departure, banging his head against the furniture like an inebriated crow, so stunned was he at having caught a glimpse of a creature more delectable to the taste than a siren uprising from the sea. He noted the figures of animals engraven above the door, and came back home again to his worthy archbishop, with a thousand consignments of devils playing high jinks in his heart and a highly sophisticated liver. Away up in his bedchamber, under the tiles, he counted his money the livelong night, but he could never make it more than

C

four angels, and as this was the sum total of his wealth,
he aspired to satisfy the fair one by giving her all he had
got in the world.

" But what ails you, Philippe ? " said the good old archbishop, who was filled with anxiety as he listened to the
sighs and groans of his little clerk.

" Ah, Monseigneur," answered the poor priest, " but
it amazes me how so lightsome and sweet a bit of woman's
flesh can weigh thus heavily on the heart ! "

" And what woman is it ? " replied the archbishop,
putting down his Breviary which he read for other folks'
sake, good worthy man.

" Ah, Jesus, but you'll be storming at me, my kind
master and protector, because I have set eyes on one who
must be the lady of a cardinal at the very least. . . . And
I was weeping because I lacked more than one rascally
crown to win me admission to her, even if you gave me
permission to convert her to a godly life."

The archbishop, deepening the circumflex accent
which he wore above his nose, breathed never a word.
Wherefore the very meek little priestling trembled in his
skin at having thus confessed himself to his superior.
But the holy man blurted out :

" Of a truth, then, is she so very dear ? "

" Verily, she hath taken down the fat of many a mitre
and worn away many a crozier."

" Well, then, Philippe, if thou wilt but renounce
her, I will give thee thirty golden angels from the poor
box."

" Ah, Monseigneur, but I should lose too much,"
answered the youngster, all aglow at the thought of the
pleasure he was going to give—and take.

" Fie on thee, Philippe," said the good old man of
Bordeaux. " Wilt thou then go to the devil and dis-
please God, like all our cardinals ? "

And forthwith the master, sore stricken with grief,
fell to beseeching St. Gatian, the patron of bully-boys,

to save his servant from perdition. He made him go down on his knees, bidding him recommend his soul to Saint Philip. But the naughty little priest implored him, under his breath, to see that he failed not, if on the morrow his lady should show herself sweet and compassionate. And the good archbishop, noting the fervour of his servant's tones, cried to him :

" Courage, my son, God will hear thy prayer."

On the morrow, what time His Grace was holding forth at the Council against the shameless excesses of the apostles of the Christian Faith, Philippe de Mala squandered the angels which he had earned with such arduous toil, in perfumes, ablutions, baths, and other fripperies. So complete a dandy did he appear that you would have taken him for the spoilt darling of some wealthy light o' love. He wandered up and down the city to find the dwelling of his heart's own Queen. And when he enquired of the passers-by asking to whom the house belonged, they laughed in his face as they replied :

" Whence cometh this scurvy loon who hath never heard tell of the Fair Imperia ? "

He was sore afraid that he had consigned his angels to the devil when he heard the name and learnt into what a terrific kettle of fish he had voluntarily fallen.

Imperia was the most precious and fantastic light o' love in the world, besides being reputed the most luminously beautiful and better able than any to ride the high horse over the cardinals, to keep the roughest men-at-arms and oppressors of the people in their places. She had, in her own private train, archers and lords, anxious to serve her in every way. She only had to whisper a word to procure the death of any folk who gave her annoyance. A fatal brawl brought but a gentle smile to her lips ; and many a time the Sire de Baudricourt, a captain of the King's guard, would jokingly enquire, when they encountered any clerics, if there was anyone he could kill for her that day. Save with the higher dignitaries of the Church,

whom Madame Imperia was cunning enough to humour,
she carried off everything with a high hand. Her manners
and her mode of making love were irresistible and reckless and prudent alike fell to her lure.

Thus she lived, petted and respected no less than the
real dames of high degree and princesses, and she was
called " Madame." " Wherefore protest ? " said the good
Emperor Sigismond to a worthy and virtuous lady who
complained thereof. " Let them, the good ladies, keep
the sage precepts of holy virtue, and Madame Imperia the
sweet vices of the goddess Venus." Christian words
which sorely scandalised the good ladies, quite unreason-
ably withal.

Philippe, then, thinking of the dainty morsel he had
beheld with his eyes the night before, was much afraid that
nothing more would come of it. And his heart was sore
within him so that, tasting neither food nor drink, he
wandered all about the city waiting for the appointed
hour, hoping, since he was well attired and of gallant
appearance, to find other damsels less difficult of access
than my Lady Imperia.

When night came, our pretty little Tourainian, all
puffed up with pride, caparisoned with desires, and
whipped to a frenzy by his sighs and groans which nearly
choked him, slipped like an eel into the abode of the
real Queen of the Council; for before her cringed and
bowed all the men of learning and all the leading lights
of Christendom. The major-domo recognised him not
and was about to throw him out, when the lady's-maid
called out from the top of the stairs :

" Hi ! Messire Imbert, 'tis Madame's little darling."

Whereupon poor Philippe mounted the staircase all
reeling with joy and excitement. The lady's-maid took
him by the hand and led him into the room where Madame
was awaiting him with impatience, tricked out like a
brave girl hoping for the best. The radiant Imperia was
seated at a table covered with a velvet cloth adorned with

gold and bearing upon it all things necessary for a brave carouse. Flagons of wine, goblets, bottles of hippocras, decanters full of the good wine of Cyprus, dainty boxes of sweetmeats, roasted peacocks, green sauces, little salted hams would all have delighted the eyes of the youthful gallant had they not been already blinded with love for Madame Imperia. She saw well enough that the eyes of her little priestling were all for her. Accustomed as she was to receiving the irregular devotions of the high dignitaries of the Church, she was now mighty content, for all through the night she had felt the pangs of desire for this humble priest, and all the livelong day the thoughts of him had been fluttering about her heart. The windows were closed, Madame felt in excellent trim and was adorned as though to receive a Prince of the Empire. Thus the young rascal, beatified by the sacred beauty of Imperia, knew full well that no one, had he been emperor, or burgrave, or even a cardinal and pope-elect, would, that night, get the upper hand of him, a humble little priest, who dwelt alone in his garret with none but Love and the Devil to keep him company. He played the *grand seigneur* and bore himself with a flourish, saluting her with a courtesy that was quite of the right breed. Whereupon the lady, warming the cockles of his heart with a passionate look, said :

" Come and sit near me, that I may see whether or not you have changed since yesterday."

" Oh, but changed I am indeed ! " was his reply.

" And where ? " said she.

" Yesterday," answered the cunning wight, " I loved you. But to-night we love each other, and instead of a needy suppliant, behold me now far richer than a king."

" Oh, you little darling ! " cried she joyously. " Yes, truly you have changed. Yesterday you were but a young priest; but now, 'tis plain, you are an old devil."

And they sate them down side by side before a goodly fire which made the warm blood of desire tingle in all

their veins. There they sate on, always about to eat
yet never eating, for they never wearied of gazing into
each other's eyes, and tasted not of the dishes. But just
when they at length settled in ease and contentment,
there arose an unwelcome din at Madame's door as
though a mob were battering thereat and shouting.

" Madame," said the waiting-woman in hurried tones,
" behold here is yet another of them ! "

" What ! " cried the lady haughtily, like one grievously
annoyed at being interrupted.

" The Bishop of Coire craves speech with you."

" The Devil flay him ! " she replied, looking at
Philippe with a languishing gaze.

" Madame, he has seen the light through the chinks
and is making a great uproar."

" Tell him that I have the fever and thou wilt lie not,
for, by my troth, I am sick with love for this little priest
who has set my head in a whirl."

But just as she was finishing her speech, tenderly
pressing Philippe's hand, while he was boiling within his
skin, the fat Bishop of Coire appeared on the scene,
puffing and panting with rage. His lacqueys followed
bearing, on a golden salver, a trout canonically roseate,
fresh taken from the Rhine, and choice sweetmeats contained in wondrous caskets, and all manner of dainties,
liqueurs and cordials compounded by the holy nuns of
his abbeys.

" Ah, ha ! " quoth he in his great deep voice, " I
shall be with the Devil soon enough without your getting
him to flay me in advance, my popinjay."

" Your belly will make a fine sheath for a sword one
of these days," she replied with a frown ; and her eyes,
a moment before so fair and gentle, grew alarmingly
fierce.

" And this choir-boy, has he come for the offertory
already ? " said the bishop, insolently turning his full-
blown ruddy countenance on the gentle Philippe.

" Monseigneur, I am here to confess Madame."

" Oh! Ho! Know you not the canon? Confessing ladies at this time of night is a prerogative reserved for bishops; so away with you! Go herd with simple monks, and return not hither under pain of excommunication."

" Budge not an inch," cried Imperia, blushing deeply, anger making her even more beautiful than love, because now love and anger were blended in her countenance. " Stay, my friend, this house is yours as much as mine."

Then he knew that he was loved indeed.

" Is it not written in the Breviary and laid down in the Gospel that ye shall be equals before God in the valley of Jehoshaphat? " asked she of the bishop.

" 'Tis an invention of the Devil, who has tampered with the Bible; yet so indeed it is written," answered that great dunderhead the Bishop of Coire, in a hurry to begin the feast.

" Well, then, be ye equal before me who am here your goddess," replied Imperia. " If not, I will have you neatly strangled one of these days betwixt the head and the shoulders. I swear it by the power and glory of my tonsure, which is as good as the Pope's I trow."

And anxious that the trout should make part of the feast, and the golden salver, the comfit boxes and the sweetmeats into the bargain, she added adroitly :

" Now sit ye down and drink."

But it was not the first time our cunning canary had been in a pass of this sort, and she winked at her darling to tell him that he need not worry about the German, for the wine would soon account for him.

The serving-woman settled the bishop comfortably at the table, while Philippe, consumed with a rage that made him speechless since he saw his good fortune all ending in smoke, consigned the bishop to more devils than there were monks in all the world. They were getting pretty nearly half-way through the repast, but the young priest had not touched a morsel, his whole and

sole appetite being for Imperia. He nestled up close
to her without saying a word but speaking that excellent
language which women understand without full stops,
commas, accents, letters, figures, characters, notes or
diagrams. The fat old bishop, sensual and careful of the
ecclesiastical skin in which his defunct mother had
encased him, suffered himself to be abundantly served
with hippocras by Madame's dainty hand, and he had
already delivered himself of his first hiccup when the
clatter of a numerous cavalcade was heard in the street.
The number of horses, the shouts of the grooms, made it
clear that some prince, red-hot with love, had just arrived.
And in sooth, soon after, Cardinal de Raguse, to whom
Imperia's servants had not dared to refuse admittance,
made his way into the room. At this melancholy sight,
the poor courtesan and her lover grew abashed and dis-
heartened like folk stricken with the leprosy, for it was
like bearding the devil to attempt to oust the cardinal,
particularly as, at that time, no one knew who was going
to be pope, the three claimants having withdrawn from
the contest for the benefit of Christendom. The cardinal,
who was a cunning, long-bearded Italian, the arch-sophist
and chief firebrand of the Council, took in at a glance
the alpha and the omega of the situation. It did not take
him long to decide what it behoved him to do to make sure
of getting what he had come for. He had arrived with
an appetite like a monk's, and to ease his craving he
would have run a brace of monks through the body and
sold his piece of the true cross—an evil thing to do.

"Here, friend," said he to Philippe, calling him to his
side.

The hapless Tourainian, more dead than alive, suspecting that the Devil himself had taken his business in hand,
rose and said, "I crave your pardon?" to his formidable
Eminence. The latter, taking him by the arm to the
top of the stairs, looked straight into his eyes and continued in no jesting tone:

"Beshrew me, you are a nice little companion, and I would not care to have to tell your superior the precise weight of your belly. Such gratification might cost me some pious foundations in my old age. Therefore, choose. Choose whether thou wilt marry thee with an abbey for the rest of thy days, or with Madame for one night, to die on the morrow."

Said the poor Tourainian to him, in desperation :

"And when your ardour is cooled, Monseigneur, may I come back again?"

This was nearly too much for the cardinal. Howbeit, he said gravely :

"Choose! The gallows or a mitre."

"Ah!" said the priest slily, "a good fat abbey for me. . . ."

Hearing that the cardinal went back into the room, seated himself at an escritoire and scribbled on a piece of parchment a memorandum for the French Envoy.

"Monseigneur," said the priest of Touraine, while he was writing down the name of the abbey, "the Bishop of Coire will not relieve you of his presence as quickly as I, for he has as many abbeys as the men-at-arms have taverns in the town, and he dwells in the bosom of the Lord. Therefore, methinks, in gratitude to you for this goodly abbey, I owe you a piece of sound advice. You know how virulent and infectious is this cursed epidemic that has of late been playing the deuce in Paris. Well, tell him that you have just come from nursing your good old friend the Archbishop of Bordeaux, who is down with it. You will make him skedaddle like thistledown before the wind."

"Ho! Ho!" cried the cardinal. "You deserve more than an abbey. Odds-bodykins, man, there are a hundred gold crowns for your journey to the Abbey of Turpenay, which I won yesterday at cards and which I now hand over to you as a free gift."

Hearing these words and seeing Philippe de Mala

disappear without giving her the quintessential glance of love which she was waiting for, the lionlike Imperia, puffing and panting like a dolphin, concluded that her priestling was a graceless coward. She was not as yet good Catholic enough to forgive her lover for laughing at her and refusing to die to satisfy her longing. And so Philippe's death was writ plainly in the venomous glance she darted at him; whereat the cardinal was right glad, for he deemed it augured that he would soon be getting his abbey back again. The Tourainian, showing little anxiety to affront the storm, slided out in silence with his tail down, like a wet dog being chased out of church. Madame sighed as if her heart would break. She would have put a singular glow on that specimen of the human race if only she could have got hold of him, for the fire that burnt within her had mounted to her head and coruscated in little flames about her. And there was good reason for it, for this was the first time she had ever been bamboozled by a priest. Then the cardinal smiled, believing that the moment of bliss was at hand. Was he not a cunning wight? That was why he had a red hat.

"Ha! Ha! my worthy brother," said he to the bishop, "I am glad to find myself in your company, and I rejoice that I was able to kick out that little nincompoop, an unworthy mate indeed for Madame here, particularly as, if you had come near him, my fair and dainty doe, you might have caught your death from contact with a common little priest."

"But how could that be, pray?"

"He is the secretary of Monseigneur the Archbishop of Bordeaux, and this very morning that worthy man was stricken with the pestilence."

The bishop opened his mouth wide enough to swallow a cheese.

"But how do you know that?" he gasped.

"By my troth!" said the cardinal, taking the good

German's hand. " I know well enough, for I have just been to administer the last rites to him. At this moment the holy man is like to be wafted by a prosperous gale to Paradise."

The Bishop of Coire gave immediate proof how light and nimble fat men are on their feet; for men with heavy paunches enjoy, by the grace of God, this recompense for their labours : their internal tubes are as elastic as balloons. So the aforesaid bishop made a mighty bound to the rear, sweating and gulping and coughing like an ox with feathers in his fodder. Then, suddenly turning deathly pale, he made off downstairs as fast as his legs would carry him, without so much as a "good-night" to Madame. When the door was shut on the bishop and he was out in the street, Monsieur de Raguse began to laugh and was fain to make merry.

"Ah, my darling, am I not worthy to be pope, ay, and better still, your sweetheart to-night ? "

But, observing Imperia's thoughtful mien, he approached her in order to take her tenderly in his arms and titillate her after the manner of cardinals, who are a race enterprising beyond all others, surpassing even military men, inasmuch as, being men of leisure, they squander not their essential spirits.

"Ha ! Ha ! " cried she, drawing back. " You would be the death of me, madman that you are ! Your chief care is your own enjoyment, and my pretty body but an instrument thereto. And if you kill me in having your pleasure of me, you will canonize me, I suppose. What ! You have the plague, and yet would tumble me ? Away with you ! Begone thou brainless shaveling. . . . And beware thou touch me not," she added seeing him advance towards her, " or verily I will puncture thy belly with this poniard."

And the cunning hussy drew from her bag a dainty little dagger whereof, when need arose, she could make wondrous skilful use.

" But, my little paradise, my darling," said the other laughing, " do you not see the trick ? Did we not have to rid ourselves somehow of that old ox from Coire ? "

" A nice story ! . . . If you love me, prove it now. I desire that you depart on the instant. If you are infected with the pestilence, my death would matter little to you. I know you well enough to realise at what price you would put a few moments' pleasure, when you came to give up the ghost. You would drown the world. Ah, ha ! You boasted about it when you were drunk. Know then that all I care about is myself, my money and my health. Go, and if the fell sergeant death hath not frozen your vitals, come and see me again to-morrow. . . . To-day, my good cardinal, I hate you," said she with a smile.

"Imperia ! " cried the cardinal on his knees, " my sainted Imperia, I beseech thee, trifle not."

" Nay," she said, " but I never trifle with what is holy and sacred."

" Out on thee, vile strumpet, I will excommunicate thee. . . to-morrow."

" Merciful God, but have you taken leave of your cardinalian senses ? "

" Imperia, hell-breed, spawn of Satan . . . my sweeting, my beautiful, my little one ! "

" You grow unseemly. . . . Kneel not to me. Oh, fie ! "

" Wouldst thou have some dispensation *in articulo mortis ?* Wouldst thou my fortune, or what is worth still more, a piece of the True Cross ? Wouldst thou. . . ."

" To-night, not all the wealth of heaven and earth would satisfy my heart," she answered with a laugh. " I should be the worst of sinners, unworthy of the sacraments, if I did not have my whims."

" I'll set fire to your house. Sorceress, thou hast bewitched me ! Thou shalt perish at the stake. Hist to me, my love, my pretty chick, I promise thee the foremost place in heaven. How ? Thou wilt not ? Then death, death to thee, thou cursed witch ! "

" Ho ! Ho ! I will slay thee, Monseigneur ! "

The cardinal foamed with rage.

" You are going mad," said she. " Now, begone . . . 'tis making you tired."

" I shall be Pope and I'll make you pay dearly for this scurvy trick."

" For all that, you must obey me."

" Now, what *must* I do to-night to please you ? "

" Depart———"

So saying, she skipped nimbly aside, and locked herself in her bedchamber, leaving the cardinal fretting and fuming outside, till at last he had nothing for it but to decamp. When the fair Imperia found herself alone in front of the fire, with the table all spread out before her, but without her little priest, she tore off her gold necklaces in a rage and said :

" By the triple horn of Satan, if the little wretch has made me thus rebuff the cardinal and put me in danger of being poisoned to-morrow, without letting me feast on the sweets of his body to my heart's content, I will never die till I've seen him flayed alive with these very eyes. Ah ! " said she, weeping, and this time her tears were genuine, " unhappy is the life I lead, and the little grains of good fortune that fall to me here and there cost me a dog's life, to say nothing of my eternal salvation."

While she was unburdening herself of these wrathful lamentations, bleating like a dying calf, she happened to glance at her Venetian mirror, and caught sight of the rosy countenance of her boy-priest, who had slipped in very dexterously, beaming behind her.

" Ah ! " she cried, " you are the most perfect monk, the prettiest little duck of a monk, the most monkified monkey-boy that ever went a-monking in this holy and amorous city of Constance. Ah, come, my gentle knight, my darling child, my bawcock, my paradise of all delight, I would fain drink deep of thine eyes, devour thee, kill thee with love. Oh, my strong, my flourishing, my everlasting god. Gadzooks, thou shalt monk it no longer; I will make thee King, Emperor, Pope, and happier than the whole tribe of them. And now, thou maggot, stab and ravage as thou wilt, for I am thine, and full plainly will I show it, for soon shalt thou be a cardinal, even if I have to shed my heart's blood to crimson thy biretta."

And so with trembling hands, all radiant with joy, she filled to the brim with Grecian wine, a golden beaker, brought by the portly Bishop of Coire, and presented it to her lover; and she was fain to serve him on her knees, she whose slipper was more delectable to princes than the Pope's.

But he looked upon her in silence with an eye so hungry for love that, trembling with delight, she said:

" There, little one, speak not—let us fall to. . . ."

THE VENIAL SIN

THE DEVIL CAME AND
WHISPERED IN HIS EAR

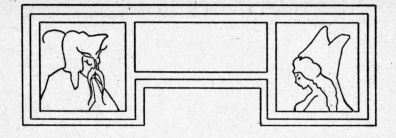

THE VENIAL SIN

How the worthy Bruyn took to Himself a Wife

MESSIRE BRUYN, he who completed the Castle of Roche-Corbon-lez-Vouvray on the Loire, was a dashing blade in his young days. When he was quite small, he was a great cruncher of maidenheads, would turn a house inside out and upside down, and was playing ducks and drakes with his substance, when he was called upon to tuck up his father in his final resting-place. Then he was free to live as riotously as it pleased him, and in sooth, he clutched at pleasure with both hands. And so, what with spending his money, with amorous dalliance, with wine-bibbing, with feasting and pampering the courtesans of the place, he found himself cold-shouldered by the worthy folk of the neighbourhood, his only friends being the pillagers and usurers. But the usurers soon became as dry as chestnut husks when he had nothing more to pledge than his aforesaid signory of Roche-Corbon, seeing that the *Rupes Carbonis* was held by him in fief from our lord the King. Then did Bruyn lay about him at random, doing much bone-breaking and picking a quarrel on the slightest pretext. Perceiving which, the Abbé de Marmoustiers, his neighbour, a man liberal of speech, said that all this was a sign that he was a worthy lord, that he was on the right road, but that if, for the glory of God, he would go and bring discomfiture to the Turks, who were defiling the Holy

Land, it would be better still, and that without doubt
he would come full of riches and indulgences either to
Touraine or to Paradise, whence, in times long past, all
the Barons had sprung.

The said Bruyn, admiring the Prelate's excellent good
sense, departed from the country, equipped by the
monastery and blest by the Abbé, to the great joy of his
friends and neighbours. Then he proceeded to sack
many a city in Asia and Africa, slaughtered the unbelievers
without so much as a word of warning; slew Saracens,
Greeks, English, and the rest, never heeding whether they
were friends or foes, and whence they sprang from;
for among his virtues he counted that of not being
inquisitive, and never made any enquiries of them till
after he had slain them. In this business, highly agreeable to God, to the King, and to himself, Bruyn won for
himself the reputation of a good Christian and a true
knight, and diverted himself greatly in that land beyond
the sea; and he would give a crown far more willingly
to a wench than six pennies to a beggar, though a goodly
beggar was far more often to be met with than a well-
made piece of womankind. But like the good son of
Touraine that he was, he turned everything to advantage.
At last, when he had had his fill of Turkish women, relics
and other products of the Holy Land, Bruyn, to the great
astonishment of the folk of Vouvray, returned from the
Crusade laden with money and precious stones, in marked
contrast to some who, though rich when they departed,
came home well ballasted with leprosy but very light in the
purse. On his return from Tunis, our sovereign lord
King Philippe made him a Count and appointed him
Seneschal in our country and in Poitou. There he was
greatly beloved and unfeignedly held in high esteem,
since, over and above his other merits, he founded the
Church of Carmes-Deschaulx in the parish of Esgrignolles, by way of paying his debt to Heaven, for he bethought him of his riotous youth. In this manner was

he right firmly established in the good graces of God and
Holy Church. Thus, though his boyhood was evil and
his manhood fraught with many ill-deeds, he became,
when his hair began to grow thin, a model of kindly
wisdom, never wantoning it save with much discretion.
In a word, he gave up quarrelling since, seeing he was
Seneschal, everyone gave in to him without a word. And
truth to tell, his desires no longer pricked him, and that
is enough to make the Devil himself calm and sober from
heel to headpiece. And then he possessed a castle
slashed at every seam like a Spanish doublet, seated on
a hill and looking down at its image mirrored in the Loire.
In the chambers within were royal tapestries, furniture
and trappings, pumps and Saracen inventions which were
the wonder of the people of Tours, and even of the
Archbishop and Clerks of Saint Martin's to whom he
handed over, as a free gift, a banner fringed with gold.
All round about the said château were a multitude of fine
demesnes, mills and noble woodlands, with fields yielding
all manner of crops; so that he was one of the most
puissant bannerets in the Province, and was able to lead
a thousand men to war in the service of our lord the King.
In his old days, if by chance his bailiff, a man right
diligent in the hanging of his fellows, should bring him a
poor peasant suspected of some misdemeanour, he would
say with a smile, " Let the fellow go, Bresdif, he will
count against those I thoughtlessly sent to glory over
yonder." True, he would often have them strung up
on an oak-tree, or fixed to a gibbet, but that was only that
justice might be done and that ancient custom should be
duly observed in his domains. So the common folk
were careful and well-behaved as new-fledged nuns, when
they were on his land, aye and tranquil, for he protected
them from highwaymen and robbers, the which he never
spared, knowing full well by experience the wounds
inflicted by those accursed beasts of prey. For the rest,
he was a very devout man, getting through everything,

both prayers and good wine, with praiseworthy dispatch.
In his capacity of judge he settled disputes with Turkish
promptitude, delivered himself of endless merry quips to
the losers and dined with them by way of consolation.
Those who were hanged he commanded to be buried in
consecrated ground, holding that they had been sufficiently punished by having their lives cut short.   Nor
did he bring pressure on the Jews till the time was ripe,
when they were swollen with usury and shekels.   He
suffered them to amass their booty like flies in a honey-
pot, saying that as tax-gatherers there were none to equal
them; and never did he despoil them save for the use
and benefit of the clergy, the King, the Province and
himself.

This debonair behaviour won him the affection and
esteem of all, both great and lowly.   If he returned with
smiling face from his judicial functions, the Abbé of
Marmoustiers, who, like him, was well stricken in years,
would exclaim, "Ha! ha! Messire, so there's been
some work for the hangman, that you are merry
to-day?"   And when, coming his ways from Roche-
Corbon to Tours, he rode on horseback through the
suburb of Saint-Symphorien, the little cottage girls
would cry, "Look, 'tis judge's day to-day, there goes old
Bruyn!"   And fearlessly they would stare at him riding
the great white charger that he had brought with him
from the East.   On the bridge of Tours, the urchins
would leave off playing marbles and shout after him:
"Good-day to you, Sir Seneschal!"
And he would answer banteringly:
"Rest you merry, my little ones, until you get a
thrashing."
"Aye, aye!   Sir Seneschal!"
And thus he made the country so contented and so
free from robbers that, the year of the disastrous floods of
the Loire, there were not more than twenty-two male-
factors hanged in the whole course of the winter, not

counting a Jew who had been burnt in the commune
of Château-Neuf for having stolen a consecrated wafer, or,
as some said, bought it, for he was passing rich.

One day, in the following year, round about the Feast
of Saint John of the Hay, or Saint John of the Mowing,
as we say in Touraine, there came thither a band of
Egyptians, Bohemians, or some such marauders, who
stole some sacred articles from the Church of Saint Martin,
and who, in place of Our Lady the Virgin, left behind
them, in token of insult and mockery of our true religion,
a shamelessly pretty girl about as full of years as an
elderly dog. Quite naked was she, a little Moorish
mummer like the rest of them. And it was agreed
between the King's men and the ecclesiastical authorities
that the girl should pay the penalty for the sacrilege
and that she should be burnt and roasted alive in Saint
Martin's Square, nigh unto the fountain where is the
grass market. Thereupon the worthy Bruyn did clearly
prove and skilfully demonstrate, in the face of all the rest,
that it would be profitable to God and pleasing in His
sight, to win over the soul of this African maiden to the
true faith ; and that, if the demon that dwelt within the
body of the said girl showed himself obstinate, faggots
would assuredly not avail to burn him, as the terms of the
said judgment did announce would be the case. And
of this the Archbishop did mightily approve, deeming it
soundly argued, highly canonical and in accordance both
with Christian charity and the teaching of the Gospel.
The ladies of Tours and other persons of weight did
loudly proclaim that they were being cheated of a brave
ceremony, for the Moorish maiden was weeping her life
out in prison, bleating like a captive goat, and she would
assuredly become a convert in order that she might live
as long as a crow, if only the chance were given her.
Whereto the Seneschal made answer that if the girl would
unfeignedly be converted to the Christian faith, there
should be held a very different and glorious ceremony,

and that he would pride himself on making it one of regal splendour, for that he himself would stand sponsor at the baptism, and that a virgin should be sponsor with him, so that the rite might be the more pleasing in God's eyes, since he himself was reputed to be a brave cockbird. This, in our land of Touraine, is the name given to lusty young lads as yet unwed or held to be so, in order to distinguish them from married men and widowers; but the girls know full well how to divine them without being told, because they are nimbler and more full of merriment than those who have been seasoned in the ways of matrimony.

The Moorish lass lost not a moment in choosing between the fire of the faggots and the water of baptism. She had liefer be a live Christian than a burnt Egyptian; for instead of frizzling for a moment, she would glow for the rest of her days. And in order that she might be more firmly established in godliness of life, she was received into a convent of nuns near to Chardonneret, where she took the vow of sanctity. The said ceremony was celebrated at the house of the Archbishop, in honour of the Saviour of men. There was such dancing and footing by the Lords and Ladies as had never been before in Touraine—a country in which there is more dancing, prancing, eating and buttock-stirring, more rich banquets and more merry-making than in any other place in the wide world. The good old Seneschal had chosen as his fellow-sponsor the daughter of the Lord of Azay-le-Ridel (since known as Azay-le-Bruslé), the which lord, having departed on a crusade, was taken prisoner before Acre, a very distant city, by a Saracen who demanded a king's ransom for him, so noble a figure did the said lord present.

The Lady of Azay, having pledged her fief to the Lombards and usurers in order to collect the necessary sum, was left without so much as a stiver, awaiting her lord's homecoming, in a poor lodging within the city, with not so much as a rug whereon to sit; but she was as proud as the Queen of Sheba and game as a dog defending his master's clothes. Beholding her great distress, the Seneschal betook himself delicately to beseech the young demoiselle of Azay to be godmother to the aforesaid Egyptian, so that he might have lawful occasion to confer a benefit on the Lady of Azay, her mother. And, indeed, he had in his possession a heavy gold chain, which had fallen into his hands at the taking of Cyprus, and which he purposed to clasp about the neck of his fair colleague; in like manner he hung there his estate, his white hairs, his besants and his saddle-horses; in short, he put everything there as soon as he had seen Blanche of Azay dancing a measure among the ladies of Tours. Although the Moorish girl, who danced for dear life, amazed the assembly by her leaps and twists and wriggles and all manner of striking poses, Blanche, in the unanimous judgment of all, carried off the palm, with such dainty and virginal grace did she acquit herself.

Thereupon Bruyn, looking with admiration on this comely damsel, whose ankles seemed to shun the floor, and who diverted herself innocently for her seventeen years like a grasshopper about to essay her first trill, was seized with an old man's longing, so apoplectic and vigorous a desire to trip, that it warmed him up from the sole of his feet to the nape of his neck; but no farther, for his poll had too much snow upon it for love to find a lodging there. Then the old fellow bethought him that he lacked a wife in his manor, and it seemed to him a sadder place than it really was. And zounds, what is a castle without a châtelaine ? You might just as well have a clapper without a bell. In short, a wife was the one thing he needed; and so he was fain to have her promptly, for if the Lady of Azay made him wait, he might quite well pass from this world to the next in the interval. During the baptismal celebrations, he bethought him little of his grievous wounds and still less of the eighty

years that had robbed him of his hair. He found his
eyesight full strong enough to take in the charms of his
fellow-sponsor who, in obedience to her mother's commands, regaled him with some meaning glances and
eloquent gestures, deeming that she ran no risk with so
old a man. And so it befell that Blanche, naïve and
comely as she was in contrast to all the other wenches of
Touraine, who are as wideawake as a spring morning,
suffered the old fellow first of all to kiss her hand and then
her neck where her dress was cut rather low; at least, so
said the Archbishop who married them the following
week. It was a beautiful bridal and a still more beautiful
bride.

The aforesaid Blanche was slender and graceful
beyond all other damsels, and more important still, such
a virgin as never was; a virgin that knew nought of love
nor how and why 'twas made; a virgin who would have
been shocked to hear that some wenches were given to
dalliance in bed; a virgin who believed that babies came
from curly greens. Her said mother had brought her
up in complete innocence, not even suffering her to
consider, even for a moment, how she sucked in her soup
between her teeth! Wherefore she was a child intact,
with all her bloom upon her, joyous and innocent, an
angel who only lacked wings to fly away to Paradise.
And when she quitted the poor lodging of her weeping
mother to crown her betrothal at the Cathedral of St.
Gatien and St. Maurice, the country folk round about
came to feast their eyes on the bride and on the carpets
which were laid all along the Rue de la Scellerie, and all
declared that never had the soil of Touraine been pressed
by daintier feet, never had lovelier eyes gazed heavenward,
or a more splendid festival adorned the streets with carpets
and with flowers. The wenches of the town, from Saint
Martin and the burg of Château-Neuf, all envied the long
auburn tresses wherewith, no doubt, Blanche had angled
for a Count's estate and landed it; but likewise, and still

THE SWEET VICES OF
THE GODDESS VENUS

HE WAS A DASHING BLADE
IN HIS YOUNG DAYS

more, did they envy the robe of cloth of gold, the jewels from distant lands, the white diamonds and the chains with which the pretty sweeting played and which bound her for ever to the Seneschal. The old warrior was put in such a glow by being with her that his happiness oozed out through all his wrinkles, shone in every look and movement. Although he was about as straight as a reaping-hook, he held himself so erect beside Blanche that you would have taken him for a guardsman on parade saluting the officer of the watch, and he laid his hand on his diaphragm like a man whose bliss is stifling and choking him. Listening to the ringing of the bells and beholding the pomps and splendours of the said bridal, the wenches longed for a harvest of Moorish girls, floods of aged seneschals and cartloads of gypsy baptisms; but this was the only one that ever took place in Touraine, for it is a land far removed from Egypt and Bohemia. The Lady of Azay received a notable sum of money after the ceremony, whereof she profited to set out, without loss of time, for Acre to meet her spouse, in company with the Lieutenant and the men-at-arms of the Count of Roche-Corbon, who provided them with everything on her behalf. She departed on the day of the wedding, after giving her daughter into the hands of the Seneschal, entreating him to use her gently. And after a while, she returned with the Lord of Azay, who was sick of the leprosy and cured him, tending him herself at the risk of contracting his disease, which conduct was greatly admired.

The wedding having at length come to an end—it lasted three days to the mighty content of the people— Messire Bruyn bore his bride, in great pomp, to his castle, and, in accordance with the custom of bride-grooms, laid her solemnly in his bed which had been blessed by the Abbé of Marmoustiers; then he came and took his place beside her in the great State Bedchamber of Roche-Corbon, the which had been adorned with hangings of green brocade richly inwrought with gold.

When the aged Bruyn, all perfumed, found himself
naked in bed with his lovely bride, he first kissed her on
the forehead and then on her pretty rounded breast, on
the very spot whereon she had suffered him to clasp
the fastening of the chain; but that was all. The old
stag had overestimated his powers in imagining he
could perform the rest. And so he gave love the go-by,
despite the joyous nuptial songs, epithalamiums and
merry jestings that were going on downstairs, where they
were still footing it in the dance. He comforted himself
with a draught of the bridal posset, which had been
blessed, in accordance with the time-honoured custom,
and which was set near them in a golden goblet. And
the spices wherewith it was compounded did marvellously
warm and comfort his stomach, but not, alas, the heart
and kernel of his fighting forces. Blanche was in no wise
taken aback at this treason on the part of her spouse since
she was pure in spirit and saw in marriage nought save
what is visible to maidens' eyes, to wit, rich raiment,
feastings, horses, playing the great lady, possessing
estates, enjoying oneself and giving orders to one's
underlings. And so, like the child she was, she sported
with the golden tassels and ornaments of the bed and
marvelled at the rich trappings amid which the flower of
her innocence was to be ensepultured. Feeling, though
somewhat late, a little abashed, and trusting to the
future, which nevertheless was bound to diminish his
capability every day that passed, the Seneschal endeavoured to make up in speech for his shortcomings
in action. Wherefore he made his bride all manner
of promises; told her she should have the keys of his
sideboards, his storerooms and his chests, and the un-
fettered control, without any interference whatsoever, of
his houses and estates. In short, he hung the better
half of the loaf about her neck, as they say in Touraine.
She was like a young war-horse full of fodder, and looked
on her goodman as the finest gallant in the world. And

sitting bolt upright upon her haunches, she began to
smile, looking more joyfully than ever on the lovely bed
with its green brocade in which henceforth it was vouchsafed her to sleep every night without sinning. Seeing
her disposed to playfulness, the cunning lord, who had
had little to do with virgins and knew from long and varied
experience how full of tricks a woman can be in bed, for
he had always had to do with strumpets, was afraid of the
little manual twiddlings and caresses, the roving kisses
and the little trimmings of love to which of yore he never
failed to respond, but which, at this time, would have
found him as cold as the memorial service for a dead
Pope. Wherefore he withdrew to the edge of the bed,
fearing what might befall and said to his too delectable
spouse :

" Well, then, my chuck, so now you're my Lady
Seneschal, and upon my life mighty generously
seneschalled."

" Oh no ! " said she.

" How, ' oh no ! ' " answered he, mightily perturbed.
" Are you not a wife ? "

" No," said she again, " nor shall be, till I have a
child."

" Did you see the meadows as you came hither ? "

" Aye, marry did I."

" Well, they are yours."

" Oh ! " she answered with a laugh, " how pleasant
it will be to go chasing butterflies there ! "

" Spoken like a good girl," said her lord. " And the
woods ? "

" Ah, I could not go there alone, and you will take me.
But," she went on, " give me a little of that liquor which
la Ponneuse compounded for us so carefully."

" And wherefore, my love-bird ? 'Twill set your
body afire."

" But I want some," she said gnawing her lips with
mortification, " because I want to give you a child as

soon as possible, and I know full well this liquor will do it."

"Phew! my little one!" exclaimed the Seneschal, knowing by that that Blanche was a virgin from head to foot, "but the favour of God is first necessary for the due performance of that office; besides a woman must be ripe for the harvest."

"And when shall I be ripe?" she questioned with a smile.

"When Nature wills it," he answered, thinking it well to laugh.

"And what is necessary to bring that about?" asked she.

"Ah, why thou must undergo a cabalistic and alchemistic operation, full of risk and peril."

"Ah," said she pensively, "'tis doubtless why my mother wept at the thought of such a metamorphosis; but Berthe de Preuilly, who is so proud of being changed into a woman, told me there was nothing easier in the world."

"'Tis all a matter of age," answered the old lord. "But, tell me, have you been to the stable and seen the beautiful white mare that is so much talked about in Touraine?"

"Marry, have I! And right gentle and pleasant is she."

"Well, now I will give her to thee, and thou art free to mount her when and as often as thou wilt."

"You are very kind, and they did not lie to me when they said——"

"My darling," he went on, "the steward, the chaplain, the treasurer, the squire, the cook, the bailiff, aye, even the Sire de Montsoreau, that young knave whose name is Gautier, who bears my banner, together with his men-at-arms, captains and all his followers, both men and beasts, all, I say, are yours and will obey your commands with all alacrity, or they shall hang for it."

" But," she said, " this alchemistic operation, can it not be performed here and now ? "

" Alas, no," answered the Seneschal. " For that, it is necessary that we should be in a perfect state of grace before God ; otherwise, we should have a sorry offspring, steeped in sin ; a thing utterly condemned by Canon Law. That is why there are so many incorrigible rascals in the world. Their parents did not wait until their hearts were clean within them, and so endowed their progeny with evil minds. Those who are fair and virtuous come of stainless sires. 'Twas for that reason that we cause our beds to be blessed, even as the Abbé of Marmoustiers blessed this bed on which we lie. But have you not transgressed the Church's laws ? "

" Oh, no ! " she replied eagerly. " Before Mass, I received absolution for all my faults, and since then, I have not been guilty of the slightest trip."

" You are perfect," said the cunning lord, " and right glad am I to have you for my spouse. But I, alas, have blasphemed like any pagan."

" Oh, but why ? "

" Because I thought the dance would never end, and because I could not have you to myself, could not bring you here and—kiss you."

Thereupon he seized her two hands and devoured them with kisses, bestowing upon her little superficial squeezes and caresses, the which rendered her mighty pleased and content.

Then, being worn out with the dancing and all the ceremonies, she lay herself down to sleep.

" I will see to it that to-morrow you come to bed without sinning," she said.

And she left her old husband madly in love with her fair loveliness and her delicate nature and as much puzzled to know how to deal with her in her innocence as he would have been to explain why oxen chew the cud. He was sore perplexed, yet so inflamed was he, as he looked on Blanche's exquisite charms, as she lay there in soft and innocent slumber, that he made up his mind to keep and defend so lovely a jewel. He kissed her with tears in his eyes, kissed her lovely golden tresses, her beautiful eyelids, her fresh red mouth, but very gently lest he should awaken her. And that was his sole fruition, silent pleasures which set his heart on fire while Blanche lay lapt in sweet unconscious slumber. And so he bemoaned the winter of his old age and saw, well enough, that God had amused himself by providing him with nuts when he had no longer any teeth to crack them.

How the Seneschal did Battle with his Wife's Virginity

During the early days of his marriage, the Seneschal invented some wonderful tales wherewith to gull his wife, thus abusing her most unsuspecting innocence. To begin with, his duties as justiciary supplied him with valid excuses for leaving her sometimes alone; then he occupied her with country matters, took her a-harvesting in his vineyards at Vouvray; and finally bamboozled her with countless cock-and-bull stories.

Sometimes he would tell her that noble lords did not comport themselves like humble folk; that the offspring of counts did only germinate at certain conjunctions of the heavenly bodies of which learned astrologers possessed the secret; sometimes he would tell her that it was forbidden to make children on saints' days, because it was toilsome work; and he observed the saints' days with the scrupulousness of a man who wanted to go straight to heaven. And sometimes he would tell her that, if the parents did not happen to be in a state of grace, children conceived on Saint Claire's day would be born blind; on Saint Genou's, gouty; on Saint Aignan's, bronchial; on Saint Roch's, liable to the plague. And then he would tell her that February children were delicate;

March children too boisterous; while an April child was no good at all, and that all the really nice boys were born in May. In a word, he wished his child to be perfect in every respect, and for that it was necessary that all the requisite conditions should coincide. And sometimes, again, he told Blanche that it was the man's right to give his wife a child just when his own sole will prompted him so to do; and that if she would prove herself a woman of virtue, it was her duty to conform to the wishes of her husband; and lastly, he gave out that they must await the return of the Lady of Azay in order that she might be present at the childbirth. From all this, Blanche concluded that the Seneschal had been vexed by her solicitations and that he was possibly in the right, being an old man and full of experience. Therefore she submitted, and thought no more about this much-longed-for child; that is to say she thought of it continually, as a woman does when she gets a whim into her head, never thinking that she was acting like a strumpet begging for a sweetmeat. One night, by chance, Bruyn fell to talking about children—a subject which, as a rule, he shunned as a cat shuns water. Howbeit, he was complaining about a lad condemned by him that very morning for gross misdeeds, saying that, of a surety, he had been born of parents laden with mortal sin.

"Alack!" said Blanche, "if you will but give me one, even if you yourself have not been shriven, I will train him and correct him so thoroughly that you will have no cause to complain of him."

Then the Seneschal saw plainly that his wife was devoured by hot desire, and that it was time to give battle to her maidenhood in order to master, exterminate, override and dominate it, or at least, to lull and distract it.

"How now, would you become a mother?" he asked. "Nevertheless, you know not yet how to act the great lady, and you are not accustomed to playing the mistress in the house."

" Oh, oh ! " said she. " To be a perfect countess and to harbour a little count in my loins, must I act the great lady ? 'Zounds, I will do it, and with a will."

And so Blanche, in order that she might have issue, devoted her energies to hunting the stag and the doe. She leapt ditches, rode her hunter up hill and down dale, through woods and across country, taking great delight at seeing the falcons fly and at loosing them from their leash. And she bore them gaily on her dainty wrist all through the hunt. This was exactly what the Seneschal had wished. But this exercise gave Blanche an appetite big enough for two, and those two of different sexes, that is to say, it made her long to procreate, it gave edge to her forces, and she could scarce restrain her longing when, returning from the hunt she set her teeth to work. Thus by dint of reading the legends written along the roads, and of interrupting by death the loves of birds and wild things, she performed a miracle of natural alchemy by colouring her cheeks and exciting her nutritive spirits ; all of which had little effect in calming her nature and greatly fomented her desires which laughed, prayed and gambolled more than ever. The Seneschal had endeavoured to disarm the dangerous longings of his wife by sending her to sport in the fields, but his plot went awry, for the secret love which circulated in Blanche's veins, issued from these exercises more untamed than ever, challenging to joust and tourney like a page who has won his spurs. The worthy lord then saw that he was on the wrong track and that there was no place you could call safe on a gridiron. And so he was at his wits' end to know what sort of pasture to give to such lusty virtue : for the more he tried to weary her the more lively she became. In this combat, one was bound to be worsted, and one would be stabbed, and stabbed in so diabolical a manner, that he prayed that, with God's aid, he might banish the sight of the wound,

SITTING BOLT UPRIGHT
SHE BEGAN TO SMILE

until after his death. The unhappy Seneschal had already
much ado to follow his lady in the chase, without
being unseated ; he sweated unconscionably beneath his
harness and was nearly done to death by a sport in which
his mettlesome dame found the comfort and joy of her
existence. Oftentimes, of an evening, she was fain to
dance ; and then the old fellow, all muffled up in his heavy
clothes, would be reduced to his last gasp by the giddy
pranks in which he was obliged to take part, either by
giving her his hand when she danced her Moorish
fandangos, or holding the lighted brand when she took it
into her head to dance the torchlight dance ; and, despite
his sciaticas, his imposthumes and his rheumatisms, he
was compelled to smile and say nice gallant things to her
after all the twistings, mummeries and comic buffooneries
which she practised for his amusement ; for he loved
her so madly, that if she had asked him for an oriflamme,
he would have gone wandering up and down the world to
find her one.

Nevertheless, one fine day, he realised that his loins
had grown too weak to struggle with her lusty nature, and
humbling himself before the said Sire Pucelage, he determined to let matters go as they would, relying a little on
the seemly piety and devout modesty of Blanche ; nevertheless, he always slept with one eye open, for he deemed
that God had made hymens to be captured, as he had made
partridges to be grilled and roasted. One damp morning—the sort of weather when snails love to go a-wan-
dering—melancholy weather and favourable to day-
dreaming, Blanche was at home sitting languidly in her
easy-chair. Now there is nought that produces such a
calefaction of the substantific essences, no recipe, specific
or philtre that is more penetrating, incisive, permeating,
exciting, than the subtle warmth which forms like warm
dew between the down of an easy-chair and the down of
a maiden who sits in it for any length of time. So,
though she knew not why, the Countess was strongly

E

inconvenienced by her maidenhead, which metagra-
bolised her brains and teased and gnawed at her all over.

Then the old fellow, sorely grieved to behold her thus
languishing, did his best to drive away those thoughts
which are the fount and origin of extra-conjugal love.

" Whence comes your sadness, my pretty one ? " said
he.

" From shame."

" What makes you ashamed ? "

" Not being a good woman ; because I am without a
child and you without an heir. Can you show me
another lady without offspring ? Never a one. For
look you ! All my neighbours have children ; and I
married in order to have one, just as you married to give
me one. The Lords of Touraine are all of them well
provided with children, and their wives produce them in
swarms ; you alone have none. People will laugh at you.
Go to ! What will become of your name, your fiefs and
your estates ? A child is our natural companion. It
is our special joy to swaddle and swathe and coddle him,
to dress and undress him, pat and pet and sing him to
sleep, pick him up and lay him down, and give the little
darling his pap ; and well I know that even if I only
had half a one, I should kiss him and fondle him, put on
his little clothes and take them off, and make him laugh
and dance the livelong day, as other women do."

" Were it not that women sometimes die when they
bring forth children, and that you are still too slender
and too closely sealed, you would be a mother already,"
answered the Seneschal dazed by this torrent of eloquence.
" But say, will you buy one ready made ? It will cost you
neither pain nor trouble."

" By my troth," said she, " I would have both the pain
and the trouble, for without them the child would not
be ours. I know well that it ought to issue from me
because in Church they say that Jesus was the fruit of the
Virgin's womb."

" Ah well, then, pray God it may be so," cried the Seneschal, "and let us pray to the Virgin of Esgrignolles. Many women have conceived after a novena : we must not omit to make one."

Therefore the same day, Blanche betook herself to Nôtre Dame de l'Esgrignolles, arrayed like a queen, mounted on her beautiful palfrey, with her robe of green velvet, trimmed with a lace of gold, open at the bosom, with sleeves of scarlet, little shoes, a high hat adorned with gems and a golden belt which set off the slimness of her waist.   She wished to give her raiment to Madame the Virgin and did in fact promise it for the day she should rise up from childbed. . . . The Sire de Montsoreau rode on before her, his eye glittering like a hawk's, clearing the way through the crowd, his horse-men keeping a sharp look-out against the perils of the way.   Near Marmoustiers, the Seneschal, being ren-dered sleepy by the heat—for it was in the month of August—was swaying about on his charger like a fillet on a cow's head.   And beholding so gamesome and comely a lady beside so aged a sire, a certain woman of the countryside, who was crouching beside a tree trunk and drinking water from her cruise, enquired of a toothless old crone, who was wailing out her woes as she gleaned among the stubble, whether the princess yonder was taking Death along with her to drown him.

" Nay," answered the old hag.   " That is the Lady of Roche-Corbon, the wife of the Seneschal of Poitou and Touraine, and she is going in search of a baby."

" Ah, ha ! " quoth the wench with a mocking laugh. And then, pointing to the sleepy old lord who was riding along at the head of the cavalcade, " If he who is riding in front there gets to work on her, she'll have no need of prayer or taper."

" By my troth, darling," answered the old vagabond, " but I am amazed that she should betake herself to Our Lady of Esgrignolles, seeing that the priests there are but sorry fellows. But it might richly profit her to halt a while beneath the shadow of the church tower at Marmoustiers. There the good fathers are right lusty men and she would soon bear fruit."

" A fig for your clerics ! " said a gleaner, waking from her slumbers. " The Lord of Montsoreau, look you, is ardent and comely enough to find a way into the lady's heart, especially as it has been cleft already."

Then they all burst out laughing. The Sire de Montsoreau was for taking them and stringing them up to a tree by the wayside as a punishment for their insolent language ; but Blanche would have none of it.

" Good, my lord," said she, " hang them not yet. They have not yet said their say, and we will see about them as we come back."

She blushed, and the Lord of Montsoreau gave her a right meaning glance as though to permeate her with the mystical wisdom of love. But the quickening and unlocking of the secret chambers of her mind were already begun by the things the peasant women had said, which were germinating in her understanding. Her maiden-head was like tinder and lacked only a spark to set it ablaze.

Thus Blanche forthwith perceived notable differences of a physical order between the characteristics of her old husband and the perfections of the said Gauttier, a gentle-man who was by no means weighed down by his three-and-twenty years, who sat his horse as upright as a ninepin, and as wideawake as the first tintinnabulation of the Matin bell, what time the Seneschal, on the other hand, lay grunting and snoring. Moreover, he was full of courage and address in the very place in which his master was so conspicuously lacking in those qualities. He was one of those adventurous youths who would rather sleep with a wanton than a stiff and starchy dame because they are not afraid of fleas. There be some that blame them for it ; but we should find fault with no one, for every man has a right to slumber in what manner he will.

Such were the thoughts of the lady, and they took such an imperious hold on her that, when they arrived at the bridge of Tours, she was consumed with a secret and all-possessing love of Gauttier, as a maiden loves, without really knowing what manner of thing love is. So she became a good woman, that is to say one who longs for the goods of others, those goods being the most valuable part of a man. And she fell into a love sickness, sinking forthwith into the depth of wretchedness, for all is fire betwixt the first access of desire and the final longing. And she knew not, albeit she learnt it then, that a subtil essence might flow from the eyes causing such powerful corrosions in all the veins of the body, conduits of the heart, nerves of the limbs, roots of the hair, exudations of the substance, lobes of the brain, cells of the epidermis, sinuosities of the entrails, tubes of the intestines, which, in her case, became on a sudden dilated, heated, tickled up, envenomed, set on edge, upstanding and teasing as though unnumbered needles filled her body. But 'twas the longing of a maiden, a well-behaved and seemly longing, which disturbed her vision so greatly that she could no longer see her aged husband, but only the youthful Gauttier whose nature was as ample as the glorious chin of an abbot.

When the good Seneschal arrived at Tours, the shouts of the populace woke him up; and he proceeded with great pomp, accompanied by his retinue, to the Church of Our Lady of Esgrignolles which of old was called *la Greigneur*, as who should say "the church that has the greatest merit." Blanche betook herself to the chapel, where folk pray to God and the Virgin to give them children, and she went in alone as is the custom, albeit her entry was witnessed by the Seneschal, his serving-men and certain sightseers who remained without the grille. When the Countess saw the priest coming towards her, he whose duty it was to say Mass for those who besought children and to receive their offerings, she enquired of him whether there were many barren women. Whereupon the good priest made answer that there was no reason to complain, and that the children brought in a goodly revenue to the church.

"And do you often see young women with husbands as old as my lord?" asked Blanche.

"Not often," was the answer.

"But do they have children?"

"Always," replied the priest with a smile.

"And the others, whose husbands were not so old?"

"Sometimes."

"Oh, ho!" said she. "So there is more certainty with an old man like the Seneschal?"

"Of a surety," said the priest.

"And why?" she asked.

"Madame," replied the priest gravely, "before that age 'tis only God's concern. After it, men lend a hand."

In those days, it was true that all wisdom resided in the priesthood. Blanche made her offering, which was of very great value seeing that her jewels were worth, at least, two thousand golden crowns.

"You seem in merry trim," said the Seneschal when, on the homeward journey, she made her steed prance, leap, and curvet.

"Aye marry, that am I!" said she. "I doubt not that I shall have a child, since, as the priest said, others must labour at the task. "Gauttier shall be my man."

The Seneschal would have liked to slay the monk; but he reflected that that were a crime would cost him dear, and he resolved that with the aid of the Archbishop he would devise a more subtil vengeance.

And then, or ever the roofs of the château of Roche-Corbon came in sight, he bade the Sire de Montsoreau go seek a little seclusion in his own country, which the young man did forthwith, for he knew the queer humours of his lord and master.   And in lieu and stead of the aforesaid Gauttier, the Seneschal took into his service the son of the Sire de Jallanges, a fief dependent on Roche-Corbon.   He was a young man called René, who was nearing his fourteenth year.   He made him his page until such time as he was old enough to be his squire. And the command of his men he gave to an aged man, maimed in the wars, in whose company he had roamed about Palestine and other lands.   By this means the worthy man trusted he would not be brought to put on the antlered insignia of the cuckold and would still be able to curb, rein-in and restrain the frisky longings of his spouse, the which resembled the gambols of a young mule impatient of its tether.

Wherein a Venial Sin Consists

On the Sunday which followed René's arrival at the Manor of Roche-Corbon, Blanche went forth a-hunting with her lord, and when she was in the woods, hard by Les Carneaux, she beheld a monk who seemed to be outrageously maltreating a maiden. Driving the spurs into her steed, she shouted to her retainers, " Hi, there ! See that he slay her not ! "   But when the Seneschal's lady drew nigh, she wheeled her steed aside, and the sight of what the monk was holding made her forget the chase.   She came back with thoughtful mien, and lo, the dark chamber of her intelligence was opened and received a bright light which illumined things un-numbered, such as church pictures and the like, the fables and lays of the troubadours, and the ways and habits of birds ; and on a sudden, she discovered Love's sweet mystery writ down in every tongue, even in the tongue of the carps.   And is it not a witless thing to essay to keep this knowledge from young maids ?   Soon Blanche betook herself to bed and forthwith spake to the Seneschal, saying :

"Bruyn, you have deceived me and you should labour even as the monk in the woods of Carneaux laboured with the girl."

Old Bruyn perceived how the land lay and saw well enough that his evil hour had come. He had too much fire in his eyes, as he looked at Blanche, to have any to spare for his lower parts, and answered her softly:

"Alas, my sweeting, when I took you for my bride, my love was greater than my strength, and I counted on your compassion and your virtue. The great sorrow of my life is to feel my power only in my heart. 'Tis a grief that is hurrying me to the grave swiftly and surely, and in a short while you will be free. Wait then, until I shall have departed from this world. 'Tis all I ask, I who am your master and might put my entreaties into command but yet am fain to be your minister and slave. Betray not the honour of my white hairs! In junctures such as this, lords have been known to slay their wives."

"Ah me! Thou wilt not slay me?"

"No," answered the old man. "I love thee too well, my sweet one. Behold, thou art the flower of my old age, my heart's delight. Thou art my beloved daughter. The sight of thee brings gladness to my eyes, and from thee I could endure anything, were it grief or were it joy. I give thee full licence in all things, provided thou scold not too severely poor old Bruyn who hath made thee a great lady, both rich and honoured. Wilt thou not be a lovely widow? Thy happiness will soften the pangs of my departure."

And in his shrunken eyes he found yet one tear more, which rolled down all hot upon his sere and yellow cheek and fell on Blanche's hand. And she, moved with compassion when she beheld the great love of her spouse, who was fain to lay himself in the grave to please her, said laughingly:

"There, there, weep not! I will wait."

Thereupon the Seneschal kissed her hands and petted her with little pats and fondlings.

"Didst thou but know, Blanche, my love, how I devoured thee with caresses in thy sleep; now here, now there."

And the old rascal paddled about her with both his hands, which were only skin and bone.

"And then," he kept on saying, "I did not dare to rouse the cat that would have strangled my honour, seeing that at this love-making business my heart was the only part of me that I could warm."

"Ah!" she made answer, "you can fondle me like that even when I have my eyes open, it moves me not."

On hearing these words, the poor Seneschal took up the little dagger that lay on the table beside the bed and handed it to her, saying in a tone of desperate mortification:

"Kill me, my beloved, or at least let me think that you love me a little."

"Yes, yes!" she cried beside herself with fear. "I will see to it that I love you!"

'Twas thus the girl made herself master of the old man and moulded him to her will. For in the name of that fair territory of Venus, which was then lying fallow, Blanche, with those cunning arts that are the natural heritage of woman, made her old Bruyn come and go with the docility of a miller's mule.

"Here, Bruyn dear, fetch this; Bruyn dear, fetch that. Come, Bruyn! Bruyn!" And it was Bruyn, Bruyn, all the time. The result was that Bruyn suffered more from his wife's kindness than he did from her ill-humour. She turned his poor old brain, wanted everything her own way, and at the slightest movement of her eyebrow he would rush off and turn the whole place upside down. And when she was sad, all the old Seneschal could say, as he sat on the Seat of Justice, was "Let the fellow hang!" Anyone else would have been squashed like a

fly, but Bruyn was such a stubborn old wight that it was
no easy matter to get the better of him. One night
when Blanche had turned everything in the place upside
down and inside out, ill-treated the men and ill-treated
the beasts, and with her unbearable temper would have
worn out the patience of God Almighty himself, Who
must have untold treasures of it since He puts up with
us—that night, I say, as she was getting into bed, she
said to the Seneschal :

"My good Bruyn, I have in the lower parts of me
fancies that prick and sting me ; thence they rise to my
heart, set my brain on fire and incite me to naughty
deeds ; and when the night comes, I dream about the
monk of Carneaux."

"My sweet one," replied the Seneschal ; "these are
temptations and bedevilments against which monks and
nuns are endowed with sure means of defence. Wherefore, if you would walk in the way of salvation, go and
confess to the worthy Abbot of Marmoustiers, our
neighbour. He will give you good counsel and will
guide your feet into the path of righteousness."

"I will get me to him on the morrow," she cried.

And true to her word, as soon as it was light, she tarried
not, but straightway hurried off to the monastery of
reverend monks, who, marvelling greatly at seeing so
dainty a lady come amongst them, committed more than
one sin that night, and then and there did lead her with
great joy into the presence of the Reverend Father Abbot.
Blanche found the old man in a secluded garden, hard by
a rock, beneath a verdant bower, and stood there filled
with awe at the sight of the saintly man, albeit she was
not wont to be greatly moved at the sight of white hairs.

"God keep you, Madame," said he. "What come
you to seek of one so near to death, you who are so
young ? "

"Your precious counsel," she replied with a curtsey.
"And if it please you to guide a stubborn sheep along the

narrow path, I shall be right glad to have so wise a
confessor."

" My daughter," answered the monk, with whom old
Bruyn had plotted this piece of hypocrisy and arranged
the part he should play, " were it not that I had the
chills of a hundred winters on this old bald head, I could
not give ear to your sins.   But as it is, say on, and if you
go to heaven, 'twill be through me."

Thereupon the lady produced her stock of peccadilloes,
and when she had purged her conscience of her little faults,
she came to the postscript of her confession.

" Ah, Father," said she, " I must now confess to you
that never a day goes by but I am tormented with the
desire to make a baby.   Is that an evil thing ? "

" Nay," said the Abbot.

" But," answered she, " Nature has enjoined my
husband not 'to wear out the material by too much
rubbing,' as the wayside gossips say."

" Then," answered the priest, " you must live a godly
life and abstain from all thoughts of that kind."

" But I have heard it laid down by the Lady of Jallanges
that there was no sin in it when you derived from it
neither profit nor pleasure."

" There is always pleasure," said the Abbot.   " But
look not on the child as profit. Now fix this firmly in
your mind, that it is always a mortal sin before God and
a crime before men to get oneself a child by contact with
a man to whom you have not been joined in wedlock by
the Church.   And therefore such women as contravene
the sacred laws of marriage are stricken with dire
penalties in the next world, where they are a prey to dreadful monsters with sharp tearing claws, who thrust them
into many a furnace, for that here below they warmed
their hearts a little more freely than was lawful."

Whereupon Blanche scratched her ear, and having
pondered a little while, said to the priest :

" How then did the Virgin Mary contrive ? "

" Ah," replied the Abbot, " that is a mystery."

" And what mean you by a mystery ? "

" Something we cannot explain and must believe without question."

" Well then," she retorted, " can I not perform a mystery ? "

" That miracle," said the Abbot, " happened but once, because it was the Son of God."

" Alas, Father, is it God's will that I should die, or that, sensible and sane in my understanding, I should have my brains all jangled and bewildered ? For there is great danger thereof. Things move and grow warm within me ; I am no longer mistress of my senses, and I think and care for nothing. To come to a man, I would leap over walls, I would rush across country without shame, nay I would give everything over to rack and ruin merely to set eyes upon the thing which was so incommoding the monk of Carneaux with its heat. And when these furious fits are on me, stinging and giving me no rest of body or soul, there's no God, nor devils, nor husband for me. I stamp my feet, I rush about, I break down the box trees, I smash the pottery, I play havoc with the ostrich house, the poultry yard, the household furniture and things more numerous than I can tell you. But I dare not tell you all the misdeeds I commit because the mere mention of them makes my mouth water and the thing, God curse it, gnaws at my vitals. What though this madness strike me and spur me and destroy my virtue, well, will God, who has lighted this great fire of love in my body, send me to perdition . . .?"

When he heard this, it was the priest's turn to scratch his ear, for he was utterly amazed and dumbfounded at the lamentations, wise utterances, polemical discourses and shrewd understanding that had lain hidden within this slip of maidenhood.

" My daughter," said he, " God has distinguished us from the beasts, and set before us a paradise to be won ;

wherefore he hath endowed us with reason to serve us as
a helm to guide us against the tempest of our ambitions
and desires; so that one may transfer one's energies to
one's brain by fasting, excessive labour and other wise
courses. Thus, instead of dancing and prancing like a
bear let loose, you ought to say your prayers to the Virgin,
sleep on a plank bed, busy yourself about the house and
never have an idle moment."

"Oh, but, Father, when I'm in church, in my pew, I
see neither priest nor altar, because the Child Jesus makes
the thing run in my head so. But tell me this: suppose
I went mad, and suppose when my wits were wandering,
I fell into the snares of love?"

"If such a thing befell you," was the Abbot's in-
cautious answer, "you would be in the position of that holy
woman, Saint Lidoire, who being one day wrapt in profound slumber, one leg here and one leg there, for it was
mighty hot, she, I say, being very lightly clad, was
approached by a young man, whose head was filled
with naughty thoughts, and that young man, in the calmest
possible manner, proceeded to make her with child.
And sith the saint was wholly ignorant of the mischance
that had befallen her and was sore amazed when she was
brought to bed of a child, having thought all the while
that the swelling in her stomach-part was due to some
grievous malady, she did penance as for a venial sin inasmuch as she had tasted no pleasure from her accident;
a statement that was borne out by her seducer, who said
on the scaffold, to which he was brought for his misdeed,
that the saint had made not the slightest movement."

"Well, Father," said she, "you may be sure, I should
not move any more than she did."

So saying, she gaily tripped away, thinking in what
manner she too might commit a venial sin. When she
came home from her visit to the great monastery, she
beheld in the courtyard of her castle the little page
Jallanges, who, under the direction of the aged squire,

was turning and curveting about on a noble steed, cantering up and down, holding himself very erect, and acquitting himself right skilfully. And so comely, graceful and lively was he that he would have fired the heart of Queen Lucrece with longing, though she slew herself for having been tumbled, against her will.

"Ah," said Blanche to herself, "if only this page were fifteen years old, I would sleep with him with great pleasure."

And so, despite the tender years of this comely young servitor, at collation and at supper, she gazed gloatingly on the black hair, the white skin, the graceful movements of René, and especially on his eyes which were instinct with limpid warmth and fire of life, which, poor innocent, he was afraid to reveal.

Now at eventide, seeing his lady sitting pensively in her great chair beside the hearth, old Bruyn enquired of her what it was that preyed upon her mind.

"I am thinking," said she, "that you must have begun jousting in the lists of love very young, to have come now to your present pass."

"Why," he answered, smiling with pleasure, like all old men when they are asked about their love-making exploits, "by the time I was thirteen and a half I had already got my mother's tire-woman with child."

Blanche, who wanted no less herself, thought that René the page would doubtless be sufficiently well supplied, and so she rejoiced greatly, teased her goodman with all manner of little tricks and wallowed in her mute longing like a cake rolling about in a flour bin.

How and by whom the Child was Made

The Seneschal's lady did not waste much time in thinking out the best way to awaken the page's love: she soon discovered the natural ambush into which the unsophisticated always fall. It befell on this wise.

About the hot hour of noonday, the old lord was taking his siesta after the manner of the Saracens, a custom he had never failed to observe since his return from the Holy Land. During that time Blanche would be alone in the meadows, or working at some task of embroidery or sewing as women are wont, to give employment to their hands; or more often, she would linger on in the hall, giving an eye to the washing, folding up the linen, or wandering whither her fancy took her. So on the morrow, when on the stroke of midday the Seneschal fell asleep, having succumbed to the sun that warms with its bright rays the hill slopes of Roche-Corbon, so that a man cannot but slumber save when he is worried, vexed, teased and pestered by some little demon of a maid—when, I say, the Seneschal was sound asleep, Blanche sate herself very gracefully in her lord's big chair, which was not a whit too high, for she was counting on the glimpses that the perspective would afford. The cunning jade settled down in it like a swallow in the nest, and leaned her mischievous little head on the arm like a sleepy child; but in making her preparations, she opened her greedy eyes which smiled as they gloated, in anticipation, on the little secret thrills, gulps, sidelong glances and swoonings of the page, who was about to lie at her feet, and no farther away from her than an elderly flea could jump. Indeed she placed the square of velvet on which the poor child was to kneel so close to the chair, that if he had been a saint carved out of stone, his eyes could not but follow the folds of her dress, so that he would be bound to see and admire the beauty of the lovely leg which the lady's white stocking encased. Thus a weak child could not but wander into a snare to which the doughtiest knight would readily fall a victim. When she had turned and turned about, put herself here and put herself there, and finally fixed on the position in which it would be best for the page to lie, she called softly, "Oh, René!" René, who, as she knew, was in the guardroom, hastened to obey her summons and, in a flash, poked his brown head between the hangings of the entrance.

"What is your ladyship's pleasure?" said the page.

And he stood there in an attitude of profound respect, holding in his hands his bonnet of crimson velvet, which however was not so red as his own fresh, dimpled cheeks.

"Come hither," she said in a faint voice, for so greatly did the child attract her, that she could scarcely breathe.

Truth to tell, there were never jewels that shone so brightly as René's eyes, nor vellum so white as his skin, nor woman with more softly rounded limbs. And, seeing how hot was her desire, she deemed him still more beautifully made; and you may rest assured that love's pleasant business took on a warmer glow from all this youthfulness, from the kindly sun, the quiet hour, and other things beside.

"Now read me the Litany of Our Blessed Lady," said she pushing towards him a book that lay open on her prie-Dieu. "I want to see whether your master knows how to teach. Think you not the Virgin is lovely?" she asked him smilingly as he took the prayer-book all bright with illuminations of gold and azure.

"'Tis but a painting," said he with a little hurried glance at his mistress in all her loveliness.

"Read, read!" said she.

Then René fell to reading the sweet and mystic invocations of the Litany; but you will believe me when I tell you that the responses were uttered by Blanche in a voice that grew ever fainter and fainter, like the sound of a horn heard in the open country and dying away in the distance. And when the page, with renewed ardour, began to recite "O Rosa Mystica," Blanche, who certainly heard well enough, only answered with a gentle sigh. Whereupon René never doubted but the lady was asleep. And so he began to gaze his fill upon her, gloating over her to his heart's content and

THE LOVES OF BIRDS
AND WILD THINGS

quite unconscious of any desire to sing hymns unless it were the hymn of love.   His good fortune made his heart leap into his very mouth.   So, as might well be supposed, these two pretty young things were on fire for one another, and had you seen them, you would have sworn that never had such a pretty couple come together.   René feasted his eyes upon her, pondering in his mind on countless ways of enjoying this fair fruit of love, which so made his mouth to water.   In his ecstasy he let fall the book, whereat he looked as sheepish as a monk caught out in some childish misdemeanour.   But by the same token he knew that Blanche was sleeping well and soundly, for she did not stir.   The cunning jade would never have opened her eyes for a far more startling thing than that, and she counted that something else would be descending on her far more exciting than a prayer-book.   You see there is no desire so maddening as the desire of a woman for a baby.   And now the page's eye lighted on his lady's foot, which was daintily encased in a slipper of the softest blue.   She was ostentatiously resting it on a stool, because the Seneschal's chair was too high for her. The foot in question was very tiny and slightly curved, about as broad as two fingers placed side by side and as long as a hedge-sparrow, tail included, small at the tip, a really delicious foot, a virginal foot that deserved a kiss as thoroughly as a thief deserves the rope; a frolicsome foot, a foot so wanton, 'twould have tempted an archangel, a foot of presage, a devilishly luring foot, the sort of foot that would make you want to make two more like it, so as to perpetuate here below such a beautiful specimen of God's handiwork.   The page was sorely tempted to slip off the shoe from the persuasive foot, and his eyes, aflame with all the fires of youth, glanced swiftly to and fro, like the tongue of a bell, from the lovely foot to the countenance of his sleeping mistress, listening to her slumber, inhaling her breath again and again.   And he could not make up his mind where it would be sweetest

F

to plant a kiss—whether on the fresh young lips of the
Seneschal's wife or on this most eloquent foot. To be
brief, out of respect or fear, or maybe, by reason of the
great love he bore her, he chose the foot and kissed it
quickly, like a maiden affrighted at her own daring.
Then forthwith he resumed his book, feeling himself still
as red as red could be, and, all excitement with his
delightful experience, he bawled out like a blind beggar
" *Janua coeli*," the gates of Heaven. But Blanche never
woke, for she trusted that the page would go as far as the
knee and thence into heaven itself. Great then was her
disappointment when the Litany came to an end without
any further assault being made upon her, and when
René, who deemed he had had too much good fortune
for one day, stole from the chamber like one treading
upon air, made richer by his bold kiss than a thief who
has robbed the poor-box.

When the Seneschal's lady was thus left alone, she
bethought herself in her inmost mind that the page
would certainly be a considerable time over the task,
if he thus amused himself by singing the *Magnificat* at
Matins. So, for the morrow, she decided to lift her
foot a little higher in order to afford a glimpse of that
particular piece of loveliness which, in Touraine, is called
perfect because it is never exposed to the air, and so
always remains fresh. You may well imagine how
impatiently the page, who was fairly roasted by desire,
and white hot with his recollections of the previous day,
awaited the moment when he should be able to resume
his readings from the Breviary of Love. At last he was
summoned. Then the reading began over again. This
time René lightly caressed her pretty leg and even made
so bold as to confirm whether her polished knee, aye
and other things besides, were made of satin. At the
sight of these good things the poor child, who was armed
to combat his desire, only dared venture on brief devotions and minor titillations. And even while he kissed,

albeit very gently, this lovely stuff, he kept himself within bounds. Feeling by psychical intuition as well as by her bodily senses that this was so, the Seneschal's lady, who was trying her hardest not to move, cried out:

" To it, then, René, I am fast asleep."

On hearing her utter what he took to be a grave reproach, the page fled, panic-stricken, leaving his books scattered about and his task undone. Whereupon the Seneschal's lady added this sentence to the Litany:

" Holy Virgin, how difficult a thing this baby-making is ! "

At dinner the sweat was running down the page's back when he came to wait on his lord and lady ; but he was mightily surprised when Blanche gave him one of the bawdiest glances that ever came from a woman's eyes ; and right pleasant and powerful it was since it put heart into the child and transformed him into a man of courage. And so that same night, Bruyn having stayed at his judicial duties a little longer than his wont, the page made search for Blanche and found her asleep. Lovely was the dream he made her dream. He took from her that which had been galling her so long, and so lustily did he drench her with baby-seed that she had enough and to spare to make two others. And so the jade, clasping the page's head between her two hands and pressing him to her bosom cried:

" Oh, René, you woke me up ! "

Indeed 'twas a thing nobody in the world could have slept through ; and they came to the conclusion that women-saints must sleep with grim determination. And so as a result of this encounter, and in accordance with that benign propriety which is the great conserver of connubial bliss, the sweet and gracious plumage so becoming to cuckolds, was placed upon the head of the worthy husband without his being in the least suspicious.

Ever after that magnificent entertainment, Madame la Senneschale was only too eager to take her siesta *à la*

française, what time Bruyn was taking his *à la sarrazine.*
Now from these siestas she came to realise how far more
delightful to the taste was the vigour of a young page
than the ineffective titillations of any number of old
seneschals, and of a night she would cower away among
the bedclothes as far as might be from her old husband
whom she found as rank and musty as the Devil himself.
Then, by dint of indulging these fits of sleeping and waking in the daytime, by dint of taking siestas and reciting
litanies, the Seneschal's lady began to feel within her
dainty body the premonitory symptoms of that travail
after which she had hankered for so long; but by this
time she had come to love the process better than the
result.

Now consider too that René was able to read, not only
in books but in the eyes of his fair lady, for whom he
would have cast himself into a raging fire, if such had
been her wish. When they had so enjoyed themselves
generously and to the full, more indeed than one hundred
times at the lowest computation, the Seneschal's lady
began to take thought for the soul of her beloved page
and for his future welfare.   So it befell that one morning
when they were playing touch like two sweet innocents,
Blanche, who always managed to be caught, said to him :

" Come hither, René.   Knowest thou that whereas the
sins that I committed were venial because I slumbered,
the sins that thou hast committed are mortal ? "

" 'Zounds ! Madame, then prithee, tell me where God
will stow all the damned, if you call that sinning ? "

Blanche burst out laughing and kissed him on the
forehead.

" Peace, thou rogue ! 'Tis Paradise that is at stake,
and we must dwell there together, if thou wouldst always
be with me."

" Oh, but my Paradise is here ! "

" Enough of that ! " she said.   " You are a miscreant,
a rascal that takes no heed of what is dear to me ; to wit,

yourself. Know you not that I am with child and that
in no long time it will be as impossible for me to hide
it as to hide my nose? Now what will the Abbot say,
what will my lord say about it? It may be all over with
you, if he flies into a rage. By my advice, little one,
thou wilt go to the Abbot of Marmoustiers to confess thy
sins, begging him to consider what it were best to do
as touching my lord the Seneschal."

"Alas!" said the cunning page, "if I impart to him
the secret of our delights, he will put a stop to our
intercourse."

"Beshrew me, 'tis like enough! But your welfare in
the world to come is to me a thing most precious."

"Dost thou then wish me to go, my sweet one?"

"Yea, verily!" said she, a little quaveringly.

"Well, then, go I will; but fall asleep just once again
so that I may bid thee a fitting farewell."

And the pretty pair recited their farewell litanies as
though they both knew that their love was to come to an
end in the April of its prime. Then, on the morrow,
more for his lady-love's sake than for his own, René de
Jallanges set out for the great monastery.

How for these Sins of the Flesh Grievous Penance
was exacted and how Great Sorrow did befall

"Gracious God!" cried the Abbot, when the page had
told the tale of all his sins, "thou art a partner in a terrible
crime; thou hast betrayed thy lord. Knowest thou, O
most evil-minded page, that, for thy sins, thou wilt burn
in everlasting fire? And knowest thou what it is to be
deprived of heaven merely for the sake of a moment of
vain and fleeting pleasure here below? Unhappy boy!
I see thee cast for ever into the pit of damnation unless
thou payest God, in this world, all that thou owest Him
for so grievous a crime."

And thereupon, the good Abbot, who, certes, was of

the stuff that saints are made of, and exercised great authority throughout Touraine, struck terror into the young man by overwhelming him with an avalanche of admonitions, Christian discourses, reminders of the Church's commandments and countless passages of eloquence, putting himself to as much trouble as some devil might have taken in six weeks to seduce an innocent maid from the path of virtue. And little by little, René, who was warmed by the fervour of innocence, made his submission to the good Abbot. Then the Abbot desiring to make a saintly and ever virtuous man of this child who bade so fair to become an evil one, charged him to go and made a clean breast to the Seneschal of all the wrongs he had done him : then, if he was still alive after that confession, to become a crusader forthwith and straightway to depart for the Holy Land, where he was to remain for fifteen years, warring against the infidels.

" Alas, reverend Father," said he, quite taken aback, " will fifteen years suffice to pay my score for so many pleasures ? Ah, if you only knew : they brought me such delight that a thousand years were not too dear a price."

" God will be merciful," replied the old Abbot. " Go and sin no more. On that condition, *ego te absolvo*. . . ."

Thereupon poor René returned, in deep contrition, to the château of Roche-Corbon ; and lo, the first person he met was the Seneschal, who was superintending the polishing of his arms, morions, brassarts, and the rest of his paraphernalia. He was sitting on a great marble seat in the open air, and was rejoicing his heart with the sight of his harness gleaming in the sunlight, a sight which brought back to his mind the happy days he had spent in the Holy Land, the shrewd thrusts, the wenches, and I know not what besides. When René drew near and fell on his knees before him, the good Seneschal was much amazed.

" What meaneth this ? " said he.

" My lord," answered René, " pray bid these people here withdraw."

And when the servants had retired, the page confessed his misdeed, relating how he had assailed his lady during her sleep, and how, for a surety, he had put her with child, even as the man had done with the saint; and now, he was come, as he had been commanded by his confessor, to throw himself upon the mercy of him whom he had wronged. Having spoken thus, René de Jallanges lowered those beautiful eyes of his, whence all the mischief had sprung, and awaited the issue, bowed down but fearless, his arms drooping at his side, his head uncovered, awaiting his doom, submissive to the will of God. The Seneschal was not so pale that he could not turn paler still; and indeed he went as white as a newly washen sheet, and stood there transfixed with anger. Then the old man, albeit in his veins he had not vital energy enough to make a child, discovered, in that moment of fury, more than enough to unmake a man. With his hairy right hand he grasped his massy club, raised it aloft, brandished it, and whirled it about, with such ease that you would have taken it for something about as heavy as a skittle-ball, with intent to bring it down upon the pale forehead of our René who, knowing full well the wrong he had done his lord, remained quite calm and stretched forth his neck deeming that he was then about to atone for all the sins of his beloved one in this world and the next. But the youthful grace and natural seductiveness of this charming crime pleaded and won compassion in the old man's heart, albeit he was severe. And so, hurling his club afar at a dog which it crushed to death, he shouted :

" A thousand million scorpions bite for all eternity the nether parts of the woman who brought forth the man that planted the oak whereof the chair on which thou madest me a cuckold was wrought. And the like befall them that begat thee, thou cursed whelp of calamity. Get thee to the Devil from whom thou camest. Away with thee, out of my sight, begone out of my castle, out of the country, and linger not an instant longer than thou must; or, I promise thee, I will burn thee to death by a slow fire that shall make thee curse, twenty times to the hour, thy foul misdeed!"

Hearing these preliminary observations of the Seneschal who, so far at least as cursing was concerned, had recovered his lost youth, the page spared him the rest and took to his heels. And 'twas well he did. Bruyn, boiling with rage, dashed with mighty strides into the gardens, cursing at everything that came in his way, laying about him, venting blasphemies. He even overthrew three pans borne by one of his servants who was carrying food to the dogs. Right soon he perceived his deflowered maiden, who was anxiously gazing along the monastery road looking for the page and little knowing that she would never behold him more.

"Ah, ha! my lady, by the Devil's ruddy trident, do you think I am such a nincompoop and a baby as to believe that your passage is so wide that a page may enter there without awakening you? 'Sdeath! 'Zounds! 'Sblood!"

"By my troth," answered she, seeing the game was up, "I felt a right pleasant sensation; but since you had never told me about the matter, methought it was a dream."

Then did the great wrath of the Seneschal melt like snow before the sun, for the mightiest anger of God himself would have faded away at a smile from Blanche.

"Ten thousand devils take your misbegotten whelp! I swear that . . ."

"Nay, nay, swear not at all," said she. "If he be not yours, yet he is mine; and did you not say a night or two ago that you would love anything that came from me?"

Thereupon she let loose such a torrent of pleadings, golden speeches, plaints, upbraidings, tears and all the

SHE BEHELD A MONK, WHO SEEMED
TO BE OUTRAGEOUSLY MALTREATING
A MAIDEN

A VIRGINAL FOOT THAT
DESERVED A KISS

rest of the female armoury, telling him, to begin with, that his lands would not have to revert to the King; that never was child more innocently poured into the mould, and so on and so forth; in a word, she urged her case so persuasively, that the good old cuckold was appeased. Then Blanche, taking advantage of a propitious pause, said:

" And where is the page ? "

" Gone to hell ! "

" What, you have killed him ? "

She went as pale as death, tottered and nearly fell.

Bruyn knew not what would become of him when he saw all the hope of his ancient days like to fall, and he would have bartered his eternal salvation to have given her a sight of the banished page. He sent to seek him; but René was fleeing with all the speed he could command, for he feared lest he should be undone; and he departed for the land beyond the seas in order that he might fulfil his solemn vow. And when Blanche had learnt from the Abbot what penance he had laid upon her well-beloved, she did fall into a deep melancholy, saying from time to time:

" Where is he, poor hapless one, who hath plunged into the midst of danger for the love of me ? "

And this question she would ask again and again, like a child that will let its mother have no peace till it has got the thing it craves for. And as she moaned and lamented thus, the unhappy Seneschal, whose conscience began to prick him, strove to do everything, bating only one, to make Blanche happy; but alas, nothing made up for the sweet attentions of the page.

Howbeit, one day, she had the babe she had so ardently longed for. It may be imagined what a happy day this was for the worthy cuckold; for the father's likeness was graven unmistakably on the features of this little fruit of love. 'Twas a great consolation to Blanche, and she regained a little of that sweet and innocent gaiety

which rejoiced the declining days of the old Seneschal.
Seeing the little one running hither and thither, seeing
how the Countess and her offspring loved to laugh and
play together, he came, in the end, to love the child himself, and would have been very wroth if anyone had not
believed he was the father.

Now, since the adventure of Blanche and her page had
never leaked out beyond the castle, it was held, throughout all the land of Touraine, that Messire Bruyn still
possessed the wherewithal to make a child. All unsullied
remained the reputation of Blanche, who, with the
quintessence of good sense she drew from the reservoir
of feminine wisdom, realised how needful it was to conceal the venial sin with which her child was covered.
Therefore she showed herself prudent and well-behaved,
and was accounted by all a veritable piece of virtue. Then
in order to profit by it, she made trial of her husband's
generosity. And, though she would not give him leave
to go farther than her chin, seeing that she still looked
upon herself as belonging to René, Blanche in return for
the favours which the old man bestowed upon her,
fondled him, smiled on him, kept him happy, pampering
him in all those pleasant ways employed by women who
deceive their husbands. And all went so well that
the Seneschal would not entertain the idea of departing
this life, but settled himself in his chair ; and the longer
he lived, the more enamoured he became of life. But at
last, one night he passed away without knowing whither
he was going ; for he said to Blanche :

" Oh, ho ! my beloved, I cannot see thee now. Can
it be that the night has come ? "

He died the death of the just, and well had he merited
it, because of his good works in the Holy Land.

After her lord's decease, Blanche lived a life of deep
and sincere mourning, weeping for him as a daughter
weeps for a father. She passed her days in sadness and
would not lend an ear to the seductive music that sang to

her of a second marriage. Wherefore she was much belauded by righteous folk who knew not that she had a husband in her heart and that she lived in hope. Howbeit, for the most part, she was a widow both in fact and feeling, for that being without tidings of her friend the crusader, the poor Countess believed him dead; and when some nights in her sleep, she beheld him sore stricken with grief and lying helpless afar off, she awoke in fear. Thus she lived fourteen years nursing the memory of one single day of happiness. At length, one day when she had round about her certain ladies of Touraine, and they were all talking together after dinner, behold her little boy, who was then about thirteen and a half and resembled René more closely than a child should resemble his father, having nothing of Bruyn about him but the name, behold, I say, this little one, grave and comely like his mother, came running in from the garden, sweating, heated, breathless, overturning everything that came in his way, as children will do, and running straight to his beloved mother, flung himself into her lap, and, breaking in upon the talk, shouted :

"Oh, Mother! I've something to tell you. Out in the courtyard there I have seen a pilgrim who clasped me to him very tight."

"Ha!" cried the châtelaine, hastening to one of her servants whose duty it was to attend the young Count and watch over his precious days, "I forbade you ever to leave my son in the hands of a stranger, even if he were the holiest man in the world. You will quit my service. . . ."

"Alas, my lady," answered the old squire, quite crestfallen, "this stranger wished him no ill, for he wept and kissed him tenderly."

"He wept?" she exclaimed. "Ah then, 'tis his father!"

So saying she leaned her head down upon the chair on which she had been sitting and which, as you may well guess, was the chair whereon she had sinned.

Hearing her strange exclamation, the ladies were so taken aback that, at first, they did not see that the Seneschal's lady was dead; and none ever knew whether her death was brought about by grief at the departure of her lover who, faithful to his vow, would not look upon her; or whether by great joy at his return and the hope of procuring the removal of the interdict, which the Abbot of Marmoustiers had laid upon their love. And great was the mourning that followed her decease, for the Sire de Jallanges lost his wits when he saw his lady laid in the ground, and became a monk at Marmoustiers, which, in those days, was by some called Maimoustiers, as who should say *Maius monasterium*, the greatest monastery, and in truth it was the finest in the whole of France.

THE KING'S MISTRESS

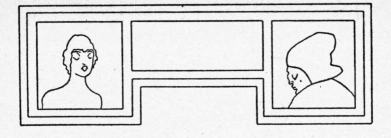

THE KING'S MISTRESS

ONCE upon a time there lived a goldsmith who had his dwelling in the forge hard by the Pont au Change. His daughter was much talked of throughout Paris by reason of her great beauty and was, above all things, held in high repute for her good behaviour. And it so came to pass that many laid siege to her in the manner usual with lovers; and some of them would have gone the length of making over money to the father in order that they might have the aforesaid damsel for true and lawful spouse. Whereat he rejoiced more than words can tell.

Now one of his neighbours, an advocate in parliament who, by dint of selling his jaw to his fellows, had enriched himself with as many estates as a dog has fleas, took it into his head to make offer to the goldsmith of a mansion, if only he would give his consent to the marriage which he had so much at heart. Whereupon the goldsmith did not think twice. He handed him his daughter, caring not a whit that the fur-lined hood contained a face like a monkey's, that the teeth in his jaws were few, and those few loose; and never so much as smelt him, though he reeked and stank like all justiciars who vent their eloquence on the Paris dunghills.

No sooner did the fair damsel clap eyes on him, than she straightway exclaimed:

" God-a-mercy, I want none of him ! "

" That will not suit me ! " said her father, who was

75

already in love with his new house. " I give him to you for a husband. Make the best of it between you. The affair henceforth rests with him, and 'tis his business to make himself pleasing in your sight."

" Sits the wind in that quarter ? " said she. " Well, then, before obeying you, I'll tell him to his face how the matter stands."

And that same evening, after supper, when the lover began to tell her how he was on fire with love for her, declaring his passion and promising that she should lack for nothing for the rest of her days, she answered him shortly thus :

" My father has sold you my body ; but if you take it, I promise you will make a strumpet of me, for I would rather give myself to the passers-by than to you. I swear to you a most unmaidenly oath : I promise you a disloyalty that death alone shall terminate ; your death or mine."

Then she fell a-weeping after the manner of all wenches before they get used to the bit. For afterwards they weep no longer with their eyes. The worthy advocate took this behaviour to be the sort of lure and bait whereof women are wont to make use to make the fire of love burn still more fiercely, and to convert the homage of their suitors into dowries, marriage settlements, and other bridal perquisites. Wherefore the sly fellow paid no heed to them and laughed at the fair damsel's vapourings, saying :

" When shall the wedding be ? "

" To-morrow, if you will," she answered ; " for the sooner I am married the sooner shall I be able to have my gallants and to live the joyous life of those who give their love to whom they will."

Thereupon, this mad advocate, like a finch caught in a booby trap, goes his ways, makes his preparations, babbles at the law courts, trots off to Doctor's Commons, gets him a licence, puts the matter through with greater

RENÉ DE JALLANGES LOWERED
THOSE BEAUTIFUL EYES OF HIS

expedition than he had ever displayed in any other case; for his head was full of the beautiful damsel. Meanwhile the King had returned from a long journey, and hearing everyone in his Court talking of nothing save this beautiful girl, who had refused a thousand golden crowns from one suitor, haughtily disdained another, and who, in a word, would put herself beneath the yoke for no man and rejected all the eligible youths who would have made God a present of their share of Paradise if only they could have enjoyed the favours of this fair dragon for a single day—hearing, I say, all this, the good King, being mightily fond of such game, went forth into the city, betook himself to the forge by the bridge, made his way into the goldsmith's shop in order to purchase jewels for the lady of his heart, but really to bargain for the most priceless gem in the shop. The King found nought to please him among the jewellery, and at last the good goldsmith fell to searching in a hidden tray for a big white diamond to shew unto His Majesty.

"My sweet one," said he to the fair maiden, what time her sire had his nose buried in the tray, "you were never made to sell jewels, but rather to receive them, and if among all the gems that I see before me, I were given leave to choose, I know one here which everyone is mad about; one which pleases me mightily, one whose submissive slave I shall ever be; one for whom the Kingdom of France were all too small a ransom."

"Ah, Sire," answered the fair one, "I wed me to-morrow; but if you will give me the dagger that hangs at your girdle, I will defend the flower of my virginity and keep it for you so as to obey the Gospel wherein it is written, 'Render unto Cæsar the things that are Cæsar's.'"

Straightway the King handed her the little poniard, and her gallant reply made him so deeply in love with the girl, that he lost his appetite in consequence. He took steps to have his new sweetheart lodged in one of

G

his great houses in the rue de l'Hirundelle. And now
behold our advocate in a mighty hurry to bridle his filly!
His rivals look on in a rage, as he leads his bride home
amid the ringing of bells and the crashing of music.
And there was feasting enough to give one the diarrhœa.
At night, when the dancing was over, he betook him
to the room in his dwelling, where he expected to find
the fair damsel in bed. Alas, she was a fair damsel
no longer, but a little hell-cat, a proper she-devil.
She refused point-blank to get into the lawyer's
bed, and was sitting in front of the fire, nursing her
anger and her grievances. The good husband, quite
taken aback, fell on his knees before her, begging and
praying her to enter the lists for love's first tourney.
But she answered never a word; and when he essayed
to lift her petticoat, so that he might, at least, catch a
glimpse of what had cost him so dear, she dealt him a
blow hard enough to break the bones in his body, and
still kept silence. The lawyer entered into the spirit of
the game, which he sought to bring to an end in the
manner you wot of. And he played valiantly, and in
good faith, receiving some hard knocks from the spiteful
wench. At last, by dint of groping and tearing and
driving straight ahead, he tore now a sleeve, now her
skirt, and at last managed to get his hand on the longed-
for goal. Whereat the fair one flew into a mighty
passion, sprang to her feet, and drew forth the King's
dagger, shouting:
"What would you have of me?"
"I would have all," was his reply.
"And a nice sort of whore I should be, to give myself
against my will. If you thought that you would find
the way open to my virginity, you made a great mistake.
See, here is the King's dagger. I will kill you with it,
if you dare come nigh me!" So saying, she took up a
piece of charcoal, still keeping her eye fixed on the
lawyer. Then she drew a line along the floor, saying:

" Behold the boundaries of the King's dominions. Enter not within them. If you pass beyond them, you are dead."

The lawyer, in no mood for amorous dalliance with this dagger, knew not what to do, but while he was listening to the cruel verdict, for which he had had to pay the costs, the good husband saw, through the rents in her garments, such an enticing sample of rounded thigh so white and so fresh, and such a lovely lining stopping up the holes in the dress, *et cetera*, that it seemed to him sweet to die, if by dying, he might only taste thereof. And straightway, he rushed into the King's domain, saying:

" What care I for death ? "

And of a truth, he flung himself upon her with such force that the fair damsel fell with some violence on the bed. But she never lost her wits, and defended herself so nimbly, that the lawyer could no more than touch his prey. And even so, she cut a goodly rasher along his spine. The wound was not mortal, and he deemed not he had paid too dearly for his irruption into the King's dominions.

And once more he returned to attack the royal preserves. The beautiful damsel, whose head was full of the thoughts of her King, was not a whit moved by this great love, and said gravely:

" The moment you come near to capturing *that* in your pursuit of me, it is not you, but myself that I shall slay."

So wild was her look, that she struck terror into the poor man. He sat him down and bewailed his evil chance, and spent the first night—so happy to those whose love affairs go well—in lamentations, prayers, interjections, and all manner of promises, as for example: how she should be waited upon; how she might squander and spend to her heart's content; wallow in money; be a great lady with vast estates; and, finally, if she would suffer him to break a lance in Love's honour, he would absolve her from all else and depart this life in such manner as it might suit her to ordain.

But she, fresh as ever, told him in the morning, that she would allow him to die; but that was the sole favour she could grant him.

" I have never deceived you at all," said she. " And now, contrary to all the vows I made, I give myself to the King, and make you a present of the passers-by, the lewd fellows and carters with whom I threatened to make you a cuckold."

Then when the day was come, she donned her petti-coats and nuptial vesture, waited patiently till her worthy husband, whose advances she had rejected, should depart from the house to attend to some client's business, and then made her way, with all speed, into the city, seeking for the King. But she did not fare farther than you may shoot an arrow from a bow, because her lord the King had set a servitor to watch for her, and he was pacing round and round the house. And straightway, he accosted the bride, who was still in all her nuptial finery, and said to her:

" Are you not looking for the King ? "

" Yea," said she.

" Well, I am your best friend," said the cunning fellow and subtle courtier; " I ask your aid and pro-tection, as I will give you mine."

Thereupon he told her what manner of man the King was; how it behoved one to take him; that he would be mad with love one day, and the next, never utter a word; and all about this, and all about that; that she would have to be well attired, beautifully adorned; but that she should keep the King within bounds; in short, he spoke to such good purpose on the way, that he had made her a most accomplished strumpet by the time she reached the hôtel de l'Hirundelle, which Madame d'Estampes afterwards made her abode.

The poor husband wept like a dying stag when he returned home and found his fair wife no longer there; and straightway he fell into a deep melancholy. His brother lawyers heaped as much mockery and shame upon him as Saint Jacques gets honours in Compostella. But the cockbird fretted and withered so lamentably in his grief, that at last the others were fain to give him consolation. So these behooded pedants, with subtle chicanery, laid it down that the grief-stricken worthy was not a cuckold, because his wife had, from the first, refused to joust with him. And if the bestower of horns had been any other than the King, they would have undertaken to dissolve the marriage. But the husband was nearly dying of love for this wanton of his, and so he abandoned her to the King, trusting that one day he would have her for himself, for he deemed that a night with her was not too dear at the price of a lifelong shame. A man must indeed be in love to do such a thing as that. But he was for ever thinking of her, neglecting his cases, his clients, his robberies and everything. He wandered about the Courts of Justice like a miser looking for his lost treasure, careworn and hollow-cheeked. Aye, and one day he pissed on a counsellor's robe, thinking he was against the wall where the advocates are wont to let flow their eloquence. Howbeit the beautiful girl was loved, morning and night, by the King, who could not assuage his longing for her; for in the matter of love-making, she had special taking ways with her, knowing how to kindle the fire as well as how to quench it. To-day she would keep him at arms' length; to-morrow, caress and fondle him; never the same for an hour together, with a thousand fantasies at her command. Yet, at bottom, her heart was kind, and she knew her business as no one else knew it, smiling of countenance and fertile in all manner of gambols and little tempting tricks.

A lord of Bridoré killed himself for her because it was

denied him to taste of her love, even though he offered
her his demesne of Bridoré in Touraine.   But of those
brave men of Touraine, who would barter an estate for
a bout with the lance of love, there are none left now-
adays, and for that her confessor imputed to her the
blame for the death of the said lord, she vowed in secret
to herself that, although she was the King's leman, she
would in future accept the demesnes thus offered, in
order that she might save her soul.   Thus it was she
laid the foundations of that great fortune which won for
her much consideration in the city.

But in this way she saved the lives of many noble
gentlemen, playing her part so well and drawing so
skilfully upon her imagination that the King never suspected the aid she was giving him in compassing the
happiness of his subjects.   And in sooth, he loved her
so dearly, that she might have made him believe that
upstairs was downstairs ; which it was easier to do with
him than with any other man, since in this hôtel de
l'Hirundelle the King was always a-bed, so little was he
able to distinguish upstairs from down ; and he was for
ever rubbing her as if he were fain to discover whether
the beautiful material of which she was made would
ever wear out.   But, poor dear man, it was only himself
that he wore out, for he died of love.   Although she
took heed never to give herself but to noblemen, the
most considerable at the Court, and though her favours
were as rare as miracles, her envious rivals averred that
for ten thousand crowns an ordinary gentleman might
taste of the joys of a King, which assertion was utterly
and entirely false, seeing that at the time of her rupture
with her lord, when he levelled this reproach against
her, she answered proudly :

" I abhor, I execrate, I cry thirty thousand to those
who have put such a nonsensical idea into your head.
I have never had any man who did not pay down more
than thirty thousand crowns for me at the entrance."

The King, angered as he was, could not forbear to smile, and kept her with him a month longer, in order to silence the scandal-mongers. At last the demoiselle de Pisselieu took it into her head that she could not be lady and mistress of the King until she had compassed her rival's ruin. But many a woman envied her such ruin, for she next wedded a young lord. He too was happy with her, for she still had love and fire enough, and to spare, for such as erred from too much innocence. But to resume. One day, as the King's sweetheart was faring about the city, in her litter, in order to purchase laces, shoes, collarets, and other articles of Love's armoury, being so fair and well attired that all who saw her, particularly the clergy, believed that the heavens had opened, behold, her husband encounters her face to face hard by the Croix du Trahoir. She, who was just about to thrust her dainty foot out of the litter, quickly drew back her head as though she had seen an adder. She was a good wife, for I know some who would have passed by, head in air, to flout their husbands, showing great contempt for their conjugal authority.

" What ails you ? " asked M. de Lannoy, who as a mark of respect was accompanying her.

" Oh, nothing," said she in a low tone ; " but that man going along there is my husband. Poor man, he's terribly altered. He once used to look like a monkey, but now, I think, he is the image of Job."

The unhappy advocate stood there dumbfounded, feeling as though his heart were being riven asunder when he saw that dainty foot and the wife he loved so dearly.

Seeing his plight, the Sire de Lannoy addressed him in a tone of angry hauteur, and said :

" Because you are the lady's husband, is that any reason why you should block her passage ? "

At this, she burst out laughing and the worthy husband, instead of slaying her bravely, wept as he heard that laugh which cleft him asunder, head, heart, soul, and everything, so that he nearly fell upon an aged citizen who was trying to warm his desires by contemplating the royal sweetheart. The sight of this lovely flower, whom he had had in bud, which was then in full bloom and sweetly perfumed, and her white and lovely bosom, her fairylike form—all this did but increase the lawyer's sufferings and made him more madly in love with her than any words can tell. And one must know what it is to be drunk with love for a woman who refuses to give herself, in order to realise how mad this poor man was. Even so, it is rare for a man to be as red-hot as he was. He swore that life, fortune, honour— all might go by the board—but that, once at any rate, he would be flesh to flesh with her and that he would make such a mighty feast of love that, peradventure, he would slip his codlings and his kidneys. All night long he kept saying to himself, " Yes ! Yes ! I *will* have her ! I will have her ! God's death, am I not her husband ? What the devil ! " Thus he kept on raving, banging his forehead and striding incontinently up and down.

Now in this world of ours there sometimes happen coincidences so strange that narrow-minded folk refuse to credit them, because they seem to be supernatural ; but men of lofty imagination hold them to be true because it would not be possible to invent them. To this order of things belongs the event that befell the poor advocate the very day after he had so bitterly chewed the cud of unrequited love. A certain client of his, a man of great name, who from time to time had the entrée to the King's society, came betimes to inform our worthy husband that he needed a large sum of money without delay, as much, indeed, as twelve thousand crowns. Whereupon the wily man of law replied that twelve thousand crowns are not to be picked up at the street corner as easily as other things you may find there ; and

that it was necessary, in addition to sureties and guarantees
for the payment of interest, to discover a man who had
twelve thousand crowns he didn't know what to do with,
and that, big city though it was, there were few such
men in Paris, and delivered himself of a lot more of
such claptrap as these cunning worthies are wont to put
forth.

" By my troth, Monseigneur, this creditor of yours
must be greedy and extortionate," quoth he.

" Aye, in sooth," replied the nobleman ; " 'tis to do
with the King's sweetheart. Breathe not a word of the
matter, but to-night, in return for twenty thousand crowns
and my estate at Brie, I am going to take her measure."

At this the lawyer grew pale, and the courtier perceived that he had made a false move. As he was only
just back from the wars, he did not know that the King's
lovely mistress had a lawful husband.

" You look ill ! " said he.

" I'm feverish," answered the financier. " But," he
went on, mastering his emotion, " is it to her that you
are handing over the contracts and the money ? "

" Aye, marry, is't."

" And who is the bargainer ? She likewise ? "

" No," answered the nobleman ; " but these major
and minor arrangements are carried out through a
serving-wench who is by far the cleverest lady's-maid
that ever was. She is keener than mustard, and she
gets some very handsome pickings out of these nights
stolen from the King."

" There is a usurer of my acquaintance who could
accommodate you ; but nothing will be done, and of
the twelve thousand crowns you will touch not a single
farthing, unless the chambermaid come to receive the
price of this commodity which is so great an alchemist ;
for 'tis God's truth that it transmutes flesh into gold."

" Oh, you'll have a good time if you make her give
you a voucher," answered the nobleman with a laugh.

The serving-woman duly presented herself at the house of the lawyer, who had asked the nobleman himself to bring her. And behold, the lordly ducats were well and truly ranged like so many nuns filing off to Vespers. They were all set out upon a table and would have brought a smile to the features of an ass about to be gelded, so fair and glittering were the brave, the noble, the shining piles. But it was not for asses to contemplate that the worthy lawyer had arranged this fair display. The little serving-woman licked her lips very greedily and curtsied low before the rows of crowns; seeing this, the husband whispered in her ear words that simply sweated gold:

" All this is for you! "

" Oh! " said she, " I've never before been paid such a price as that! "

" My sweet," answered the dear man, " you can have it without taking the impression of my seal."

Then twisting her about a little, he said:

" What, hasn't your client told you what my name is, eh? No! Well, then, know that I am the true and lawful husband of the lady whom the King has debauched, and whose serving-woman you are. Take him these crowns, and then return to me. I will hand you over yours on terms you will find to your taste."

The wench banished her alarms and was mighty curious to know how she was going to earn twelve thousand crowns without yielding herself to the lawyer. So she was back again in no time.

" Ah, ha, sweetheart mine! " said the lawyer. " Here be twelve thousand crowns. Now with twelve thousand crowns, one may buy estates, men, women, and the consciences of, at least, three priests; so, methinks, for these twelve thousand crowns, I ought to have you body and soul and entrails into the bargain. Now I shall trust you—in true lawyer fashion—giving, ever giving. I want you to go straightway to the nobleman who thinks my wife is going to give him of her love to-night.   Bamboozle him and tell him that the King is coming to sup with her and that, for to-night at all events, he must indulge his fancy somewhere else.   In this way, I shall take his place and the King's as well."

" And how ? " she asked.

" Oh ! " he answered, " I've bought you, lock, stock, and barrel ; and in about as long as it takes you to give two winks at this money, you will find out some plan to get me into bed with my wife.   For in doing a thing like that, you commit no sin.   Is it not a pious act to labour at consummating the union of a husband and wife who have hitherto only joined hands before the priest ? "

" By my troth, now, you shall come to it ! " said she. " After supper the lights will be out and you can slake your passion on my lady to your heart's content provided you say not a word.   Fortunately, at these moments of delight, she utters more cries than words, and puts her questions by gestures rather than by speech, for she is exceeding modest and likes not libidinous talk as do the ladies of the Court."

" Oh," said the lawyer, " come take the twelve thousand crowns, and I promise you twice that sum if I obtain by stratagem the treasure that belongs to me by right."

Thereupon they arranged time, place, signal, and everything ; and the wench departed in good company, carrying off the precious coins, dragged one by one from widows, orphans and others, which coins were now all bound for the little place wherein everything melts away ; even our life, which likewise issues from it.   Now behold our lawyer shaves, scents himself, puts on his finest linen, abstains from onions so that his breath may smell sweet, plucks up his courage, trims himself up, and does everything an ill-favoured scab of a lawyer could do to make himself look like a gentleman.   He tries to act the dandy; does his best to cut a dash, and endeavours to disguise his ugly face. But do what he may, he still smells like a musty lawyer.

And swiftly and tightly, he put his rustic cripsimen round his belly-part which prevented any dilatation. Now our crafty gentleman deemed himself the handsomest beau in the world, whereas of all its vermin, he was the filthiest. Well, to cut a long story short, he donned his lightest clothes, though the cold gripped him like a hempen rope, and went forth, making as quickly as possible for the rue de l'Hirundelle. There he hung about a weary while, but just when he was beginning to think they had sold him a packet, the lady's-maid came and opened the door, and the worthy bridegroom slipped in mighty pleased to find himself in the royal abode. The servant led him cautiously to a cupboard near the bed in which his wife lay, and through the chinks he could see her in all her beauty, for she took off her clothes before the fire and put on her robe of battle which was so thin, you could see everything beneath it. Then, thinking she was alone with her maid, she began to deliver herself of the sort of prattle which women usually indulge in when they are about their toilet.

" Am I not worth a good twenty thousand crowns to-night ? And are these not lovely enough for a château in Brie ? "

So saying, she gently raised a pair of outposts, firm as bastions, and well able to endure many an onslaught, seeing how furiously they had already been attacked without growing soft.

" My shoulders alone are worth a kingdom ! " she said. " I defy the King to make their like. But, God knows, I am beginning to weary of this calling. When you're always performing, the pleasure grows stale."

The maid smiled, and the fair lady added :

" I should like to see you in my place."

This only made her laugh the more, and she answered :
" Hist, Mademoiselle ! *He* is there."
" He ? Who ? "
" Your husband."
" Which one ? "
" The real one."
" Hush ! " said the lady.
And the lady's-maid, anxious to keep her mistress's favour as well as the twelve thousand crowns, told her the whole story.

" Oh well, he shall have his money's worth," said the lawyer's wife. " I'll see that he has a merry time of it. If he touches me, may I lose my beauty and grow as ugly as a pedlar's monkey. You shall push and thrust with him in bed instead of me, and see to it that you earn your twelve thousand crowns. But tell him, he will have to pull his breeches on betimes in the morning, so that I may not discover the subterfuge, and then, a little before daybreak, I'll come and lay myself beside him."

Meanwhile the luckless husband was shivering and his teeth were chattering with cold. So, pretending to be looking for something in the linen-cupboard, the maid went back to him and said :

" Keep yourself warm in your desire. Madame is preparing for great things to-night, and you will be royally served. But wreak your passion on her in silence, or I shall be undone."

At last, when the worthy husband was completely frozen, the torches were extinguished and the maid whispered softly between the curtains to the King's sweetheart that the nobleman was there. Then she herself got into the bed and the fair lady went out, as if she had been the maid. The lawyer issued from his chilly hiding-place and nestled down between the sheets thinking to himself :

" Ah, how good it is ! "

In truth, the lady's-maid gave him a hundred thousand crowns' worth, and the good man realised the difference there is between the profusion of a royal house and the niggardly entertainment of a bourgeois establishment. The maid, laughing softly to herself, played her part to a marvel, regaling the man of law with soft moans, and many a turn and twist and convulsive leap like a carp fresh landed on the grass, and murmured little " oh's " and " ah's " that dispensed her from more explicit observations. And many as were the demands she made on him, he answered them all in generous measure, till at last he fell asleep like an empty pouch, but before he had finished with her, wishing to preserve a memento of this delicious night of love, he took advantage of one of the lady's capers, to pull out a wisp of hair from I cannot tell where (since I was not present), and kept this precious pledge of the girl's hot valour in his hand. Next morning, at cock-crow, the King's mistress slipped in beside her husband and pretended to be asleep. Then the maid came and tapped gently on the happy man's forehead, whispering in his ear:

" The time is up. Pull on your breeches and be off ! 'Tis morning."

The good man, sore unwilling to leave his treasure, insisted on giving one last fond look at the source of his vanished bliss.

" Oh, ho ! " exclaimed he, " the hair I have here is fair, and that is dark."

" What have you done ? " said the maid. " Madame will see where you have robbed her."

" But look, I tell you ! "

" Well," she answered with a contemptuous air, " don't you know, Mr. Knowall, that things which are uprooted fade and lose their colour ? "

So saying, she flung him outside ; and she and her mistress burst out laughing. The story got abroad. The poor lawyer, whose name was Féron, died of grief and rage when he realised that he was the only man who never had his wife; while she, who came to be known as la Belle Féronnière, married, when she had left the King, the young Count of Buzançois.

And when she was an old woman, she used to tell the story of this little trick and laughed about it, for she could never abide the smell of that lawyer fellow.

From all this we learn never to grow too deeply attached to women who refuse to bear our yoke.

THE LAWYER, IN NO MOOD FOR AMOR-
OUS DALLIANCE WITH THIS DAGGER

THE DEVIL'S HEIR

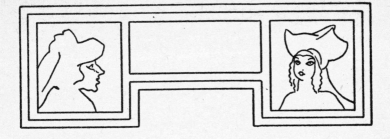

THE DEVIL'S HEIR

ONCE upon a time there was a good old Canon of Notre Dame in Paris who dwelt in a fine house of his own near Saint Pierre aux Bœufs within the precincts. This same Canon, when first he came to Paris, was just an ordinary priest, naked as a sheathless dagger. But, seeing that he was a well-set-up man, generously endowed by nature, indeed so sturdy and stalwart that, if need were, he could do several men's work without overtaxing his powers, he devoted himself, with great energy, to hearing the confessions of the ladies; giving to the melancholy sweet absolution; to the morbid, a dram of his balm; to all, some succulent tit-bit. So renowned was he for his discretion, his benefactions, and other ecclesiastical qualities, that he numbered many Court ladies among his penitents.

Now, in order not to awaken the jealousy of the authorities, such as husbands and others; in a word, to endue with sanctity his benevolent and profitable ministrations, the Maréchale Desguerdes presented him with a bone of Saint Victor, by virtue of which bone, all the miracles of the Canon were carried out. The inquisitive were told,

"He has a bone that cures of every ill."

Of this no one could complain; for it were unseemly to harbour suspicion of relics. Beneath the shelter of his cassock, the good priest enjoyed the best of reputations;

that of a man of valour under arms. So he lived like a king, coining money with his sprinkler and turning holy water into good wine. Moreover, he always figured advantageously in the accounts of the testamentary notaries, or in caudicils, which some people erroneously spell codicils, whereas the word is derived from *cauda*, as who should say the tail, or appendix, of the legacy. Finally, the worthy shaveling would have been made an archbishop, if he had said, were it only in jest, that he wanted a mitre just to keep his top-knot warm. But as it was, of all the benefices offered to him, he only chose an ordinary canonry, so that he might continue to enjoy the delectable profits of his confessorship. But a day came when the courageous Canon found his back was wilting, for you see he was full sixty-and-eight years old, and, in truth, he had worn out many a confessional. Now, when he bethought him of all his good works, he deemed he had a right to cease from his apostolic labours, more especially as he possessed about a hundred thousand crowns which he had earned by the sweat of his body. From that day forth, he only confessed women of high lineage and the pick of their sex. Thus it was currently said, at Court, despite the efforts of the best of the younger clerics, that there was still only one man who could thoroughly whiten the soul of a lady of standing, and that was the Canon of Saint Pierre aux Bœufs. At last, by the process of nature, the Canon became a handsome nonagenarian, very snowy as to the poll. His hands were shaky, but he was as sturdy as a tower. He had spat such a deal without coughing, that now he had come to coughing without spitting. He never rose from his seat, though, in his day, he had stood up so often for humanity. But he drank freely, ate heartily, said nothing and displayed all the characteristics of a very-much-alive Canon of Notre Dame. But, seeing the immobility of the Canon, and the stories of his evil living, which for sometime past had been current among the ever-ignorant lower orders; seeing too, the quiet seclusion of his life, his flourishing health, his green old age, and other things too long to describe, there were some folk who, from their love of the marvellous, or in order to injure our holy religion, went about saying that the real canon had died long ago, and that for upwards of fifty years the Devil had had lodgings in the monk's body. Indeed it seemed to his former customers that only the Devil, by the great heat at his command, could have supplied the hermetical distillations which they remembered they had so abundantly obtained from their good confessor who, in very sooth, always seemed to have the Devil inside him. But as this same Devil had been notoriously cooked and ruined by them, and as he would not have put himself out for a queen of twenty summers, thoughtful people who were not totally devoid of sense, and disputatious folk who would argue about anything, and others who would look for fleas on the pate of a bald man, enquired why the Devil should want to take on the semblance of a canon, go to Notre Dame at the hours appointed, and not stick at swallowing clouds of incense, tasting holy water, and all manner of other things besides.

To these heretical objections, some answered that he was doubtless anxious to turn over a new leaf; and others, that he retained the semblance of the Canon in order to have the laugh of the three nephews and heirs of the brave old confessor, and to make them wait until the day of their own demise for the ample estate of their uncle, whom they visited every day to see whether his eyes were still open. Truth to tell, they always found his eye very bright and lively, and disturbing as a basilisk's; a sight which made them right joyful, for they dearly loved their uncle—in words. Concerning this matter, a certain old woman would have it that the Canon was the Devil for certain, because two of his nephews, the proctor and the captain, who were coming along with their uncle by night without lamp or lantern, on their way back from supper

at the penitentiary's, had, quite accidentally, run into a
heap of stones that had been collected together to serve
as a base for Saint Christopher's statue. At first the old
fellow saw sparks, but the shouts of his dear nephews, and
the lights which they came to ask for at her house,
brought the old gentleman to his feet again and he stood
up as straight as a quill and as gay as a weaving whorl,
saying that the penitentiary's good wine had given him
courage to sustain the shock; that his bones were very
tough and had stood many a ruder assault than that.
His good nephews, thinking he was dead, were sore
amazed, and saw that it would take them a considerable
time to break up their uncle since, at this game, it was
the stones that got the worst of it. And indeed when
they called him their good uncle, they were well advised,
for he was made of right good stuff. Some spiteful folk
averred that he had found so many of these stones on his
way that he thought it better to stay at home lest he
should die of stone, and that the fear of worse things was
the cause of his retirement.

From all these statements and rumours one thing
emerges, and that is that the old Canon, devil or no devil,
stopped at home and would not die; and that he had three
heirs with whom he lived, together with his sciatica,
kidney troubles, and other things that flesh is heir to. Of
the aforesaid three heirs, one was the scurviest blade that
had ever issued from a woman's womb, and he must
have given her a rough time when he broke his shell,
since he came forth fully furnished with teeth and
bristles. When he ate, he ate in both tenses of the verb;
that is to say, he laid in enough for the present and the
future; and he had girls for his own use for whom he paid
the piper. He inherited his uncle's strength and staying
power and his skill in using the thing that is frequently
put into commission. In big engagements he aimed at
giving without receiving, which is always the great thing
to strive for in war. But he never spared himself and,

in fact, as he had no other virtue save his bravery, he became captain of a company of doughty lancers, and was a great favourite with the Duke of Burgundy, who recked little what his soldiers did when they were off duty. This particular nephew of the Devil was called Captain Cochegrue, and his creditors—yokels, citizens, and the rest, whose pockets he slit, called him Mau-cinge, since he was as spiteful as he was strong. But his back was disfigured with the congenital infirmity of a hump, and it would never have done to look as if you were going to climb up on to it to find out how far you could see, for he would most certainly have given you your quietus.

The second had studied law, and, through his uncle's influence, had become a good proctor. He pleaded in the Courts, where he undertook the business of the ladies whom his uncle had formerly shriven so faithfully. This one was called Pille-Grue by way of a joke on his real name, which was Cochegrue, like his brother's, the captain. Pille-Grue had a lean, meagre body and seemed to be a very wet blanket ; he had a pale face and a muzzle like a ferret's. Notwithstanding that, he was worth a good penny more than his brother and bore his uncle a modicum of affection. But about two years since, his heart had cracked a little and, drop by drop, his affection had oozed away, so that from time to time, when the weather was damp, he liked to dive into his uncle's breeches and finger in advance the price of that goodly inheritance. He and his brother, the soldier, found their share uncommon small since, faithfully, in law, in fact, in equity, in nature, and in reality, they were constrained to give a third part of the whole to a poor cousin, the son of another sister of the Canon. He being little beloved by the old man, remained in the country near Nanterre, where he was a shepherd. This keeper of beasts, a common chaw-bacon, came to town on the advice of his two cousins, who hoped that by his stupidity, clumsiness and brainlessness, he would be so displeasing to the

Canon, that he would cut him out of his will. So it was that this poor Chiquon (such was the shepherd's name) had been living alone with his old uncle for about a month past, and finding it more profitable to take care of an abbé than to look after sheep, became the Canon's dog, his slave, the crutch of his old age; saying " God keep you," when he parted; " God save you," when he sneezed; and " God preserve you," when he belched. He would go and see whether it was raining, or where the cat was, keeping quiet, listening, talking, letting the old man cough in his face, telling him he was the finest canon there ever had been in the world. All this he did frankly and from his heart, never dreaming that he was slobbering him after the manner of bitches licking their whelps. And the uncle, who didn't need telling which side of the bread the jam was on, rebuffed the poor Chiquon, spun him round like a die. It was Chiquon here and Chiquon there, and he was for ever telling his other nephews that Chiquon would be the death of him he was such a graceless lout. Hearing that, Chiquon tried his hardest to be kind to his uncle and cudgelled his brains to discover how he might best serve him. But as he had a rump shaped like a couple of pumpkins, with broad shoulders, fat limbs, and a slow brain, he looked much more like Silenus than a gentle Zephyr. But the poor shepherd, being a plain simple man, knew not how to remodel himself, so he remained big and fat, waiting for his inheritance to bring down his weight.

One evening the Canon was holding forth on the subject of the Devil and on the sore trials, pains, tortures, *et cetera*, which God was making ready for the damned. The good Chiquon, all ears, opened his eyes as wide as an oven door, when he heard these things, and said he believed none of them.

" How now," said the Canon, " are you not a Christian ? "

" Aye, marry I am ! " replied Chiquon.

CONSUMMATING THE UNION
OF A HUSBAND AND WIFE

ONLY ONE MAN WHO COULD
THOROUGHLY WHITEN THE SOUL
OF A LADY OF STANDING

" Well, there is a paradise for those who do good. Must there not be a hell for those who do ill ? "

" Yes, reverend sir, but the Devil is no use at all. If you had a knave in the house who turned everything upside down, would you not kick him out ? "

" Yes, Chiquon."

" Well, then, Uncle, God would be a simpleton if he permitted to remain in this world, which he has so carefully constructed, an abominable devil whose particular aim it was to ruin everything. Bah ! I will have none of your devils, if there is a good God. Make up your mind to that. I should very much like to clap eyes on that devil. I'm not afraid of his claws."

" Ah, if I thought as you do, I should have no misgivings about those youthful days of mine when I confessed as many as ten women a day."

" Keep on doing it, sir. I assure you 'twill be held highly meritorious conduct in the realms above."

" 'Sblood ! Do you mean that ? "

" I do, your reverence."

" Are you not scared, Chiquon, when you deny the Devil ? "

" I don't care a straw about him ! "

" You'll be punished for those ideas of yours ! "

" Don't you believe it. God will defend me from the Devil, because I hold God to be cleverer than the learned folk do ! "

Just then the two other nephews came in, and recognising from the Canon's voice that he was a long way from hating Chiquon and that the complaints he made concerning him were but tricks to disguise the affection he really entertained towards him, they looked at each other in great amazement.

Then seeing their uncle in jovial mood, they said to him :

" If you make a will, to whom will you leave the house ? "

" To Chiquon."

" And the quit rents of the rue Saint-Denis ? "

" To Chiquon."

" And the freehold of Ville-Parisis ? "

" To Chiquon."

" Why, then," said the captain in his heavy voice,
" Chiquon will get everything."

"No," answered the Canon with a smile, " because,
however carefully I make a will, my estate will go to the
cleverest of the three of you.   So near am I to the world
to come that I can clearly read your destinies."

And the cunning Canon gave Chiquon a look such as a
wanton might give a dandy to entice him into her toils.
The light that shone in his eye illumined the shepherd
who, from that moment had his ears, his understanding
and everything quite clear, and his mind as wide open as a
virgin after the first night.   The proctor and the captain,
taking all this for gospel, made their bows and took their
leave, quite dumbfounded at the Canon's outrageous
intentions.

" What think you of Chiquon ? " said Pille-grue to
Mau-cinge.

" I think, I think," answered the soldier with a growl,
" I think I will hide me in the rue de Hiérusalem and
put his head where his feet ought to be.   He can pick
it up again if he cares to."

" Oh, ho ! " said the proctor ; " your mode of doing
the trick would be recognised and everyone would say,
' That's Cochegrue.'   My idea is to invite him to
dinner.   Afterwards we would play at getting into sacks
in order to see, as they do at the King's, who would
move the quickest, thus accoutred.   Then, having sewn
him up, we would pitch him into the Seine, and tell him
to swim."

" That must be well thought out," answered the
soldier.

" Oh, that's all right," said the lawyer.   " Our cousin

having been consigned to the Devil, we should have all the property between us."

"Good!" said the man-at-arms. "But we must arrange to work together, like the two legs of the same body. For if you have a tongue like silk, I have a body like steel. And daggers are as good as cords, any day. Hark you to that, good brother!"

"Yea," said the lawyer, "the case has been heard. Now, is it to be rope or steel?"

"Eh, Od's bodykins, man. Is it a king we are going to put away? For a simple lout of a shepherd, what's the need of all this palaver? Come now, twenty thousand francs out of the estate to whichever of us cuts his head off first. I shall say to him, from my heart, 'Pick up your head.'"

"And I shall say, 'Swim friend,'" exclaimed the advocate, laughing like the slit of a doublet.

Then off they went to supper, the captain with his wench, the lawyer with the wife of a goldsmith whose paramour he was.

Who was knocked all of a heap? Why, Chiquon. The poor shepherd overheard the plot to kill him, though his two cousins were still walking in the Cathedral yard and talking as softly as a man muttering his prayers in church. So Chiquon was greatly exercised to know whether the words were coming up to him, or whether it was his ears that had gone down to the words.

"Do you hear anything, your reverence?"

"Yes," said the Canon, "I hear the wood a-sweating in the fire."

"Oh, ho!" answered Chiquon, "if I don't believe in the Devil, I believe in Saint Michael, my guardian angel, and I am going whither he calls me."

"Go, my son," said the Canon, "and mind you don't get wet or get your head cut off, for I seem to hear the water trickling, and street ruffians are not always the most dangerous."

At these words, Chiquon was sore amazed and looked at the Canon, who seemed very festive and bright-eyed and very crooked about the feet. But as he had to take steps to ward off the danger that threatened him, he reflected that he would have plenty of time later on to admire the Canon and to pare his nails, so he made off quickly for the town, like a woman briskly trotting along to meet her lover.

The two cousins, having no suspicions concerning the divinatory powers with which shepherds are occasionally visited, had often discussed their secret affairs in his presence, looking on him as a nonentity.

Now, one night, in order to amuse the Canon, Pillegrue had been telling how his mistress behaved when he was clipping her. She was the wife of that goldsmith of his acquaintance, whose head he had embellished with horns chiselled, stained, carved and chased like a prince's salt-cellar. According to him, the good lady was a frisky commodity, bold in the onset and so prompt that she could bring off the trick while her husband was coming up the stairs, without turning a hair, devouring the article as if she were gobbling a strawberry, her thoughts always dwelling on the fray; always merry and bright; happy as a well-conducted woman who gets all she wants; contenting her husband, to whom she was as dear as his own gullet; delicate as a perfume; and so well had she managed her household affairs and her love-affairs for the past five years, that she had an excellent reputation, the confidence of her husband, the keys of the house, the money, and all.

" And when do you play on this gentle flute ? " asked the Canon.

" Every night. And sometimes I sleep with her."

" How do you manage that ? " enquired the Canon in astonishment.

" Like this. In a little room close by there is a big chest in which I take up my abode. When her worthy husband comes home from visiting his friend the draper, with whom he sups every night, because he often performs a little business with the draper's wife, my mistress pleads a slight indisposition, lets him go to bed by himself and comes to put herself to rights in the room where the chest is. Next day, when my goldsmith is at his forge, I decamp; and as the house has two exits, one on to the bridge and the other on to the street, I always come to the door where the husband is not, on the pretext of talking to him about his cases which I always keep healthy and bright without ever letting them come to an end. It is a most profitable piece of cuckoldry seeing that the minor disbursements and major costs of the proceedings cost him as much as a team of horses that eat their heads off in the stable. He is very fond of me, as it befits a good cuckold to be fond of the man who helps him to dig, water, cultivate and till the natural garden of Venus; and he never does a thing without me."

Now these doings came back into the mind of the shepherd, who was enlightened as though by a flash from his own peril and inspired by that instinct for self-preservation, of which every animal possesses a sufficient stock to carry him to the end of his skein of life. So off went Chiquon, hot-foot, to the rue de la Calandre, where he counted on finding the goldsmith at supper with his gossip. He knocked at the door, was questioned through the grille and, having announced that he was a messenger bearing secrets of state, was admitted to the draper's house. Then coming straight to the business, he caused the merry goldsmith to rise from the table, took him apart, and said to him:

" If one of your neighbours were to embellish your forehead with horns and he were delivered unto you bound hand and foot, would you not pitch him into the river ? "

" Marry, that would I ! " said the goldsmith. " But if you are fooling me, I will make it hot for you."

" Go to," answered Chiquon, " I am one of your friends and am come to inform you that as many times as you have tickled up the wife of the draper here, just so often has your own wife been treated in the same fashion by lawyer Pille-grue ; and if, at this moment, you are minded to go back to your forge, you will find a very good fire there. On your arrival, the gentleman who plies his broom in your wife's you-know-what to keep it clean, will go and tumble into the big clothes chest. Now, give out that I am buying the said chest from you, and I will be on the bridge with a waggon, at your command."

The goldsmith seized his cloak and bonnet, quitted his gossip without a word, and rushed away to his hole like a poisoned rat. He arrives and knocks with vigour. The door is opened ; he rushes in, finds the table laid for two, hears the chest shut to, sees his wife coming out of the love-chamber, and says :

" My sweetheart, the table is laid for two."

" Well, darling, there are two of us, aren't there ? "

" No," said he, " three."

" Is your gossip coming ? " she enquired, looking down over the banisters with an expression of perfect innocence.

" No, I'm speaking of the gossip in the chest."

" What chest ?   Are you in your right mind ?   Where do you see a chest ?   Does one put gossips in chests ? Am I a woman to put gossips in chests ?   Since when have gossips taken up their abode in chests ?   Have you come home mad, that you mix up your gossips and your chests ?   The only gossip of yours I know is Maistre Corneille, the draper ; and the only chest, the chest where we keep our clothes."

" My good wife," said the goldsmith, " a wicked urchin came and told me that you suffered yourself to be bestridden by our lawyer, and that he is in your chest."

" Me ! " said she.   " I can't abide the knavish tribe !
They do their business all awry."

" There, there, my sweet one," answered the goldsmith.   " I knew you were an honest wife, and I certainly do not want to bandy words with you about a
wretched chest.   My informant is a cabinet-maker and I
am selling him the chest which I never want to see in the
house again ; and in exchange for it, he is going to let
me have two nice little ones which are not big enough
to put a baby in.   Thus the spite and gossip of the envious
will die of inanition."

" I am glad to hear it," said she.   " As for my chest,
I care not about it at all and, as it happens, there is
nothing in it now.   Our linen is at the wash.   It will
be quite easy to have the wretched thing carted away to-
morrow morning.   Are you going to have any supper ? "

" No," said he.   " I shall have a better appetite for
supper when this chest is out of the way."

" I see," she answered, " that it will be easier to get
the chest out of the house than out of your head."

" Ho, there !   Hullo ! " cried the goldsmith to his
workmen and apprentices.   " Come down, I say ! "

In the twinkling of an eye, his fellows were on the spot.
The master told them what he wanted done with the
thing, and they had the love-chest out through the hall in
a trice.   But the lawyer finding himself, during the tran-
sit, with his heels in the air—a very unusual attitude for
him—lost his centre of gravity a little.

" Go on," said the wife ; " carry on.   'Tis the lid
shaking."

" Not a bit of it, my sweet, 'tis the bolt."

And now without further discussion, the chest slid
smoothly down the stairs.

" Ho, you waggoner there ! " shouted the goldsmith.

And up came Chiquon, shouting at his mules and
shouting at the lusty apprentices to hoist the chest of
discord on to the cart.

" Hi! Hi! " shouted the lawyer.

" Master, the chest is speaking," said one of the apprentices.

" In what language ? " said the goldsmith, giving him a vigorous kick between two ornaments that luckily were not made of glass. The apprentice doubled up on the stairs and the language of chests ceased to engage his attention. The shepherd, accompanied by the worthy goldsmith, dragged the load to the water's edge, deaf to the lofty eloquence of the loquacious timber ; and having added the weight of a few stones, the goldsmith tipped it over into the Seine.

" Swim, friend," cried the shepherd derisively, as the chest touched the water and dived beneath it like a duck.

Then Chiquon continued his walk along the quay as far as the rue du Port Saint-Landry, near the cloisters of Notre Dame. There he noticed a certain house, recognised the door, and knocked loudly.

" Open," he shouted, " in the King's name ! "

Hearing this summons, an old man, who was none other than the famous Lombard Versoris, hurried to the door.

" Who's there ? " said he.

" I have been sent by the provost to warn ye to keep good watch this night," said Chiquon ; " and he, on his side, will have his archers on the alert. The hunchback, who robbed you, is back in town again. Stand stoutly to your arms, for he is quite capable of relieving you of the rest."

With these words, the worthy shepherd turned on his heel and hastened away to the rue des Marmouzets, to the house where Captain Cochegrue was carousing with Pasquerette, the prettiest wench that ever was and the most fertile in perversity, according to the testimony of all the whores in the town. Her demeanour was so enticing that she would have made heaven itself horn

COMES TO PUT HERSELF TO RIGHTS
IN THE ROOM WHERE THE CHEST IS

mad.   She was as bold as a woman with no virtue left
but insolence.   Poor Chiquon was not a little cast down
as he fared towards the quarter of the Marmouzets.   He
was greatly afraid he would not discover Pasquerette's
house or find the two pigeons roosting together.   But
a good angel brought things to pass exactly as he desired,
and this was the manner of it.   On entering the rue des
Marmouzets, he saw a great number of lights at the
windows, with night-capped heads, and good wenches,
strumpets, charwomen, husbands, damsels, all just out of
their beds and looking at each other as if a robber were
being hauled off to the gallows by torch-light.

" 'Od's-fish, but what's the matter ? " said the shepherd to a citizen, who had hastily taken his stand at the
door with a partisan in his hand.

" Oh, 'tis nothing," answered the worthy.   " We
thought the Armagnacs were descending on the town,
but it's only Mau-cinge belabouring la Pasquerette."

" But where is it ? " asked the shepherd.

" Over there, at the fine house yonder with columns
surmounted by heads of flying toads, very daintily carved.
Do you hear the varlets and the chambermaids ? "

And, in sooth, 'twas nothing but shouts of " Murder !
Help ! Hi ! Come quick ! "   Inside the house it
was raining blows, and you could hear Mau-cinge shouting in his big bass voice, " To hell with the bitch !   You
sing, you jade ?   You want crowns, do you ?   Well, take
that . . . and that ! "   And la Pasquerette was shriek-
ing at the top of her voice, " Oh ! Oh ! He's killing
me ! Hi ! Hi ! "   Then came a great blow with a
sword ; then the heavy thud of the pretty girl's slender
body, followed by a long silence.   After that, the lights
were put out and servants, chambermaids, guests, and
the rest, went back indoors, and the shepherd, who had
arrived in the nick of time, went upstairs with them.
But when they looked inside the lofty room and saw the
broken decanters, the slashed carpets, the tablecloth,

I

with all that was on it, dragged on to the floor, everyone stood petrified with amazement.

The shepherd, resolute, as a man fired by a single idea, opened the door of the beautiful room in which Pasquerette slept and found her all undone, her hair dishevelled, her breasts exposed, lying on her bloodstained carpet; there too stood Mau-cinge, quite bewildered. He was singing very low and didn't know on what note to finish out his anthem.

" Come, come, my little Pasquerette, don't make out you're dead ! Come now, let me patch you up again. Ah, you rogue, dead or alive, you look so pretty with this blood on you, that I really must have you."

So saying, the cunning blade threw her on the bed. But she fell straight and stiff as a corpse cut down from the gallows. Seeing that, her friend thought it was perhaps time to make himself scarce; however, before taking himself off, the sly customer said :

" Poor Pasquerette, how could I have come to murder so good a girl whom I loved so dearly. But yes, I have killed her, that is quite clear; for if she had been alive never would her pretty nipple have hung down like that. Heavens, you would think it was a crown piece at the bottom of a wallet."

Hearing this, Pasquerette opened her eyes and bent her head a little to snatch a glance at her breast which was white and firm; then she was restored to animation with a great slap, which she administered to the captain's cheek.

" That's for speaking ill of the dead ! " said she with a smile.

" And why did he try to kill you, coz ? " enquired the shepherd.

" Why ? Well, to-morrow the police are coming to seize everything there is in the place; and he, who has no more money than virtue, quarrelled with me because I was going to be obliging to a young nobleman who has given his word to save me from the hand of justice."

" Pasquerette, I will break every bone in your body ! "

" Well, well ! " said Chiquon, who had at length been recognised by Mau-cinge; " is that all ? Why, friend, I have got some big sums of money for you."

" Where from ? " said the astonished captain.

" Come here so that I may whisper it in your ear. If some thirty thousand crowns could be picked up after dark in the shadow of a pear-tree, wouldn't you stop to pick them up so that they should not go rotten ? "

" Chiquon, I will kill you like a dog if you are fooling me; and I will kiss you wherever you like, if you will bring me face to face with thirty thousand crowns, even if I had to kill three citizens for them, at the corner of a quay."

" You will not even have to kill so much as a bonnet. This is how it stands. My mistress—this is gospel truth I'm telling you—is servant to the Lombard who lives in the city close to our uncle's house. Well, I have just learned, beyond all shadow of doubt, that the good man left home this morning for the country, and that before he left, he hid a great heap of gold under the pear-tree in his garden, thinking that none but the angels saw him do it. But the maid, who happened to be suffering from a bad attack of toothache and was taking in a breath of fresh air at her window, happened to see the old miser at his task and told me about it, because she loved me. If you swear to let me have a decent share, I will lend you my shoulders to help you on to the wall, and then you will fling yourself on to the pear-tree which is close to the wall. Now, then, do you take me for a clown, a lout ? "

" By Our Lady, no ! You are a true and loyal cousin ; a worthy man, and if you ever have an enemy you want to get rid of, I am there, ready even to kill one of my own friends, for your sake. Henceforth, I am not your cousin, but your brother."

" Come, my love ! " cried Mau-cinge to Pasquerette,
" lay the tables again, wipe away your blood, it belongs
to me ; I pay you for it, and I will give you, my beloved,
a hundred times as much as I have taken from you.
Bring out the best we have ; dry your tears ; adjust
your petticoats ; laugh, I say ; give an eye to the stew, and
we'll resume our evening prayers at the spot where we left
off.　To-morrow, I'll make thee braver than the Queen.
This is my cousin, whom I wish to entertain, even though
we had to throw the house out of window to do it.　We
shall find it all again to-morrow in the cellars.　Come,
let us get on with it."

Thus, and in less time than it takes a priest to say his
Dominus vobiscum, the whole dovecot passed from tears
to laughter, as, a while before, it had passed from laughter
to tears.　These brothels are the only houses where love
is made with the thrusts of a dagger, and where joyous
tempests rage between four walls.　But respectable
ladies know nothing of such things.　Captain Cochegrue was as merry as five-score urchins escaped from
school, and he made his cousin drink deep.　Chiquon
gulped down his liquor in true rustic fashion, played
the drunkard to perfection, delivering himself of endless
absurdities, saying how, on the morrow, he would buy up
Paris ; lend a hundred thousand crowns to the King ; in
short, he emitted such a flow of rubbish, that the captain,
fearing he would make some untoward avowals and deeming him very cracked as to the brain, took him outside
with the laudable intention of ripping him up when the
sharing out process came on, to find out whether he hadn't
got a sponge in his belly, seeing how he had soaked up
an enormous hogshead of Suresne wine.　They went their
way discussing countless theological topics, which they
mixed up very thoroughly, and at last found themselves
just alongside the wall of the garden in which the Lombard's crowns were buried.　Cochegrue, using Chiquon's
broad shoulders as a platform, leapt on to the pear-tree

with the agility of a man expert in storming cities; but
Versoris, who was lying in wait for him, made a notch
in the back of his neck and repeated the process with such
vigour that, in three blows, Cochegrue's head fell to the
ground, but not till he had heard the shepherd shouting
to him in a loud voice:

" Pick up your head, friend."

Thereupon the generous Chiquon, in whom virtue was
receiving its reward, bethought him that it would be wise
to return to the dwelling of the worthy Canon, whose
testamentary dispositions had, by the grace of God, been
so methodically simplified. So he made good use of his
legs and arrived at the rue Saint Pierre-aux-Bœufs and
was soon slumbering like a new-born babe, quite
oblivious now of the meaning of the words first-cousin.

Next day he rose with the sun, as is the wont of shepherds, and came to his uncle's bedroom to find out
whether he was spitting white; whether he was coughing,
and whether he had had a good night's sleep. But the
old housekeeper told him that the Canon, hearing the
bell ringing for the Matins of Saint Maurice, the first
patron of Notre Dame, had piously betaken himself to
the Cathedral, where the whole Chapter were bidden to
dine with the Bishop of Paris. Whereupon Chiquon
made answer:

" Has the Canon taken leave of his senses to go out in
the cold like this to catch a chill and get cold feet? Does
he want to catch his death? I will go and light a good
fire to warm him when he comes back."

And the worthy shepherd betook himself to the room
in which the Canon best loved to sit; but to his great
amazement, he saw him there seated in his chair.

" Ah, ha! What did she mean, the old lunatic
Buyrette? I knew you had too much sense to go and
perch yourself up in your stall as early as this."

The Canon answered never a word. The shepherd,
who, like all contemplative folk, had a fund of hidden

wisdom, was aware that sometimes old men were visited
by trances of second sight, held converse with the essence
of hidden things, and managed to mumble, deep within
them, words of more than superficial import.   Therefore, actuated by a feeling of reverence and by a desire not
to interrupt the Canon's abstruse meditations, he went
and sate himself down at a distance and awaited the conclusion of his reverie, noting, in silence, the length of the
old man's nails which almost seemed as if they were
making holes in his shoes.   Next he carefully scrutinised
his dear uncle's feet and was shocked to observe how
ruddy his legs appeared, how they even reddened his
breeches and seemed all on fire through his hose.

" He is dead," thought Chiquon.

At this moment the door opened, and again he beheld
the Canon, who, with his nose all frozen, had just come
home from church.

" Oh, uncle ! " exclaimed Chiquon, " have you taken
leave of your senses ?   Now you must understand that
you cannot be there at the door, because you are already
here sitting in your chair at the chimney corner, and there
cannot be two such canons as you in the world."

" Ah, Chiquon, there was a time when I would have
given a deal to be in two places at once ; but such a thing
is not given to man ; he would be too happy.   But are
you dazed ?   I am all alone here."

Then Chiquon turned and looked at the chair and, as
you may imagine, was greatly surprised to find it empty.
He went up to it and noticed on the seat a little heap of
cinders from which an odour of sulphur was still rising.

" Ha ! " he exclaimed in accents of wonder ; " I
confess that the Devil has behaved like a gentleman
towards me.   I will pray God for him."

Thereupon he told the Canon the simple story of how
the Devil had amused himself by playing the part of
providence and had done him yeoman's service in helping
him to get rid of his wicked cousins.

This the good Canon greatly admired and well understood, for he still had a deal of good sense and many a time had observed things that did the Devil credit. And the old fellow proceeded to remark that he always found as much evil in the good, as good in the evil, and that, therefore, one should not worry too much about the other world ; the which was a grievous heresy condemned by many a council.

This was how the Chiquons became rich and were able, in these latter days, by reason of their ancestors' fortune, to help in the building of Saint Michael's bridge, where the Devil cuts a very good figure beneath the angel, in memory of the adventure thus truly and historically set down.

THE MERRIE DIVERSIONS OF KING
LOUIS THE ELEVENTH

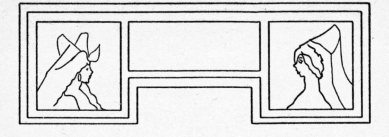

THE MERRIE DIVERSIONS OF KING
LOUIS THE ELEVENTH

KING LOUIS THE ELEVENTH was a right merry soul who dearly loved his little joke, and—save where the interests of his kingly state and the Church were concerned—he was given to good cheer and loved to give chase to little twitterers as well as to connies and other royal game. Therefore, the sorry quill-drivers who have made him out a hypocrite show plainly enough that they never knew him; for he was a good friend, a good jester, and as jovial a fellow as ever lived.

It was he who said, when he was in merry mood, that there were four things excellent and opportune in this life, to wit, keeping warm, drinking cool, standing hard and eating soft. Some folk have slandered him by saying that he consorted with trulls. This is an egregious blunder seeing that his mistresses, one of whom was legitimised, all came of great houses and kept up notable establishments.

He never indulged in wastefulness or profusion; always kept his hand on the substance and, since the oppressors of the common people never got any crumbs from him, he has been slandered by them all. But the real harvesters of the truth know that the King was a good little man in his private life, and very amiable to boot; and before beheading or punishing any of his friends, which he did right freely, they must have sore deceived him,

for his vengeance was always just. Only in our friend
Verville, have I ever read that this worthy sovereign was
once deceived. But to do a thing once is not to make
a habit of it. Moreover, on that occasion, more blame
attached to Tristan, his gossip, than to the King himself.
These are the facts, as narrated by Verville; and I
suspect that he was treating the thing as a joke. I relate
it here because there are some people who are unac-
quainted with the exquisite work of my faultless compatriot. I abridge his narrative and only give the substance of it; the details being more ample, as my learned
readers are aware.

Louis XI had bestowed the Abbey of Turpenay
(whereof mention is made in *Imperia*) upon a gentleman
who, being in enjoyment of the revenue thereof, called
himself Monsieur de Turpenay. Now it chanced that,
the King being at Plessis-lez-Tours, the real abbot, who
was a monk, came and presented himself before the King
and humbly handed him a petition wherein it was set
forth that, canonically and monastically, he was the true
possessor of the Abbey, and that the usurping gentleman
was doing him a grievous and most unjustifiable wrong;
wherefore he besought His Majesty to see justice done
to him. With a nod of his peruke, the King promised
to give him satisfaction. The monk, importunate as
every other animal that wears a cowl, came often to
intercept the King as he rose from table, and His Majesty
being thoroughly sick of such a deluge of monastic holy
water, called to his gossip Tristan and said, " Gossip,
behold here a Turpenay that galls me; see you rid the
world of him." Tristan, taking a habit for a monk or
a monk for a habit, came to the gentleman who was
known to all the Court as M. de Turpenay, and having
accosted him, contrived to take him aside, and button-
holing him, gave him to understand that it was the
King's pleasure that he should die. He did his utmost
to resist the invitation, but there was no means of getting

a hearing. He was delicately strangled between the head and the shoulders until he expired; and three hours later, the gossip informed the King that he was duly distilled. Five hours afterwards, that being the interval after which the souls of the dead return to earth, it happened that the monk entered the room where the King was sitting. When he beheld him, the King was sore amazed. Tristan was present and, summoning him to approach, the King whispered in his ear:

" You have not done as I bade you do."

" Pardon me, Sire, that have I.   Turpenay is dead."

" Eh ! but I meant this monk here."

" Oh, I thought you meant the gentleman ! "

" What then, have you done the deed ? "

" Yea, Sire."

" 'Tis well."   Then turning to the monk he said:

" Come hither, monk."

The monk obeyed.

" Down on your knees ! " said the King.

The poor monk was sore afraid.   But the King said to him :

" Give thanks to God who willed not that you should be slain as I had commanded.   He who possessed your property has been killed.   God has done justice towards you.   Go and pray God for me and budge not from your convent."

This shows how kindhearted was King Louis XI. He might quite well have consigned this monk, the cause of all the misunderstanding, to the gallows.   As for the aforesaid gentleman, he had died in the service of the King.

In the early days of his sojourn at Plessis-lez-Tours, King Louis, not wishing, out of regard for his dignity as King, to disport himself and hold his carousals in his palace (a delicacy of feeling which his successors did not share), fixed his affections on a dame called Nicole Beaupertuys, who was, to tell the truth, the wife of a city merchant. He dispatched the husband to le Ponent and placed the aforesaid Nicole in a house near the Chardonneret close to the rue Quincangrogne, because it was a lonely, unfrequented spot. Husband and wife were thus his devoted servants, and by the latter he had a daughter who died a nun. This Nicole had a beak as sharp as a parrot's. She was generously proportioned and furnished with two fine ample natural cushions, firm to the touch and white as an angel's wings, and for the rest she was known for her fertility in peripatetic resources so that in your dalliance with her you never encountered the same trick twice, so deeply had she studied the beautiful resolutions of the Science, the different ways of accommodating the olives of Poissy, the extension of the sinews and the recondite teachings of the Breviary; all of which gave great delight to the King. She was as gay as a finch, always laughing and singing. She never vexed anybody, which is the distinguishing characteristic of women of this free and open nature, who have always one occupation—to give and to take. The King often went to this house with his friends and boon companions, and in order to escape observation, repaired thither by night without an escort. But as he was mistrustful and afraid of ambuscades, he presented Nicole with the fiercest dogs in his kennel; the sort of fellows that would eat a man alive, without an instant's warning. These royal dogs knew none but Nicole and the King. When the King arrived, Nicole let them loose in the garden. The door of the house was closely barred and shut; the King kept the keys and, in perfect security, abandoned himself, together with his friends, to all manner of amusements, fearing no treachery, laughing to his heart's content, playing all manner of tricks, and getting up some pretty games. On those nights, gossip Tristan kept his eye on the game, and anyone who came to take a stroll on the Chardonneret Mall would have been pretty promptly put in a position

to bless the passers-by with his feet, unless he were
furnished with the King's pass; for Louis XI often sent
for women for his friends, or for people to enjoy themselves by contemplating the amorous subtleties invented
by Nicole or the guests. The people of Tours came
thither to look on at the minor pleasures of the King
who gently enjoined silence upon them, so that no details
of these pastimes were known until after his death. It
is said that the farce of *Kiss my arse* was invented by the
said monarch. I will tell the story of it, even though it
is not germane to the subject of this tale, for it illustrates
the comic and facetious nature of the worthy monarch.
Now in those days there dwelt at Tours three noted
misers. The first was Master Cornelius, and he is
sufficiently well known. The second was named Peccard,
and was a vendor of fiddle-faddles, knick-knacks, and
church ornaments. The name of the third was Mar-
chandeau, a very prosperous wine-grower. These three
men of Tours were the founders of good honest families,
notwithstanding their greedy ways. One night, when
the King was with his mistress, in a mighty good humour,
for he had drunk of the best, fired off his quips, and said
his prayers before Vespers in Madame's own oratory, he
turned to his gossip Le Daim, to Cardinal La Balue, and
to old Dunois who was still a good old war-horse, saying:
"Let us make merry, my friends. And I think
'twould be a pretty comedy to see how a miser would
comport himself before a sack of gold on which 'twere
forbidden him to lay hands. Hullo, without there!"
At this summons, a varlet appeared.
"Go," said the King, "and seek out my treasurer
and bid him bring hither six thousand crowns without
delay. Then go and apprehend my gossip Cornelius, the
stationer of the rue du Cygne, and lastly, old Marchan-
deau, and bring them all three hither in the King's
name."
Then they fell again to drinking and to discussing the

delicate question as to which was to be preferred, a woman with a strong smell or a woman that makes liberal use of soap and water; a woman that is thin or a woman that is well covered. And as these men represented the flower of scholarship, they decided that the best woman was the woman you had beside you, like a dish of mussels all hot, at the very moment when God sent you a pleasing notion to impart to her. The Cardinal enquired which was most precious to a woman, the first kiss or the last. Whereto la Beaupertuys made answer that it was the last, since she knew what she was losing, and that with the first she never realised what she was gaining. While these things were being discussed, and others which have unhappily been lost to us, came the six thousand golden crowns which were worth a good three thousand francs of our present currency, so greatly do we dwindle and diminish in all things. The King gave orders that the crowns should be put upon the table and well lit up. And so they shone like the eyes of the guests which sparkled involuntarily, whereat they laughed against their will. They had not long to wait for the arrival of the three misers, whom the varlet brought in pale and breathless, bating only Cornelius who was acquainted with the whims and fancies of the King.

"Now then, my friends," said Louis, "look well at the crowns on this table here."

And the three citizens devoured them with their eyes; and you may take it that even la Beaupertuys' diamond shone less brightly than their little gimlet eyes.

"All this is yours," said the King.

Whereupon they turned their gaze from the crowns and began to look fiercely at each other, and the guests soon learnt that old apes are more expert in making grimaces than anyone else, for the physiognomies before them became not a little curious, like the faces of cats lapping milk or of girls tasting the joys of marriage.

"There," said the King, "it all goes to whichever of

YOU ARE ALREADY HERE SITTING IN
YOUR CHAIR AT THE CHIMNEY CORNER

you shall say three times to the other two, ' Kiss my
arse,' putting his hand in the gold. But if he is not
grave of mien like a fly that has outraged its neighbour,
if he chances to smile as he utters this quip, he shall pay
ten crowns to Madame. Howbeit, he can have three
tries."

" That will soon be won," said Cornelius, who being
a Dutchman usually had his mouth as tight shut and
serious as Madame's affair was open and smiling.

So he bravely put his hand on the crowns to see if
they were well minted and he grasped them with gravity;
but as he turned to the others to say to them politely,
" Kiss my arse," the two misers, fearing his Dutch
gravity, answered " Good luck to you," as if he had
sneezed; whereat all the guests burst out laughing,
Cornelius included.

When the wine-grower went to take hold of the
crowns, he felt such an itching of the buttocks that his
old colander face let a laugh ooze out at every hole, like
smoke coming out through the cracks of the chimney,
and he could not utter a word.

Then it came to the stationer, who was a little bit of a
fellow with lips drawn tight like the neck of a gallows-
bird. He seized a handful of crowns, looked at the
company, including the King himself, and said in a
bantering tone, " Kiss my arse."

" Is it foul ? " asked the wine-grower.

" It is open to inspection," answered the stationer
sedately.

Whereupon the King began to feel anxious about his
money, for Peccard had said it twice without laughing,
and was about to pronounce the mystic phrase for the
third time, when la Beaupertuys made him a sign of
consent, whereat he lost countenance and his gravity
was split into fragments like a veritable maidenhead.

" How," asked Dunois, " did you contrive to keep a
serious face with six thousand crowns in front of you ? "

J

" Oh, Monseigneur, I thought, first of all, of one of
my law-cases which is coming off to-morrow; and
secondly of my wife who is a pestilent jade."

The desire to win so considerable a sum made them
try again, and the King entertained himself for more
than an hour in watching the grimaces, preparations,
and other monkey tricks, which they performed. But
it was attempting the impossible, and, for men who
loved better to close their fists than to open them, it was
a dreadful ordeal to have to count out each of them a
hundred crowns to Madame.

When they had departed, Nicole said roundly to the
King :

" Sire, would you like me to try ? "

" Gadzooks, no ! " said Louis XI.   " I would kiss
yours for much less money than that."

'Twas the speech of the thrifty man he always showed
himself to be.

One night, the fat Cardinal La Balue pursued with
gallant words and gestures and rather more freely than
canon law permitted, the dame Beaupertuys who, fortunately for her, was a smart piece of goods who knew
well enough how many beans make five.

" 'Zounds !   Monsieur le Cardinal," said she, " the
thing the King is so fond of is not yet in need of being
anointed with holy oil."

Then came Oliver Le Daim, to whom she likewise
refused to listen, and to whose tales she replied by
saying she would ask the King whether or not he preferred it shaven.

Now since the barber did not beseech her to keep
silence about his advances, she wondered whether these
little games were ruses on the part of the King, whose
suspicions had haply been aroused by his friends. So,
not being able to avenge herself on Louis, she made up
her mind, at least to have the laugh of the said lords, to
bamboozle them and to amuse the King with a practical

joke she had determined to play off on them. Now, one night, when they came to supper, she had with her a lady of the city who desired an audience of the King. This lady was a person of position who had come to ask a free pardon for her husband and, as a result of the adventure that befell, she obtained it. Nicole Beaupertuys, taking the King aside for a moment, bade him make all the guests raise their elbows and encourage them to stuff themselves with food. And she enjoined him to show himself in jovial mood and ready to laugh and make merry; but when the cloth was removed, he was suddenly to become morose and quarrelsome, to snap up their words and make them ill at ease. Then she said she would divert him by displaying all the fodder they had got entangled in their horns; finally, and most important of all, he was to show himself highly attentive to the aforesaid lady, and he was to appear unfeignedly attached to her as though she enjoyed the perfume of his favour, because she had gallantly lent herself to this excellent piece of jesting.

" Well, gentlemen," said the King, returning to the company, " let us sit down to table ; we have had a long and a fruitful day's sport."

And the barber, the Cardinal, a fat bishop, the Captain of the Scottish Guard, and a parliamentary envoy, a man of justice, a great favourite of the King's, followed the two ladies into the room set apart for the polishing up of the mandibular apparatus.

And then they set to with a will to lining the interior of their doublets. What is that? Why, paving the stomach, performing the chemistry of nature, registering the dishes, regaling your tripes, digging your grave with your molars, playing with Cain's weapon, inurning the sauces, nourishing a cuckold, or more philosophically making ordure with your teeth. Now then, do you understand? How many words does it take to knock a hole into your understanding? The King did not fail to urge his guests to partake of this most excellent supper. He stuffed them with green peas, helping them again and again from the stew; praising the plums, lauding the fish, saying to one, "How is it you eat not?" to another, "Let us drink a glass to Madame," to all, "Gentlemen, let us taste these crabs!" "Let us put this flagon out of its misery." "Haven't you tried this eel?" "And this lamprey, what about it, eh? What do you say to a little?" "And here, gadzooks, is the finest barbel ever fished from the Loire." "Come now, a slice of this pasty!" "I brought down this bird myself; I shall take it as an affront if you do not have some." Then again, "Here, drink, the King is not looking." "What say you to these preserves, Madame's own making?" "Prithee, taste of these grapes, they are from my own vineyard." "Come now, have some medlars." And so, while encouraging them to distend their intestinal tuberosities, the good monarch laughed and joked with them, and they jested and wrangled and spat and snorted and rollicked just as though the King were not there. And so it was that such a huge quantity of victuals was taken a-board, so many flagons drained and so many stews brought to nought, that the faces of the guests turned purple and their doublets looked like bursting, for they were all stuffed like Troyes hogs-puddings, from cod-piece to belly-band.

No sooner were they back in the salon than they began to sweat and puff and blow, and were already inclined to curse their gluttonous excesses. The King was glum and silent. And the others were only too glad to follow his example, because all their forces were required to perform the intestinal decoction of the dishes crammed into their bellies, the which clogged together and gurgitated very loudly. One said to himself, "I was a fool to eat that sauce." Another chid himself for gourmandising a dish of eels garnished with capers, and

another thought to himself, " Oh, ho ! That sausage-
meat is going to give me a twisting ! " The Cardinal,
who was the most corpulent of the party, was snorting
through his nostrils like a frightened horse. 'Twas he
who was first compelled to give vent to a reverberating
belch ; and then how he wished he had been in Germany
where the thing is considered a good omen, for hearing
this ventriloquial observation, the King looked at the
Cardinal with a frown.

" What do you mean by that ? " he asked. " Do you
think you're in the presence of a curate ? "

This speech aroused great alarm, for as a general rule
the King thought highly of a well-delivered borborigma.
The other guests decided to dispose otherwise of the
vapours that were already leaping and squirming in their
pancreatic retorts. At first, they endeavoured to retain
them for a space in the convolutions of their mesenteries.
It was then that, seeing them swelling like tax-gatherers,
la Beaupertuys took the King aside and said to him :

" Know that I have caused Peccard to make me two
big dolls in the likeness of this lady and myself. Now
when these guests of ours, pressed beyond endurance by
the purgative drugs which I put in their goblets, shall
betake themselves to the presidial seat where we are
going to pretend to go, they will always find the place
occupied. 'Twill entertain you vastly to behold their
writhings and contortions."

With these words, la Beaupertuys disappeared with
the lady in order to give a turn to the wheel, in accordance
with the custom of women, whereof I will tell you the
origin some other time. Then, after a certain lapse of
time, la Beaupertuys returned alone, allowing it to be
inferred that she had left the lady in the laboratory of
natural alchemy. Thereupon the King, beckoning to
the Cardinal, made him rise and began talking to him
gravely concerning affairs of State, holding him by the
cord of his cassock. To everything the King said, La

Balue answered shortly, " Yes, Sire," in order to extricate himself from the royal attentions and pull down his breeches as quickly as might be, for his cellars were full of water and he felt like losing the key of his back door. All the guests were at their wits' end as to how to stay the movement of their fæces whereto nature, even to a greater extent than water, has given the property of finding a certain level.   The said substances within them were growing soft and fluid as they worked like insects demanding release from their cocoons, raging, and straining, and caring not a jot for the King's majesty ; for there is nought to equal the ignorance and insolence of these cursed substances which are as importunate as prisoners whose time of manumission is at hand.   So every moment they were for slipping like eels from a net, and everyone had to employ all his force and skill to avoid cloutering himself in the King's presence.   Louis took great delight in putting questions to his guests, and was mightily amused at the changing grimaces of their countenances, wherein were mirrored the unseemly contortions of their fundamental physiognomies.

Said the Counsellor of Justice to Oliver :

" I would willingly resign my office for three minutes to myself in the Privy Council House."

" Aye," answered the barber, " there's no pleasure to equal a satisfactory motion.   And I no longer marvel at the everlasting droppings of the fly."

The Cardinal, thinking that by this time the lady would have duly procured her manumission from the Court House, left the tassel of his girdle in the King's hands by giving a jump as though he had forgotten to say his prayers, and bolted for the door.

" What ails you, my lord Cardinal ? " said the King.

" What ails me ?   Good God !   Everything, it seems, is on a big scale with you, Sire."

The Cardinal slipped out, leaving the others marvelling at his address.   He marched majestically towards the

privy, loosening his purse-strings a little as he went;
but when he opened the blessed door, he found the lady
enthroned upon the seat like a pope about to be crowned.
So thrusting back his ripe fruit, he hurried down the
winding staircase to the garden.   When, however, he
reached the bottom steps, the barking of the dogs made
him sore afraid of being bitten in one of his precious
hemispheres.   Not knowing where he could deliver himself of his chemical by-products, he returned to the
drawing-room, shivering all over like a man suffering
from exposure.   The others seeing the Cardinal come
back, concluded that he had emptied his natural reser-
voirs, relieved his ecclesiastical bowels, and they deemed
him a lucky man.   So up jumped the barber, as though
to take an inventory of the carpets and count the rafters,
but before anyone else could get there, he was at the
door and, relaxing his sphincter in advance, he hummed
a tune as he hastened to his retreat.   When he got
there, he had no alternative but to offer his excuses, like
Balue, to the continuous performer on the tripod, shutting
the door with as much promptitude as he had opened it.
And so he returned with his sternhold full of accumulated
molecules which greatly encumbered his internal conduits.   Similarly, in procession one after another, went
all the guests to the privy without being able to deposit
the burden of their sauces.   Back again they came into
the presence of the King, just as incommoded as before.
They looked at one another significantly and conversed
more unambiguously with their arses than they had ever
done with their mouths;   for there is never any room
for equivocation in the proceedings of the natural parts.
All is rational there and easily understood, for it is a
science that we acquire at birth.

   " I believe," said the Cardinal, " that the woman will
be functioning there till to-morrow.   What possessed
la Beaupertuys to invite such a diarrhœtic here ? "

   " She hath been a whole hour, doing what I could do

in a twinkling," said Oliver le Daim.   " May she die of
the fever ! "

All these courtiers, seized with the colic, were walking
up and down vainly endeavouring to instil patience into
their clamorous entrails, when the lady you wot of
reappeared in the drawing-room.   You may judge
whether they did not think her beautiful and gracious,
and would not eagerly have kissed her in the very place
which, in themselves, was causing them so much uneasi-
ness ; and never was the dawn of day welcomed with
greater enthusiasm than was this lady, the angelic deliverer
of their poor unhappy bellies.   La Balue rose up.   The
rest, out of honour, esteem and reverence for the Church,
yielded precedence to the cloth.   Then, renewing their
patience, they continued their facial contortions, whereat
the King laughed inwardly, and so did Nicole who helped
him to increase the tortures of these unhappy gentry.

The worthy Scottish captain, who had eaten more
plentifully than the others of a certain dish into which
the cook had put a quantity of laxative powder, cloutered
his breeches under the erroneous belief that 'twas nothing
but a harmless fart.   In great discomfiture he retired to
a corner hoping that, in the King's presence, the thing
would have the decency not to smell.   At that moment,
the Cardinal returned looking horribly blue, for he had
been to the privy and, this time, found la Beaupertuys
herself upon the episcopal throne.   Now, suffering agony,
and never suspecting she was in the room, he came
back and uttered a diabolical " *Oh* " when he saw her
beside his master.

" What means this ? " said the King, looking fire and
fury at the priest.

" Sire," said the Cardinal boldly, " matters concerning
purgatory come into my province, and I have to inform
you that sorcery reigns in this house."

" Ah, miserable priestling ; you dare to bandy jokes
with me ? " said the King.

HE WAS DELICATELY STRANGLED
BETWEEN THE HEAD & THE SHOULDERS

TWO BIG DOLLS IN THE LIKENESS
OF THIS LADY AND MYSELF

Hearing this, the rest of the company, unable any longer to distinguish lining from doublet, bejakesed themselves with terror, fit to break their necks.

" Ha ! 'Tis an insult to my sacred person," said the King in a tone that made them grow pale with fear. " Hullo, Tristan, below there ! " cried Louis starting up and flinging open a window. " Come up hither, my gossip."

The Provost-Marshal soon appeared. These people were all mere nobodies, who had been elevated by the King's favour, and a fit of the stomach-ache was quite enough to make him lay them low again, so that, with the exception of the Cardinal, who trusted to his cassock, Tristan found them all stiff with terror.

" Take these gentlemen to the Court House on the Mall, my gossip. They have cloutered themselves through over-eating."

" Am I not a good jester ? " said Nicole.

" The farce was good, but the filth was the devil," he answered with a laugh.

This utterance, as it fell from the royal lips, brought the courtiers the comforting assurance that on this occasion the King did not meditate depriving them of their heads, and for this they thanked God. Louis had a taste for this kind of joke. He was not a malevolent man, as the guests remarked, what time they eased themselves along the Mall, with Tristan who, like a good Frenchman, kept them company and escorted them to their houses. This is how it comes about that since that time the citizens of Tours have been wont to relieve themselves on the Mall of Chardonneret, sith gentlemen of the Court had so behaved.

I will not quit the subject of this great King without putting on record the quaint jest he played off on la Godegrand, who was an old maid very sour at never having discovered a lid for her pot during all the forty years she had been alive, and raged in her yellow skin at being always as virgin as a mule. This old maid had her dwelling exactly opposite the house which belonged to la Beaupertuys at the corner of the rue de Hiérusalem, so that by leaning over a balcony that ran along the wall, it was perfectly easy to see what she did, and to hear what she said, in the ground-floor room in which she dwelt. And many a time the King was vastly entertained at the goings on of this old maid, who was quite unaware that she was under the culverin of her lord and sovereign. Now it befell that one market day a young citizen of Tours was ordered by the King to be hanged because he had violated a noble lady of riper years believing her to be a young girl. In this there was nothing wrong, and it would have been meritorious for the said dame to have been taken for a virgin; but, discovering his error, he had overwhelmed her with endless insults, and, suspecting that she had been a party to the deception, had taken it into his head to rob her of a splendid silver-gilt goblet, in payment of the accommodation which he had bestowed upon her. The said young man was in the prime of his vigour and so handsome that, out of sympathy as well as curiosity, the whole town desired to see him hanged. As you may readily guess, there were more bonnets than hats at the execution. In fact, the young man was a right gallant warrior, and in accordance with the use and custom of the gallows fruit of those days, died like a man of spirit with his lance couched for action, whereof there was much talk throughout the city. Many were the ladies who swore 'twas a sin not to have preserved so fine a stuffing for a cod-piece.

"Suppose we put the fellow's corpse into la Godegrand's bed?" said la Beaupertuys to the King.

"We should frighten her to death!" answered Louis the Eleventh.

"Nay, Sire, not a whit. Be assured that she will welcome even a dead man who hath so great a longing for a live one. Yesterday, I saw her playing all manner of monkey tricks before a young man's hat that she had hung on the back of a chair, and you would have roared with laughter at the things she said and the antics she performed."

Now, while the forty-year-old virgin was at Vespers, the young citizen, who had just finished the last scene of his tragi-comedy, was cut down by the King's orders. Arraying him in a white shirt, two tall lacqueys climbed the wall of la Godegrand's garden and put the body into her bed, on the side next the wall. This done, they took their departure, and the King stayed on in the balcony room, toying with la Beaupertuys and waiting for the old maid's bedtime. La Godegrand was soon back, trotting along quick and sprightly from the church of Saint Martin, which was quite near her house, for the rue de Hiérusalem abuts on the walls of the cloister. She went in, put down her bag, her rosary, and all the other fiddle-faddles that old maids go about with. Then she stirred the fire, blew it up with the bellows, warmed herself, ensconced herself in her chair and played with her pussy-cat for lack of something more exciting. Then she went to the larder and sighed, and supped, supped and sighed, ladling it down all alone, with her eyes on the ground; and then when she had drunk her bellyful, she let a great fart which the King himself heard.

" Lord, suppose the dead man said ' God bless you ! ' to her," said la Beaupertuys.

Whereat they both broke out into muffled laughter. Keenly attentive, the Most Christian King looked on at the disrobing of the old maid, who, as she took off her clothes, kept admiring herself, pulling out a hair, or scratching a spot that had spitefully made its appearance on one of her nostrils, attending to her teeth and doing the thousand and one little things that all women, virgins or not virgins, have, to their great disgust, to see to.

But, were it not for these slight defects in nature, they would be too arrogant, and there would be no enjoyment to be had from them. Having duly performed her aquatic and musical discourse, the lady put herself between the sheets and uttered a fine, big, ample and curious cry, when she caught sight of her bedfellow and felt the chill of his poor hanged body and smelt the good odour of his lustiness. Out of coquetry, she leapt away from him, but, not knowing him to be really dead, she came back again, thinking he was playing a trick on her and only pretending to be a corpse.

" Begone, you naughty man ! " said she.

But you may take it that she pronounced these words in a tone of exceeding gracious humility. Then, seeing that he stirred not, she examined him more closely and marvelled greatly at his fine natural endowments and recognised the ill-fated young citizen. Whereupon the fancy seized her to carry out some purely scientific experiments in the interest of people who have the misfortune to be hanged.

" But·what is she about ? " said la Beaupertuys to the King.

" She's trying to restore him to life. 'Tis a work of Christian charity."

So she fell to rubbing and chafing the good young man, beseeching Saint Mary of Egypt to help her to resuscitate this husband who had fallen full of love for her from heaven, when suddenly on looking at the dead man she was so charitably warming, she thought she saw a slight movement of the eyes. Then she put her hand to the man's heart and felt that it was feebly beating. At length, from the warmth of the bed and her affectionate attentions, and by the temperature of unrequited maids which is hot as the hottest breeze that ever blew from an Arabian desert, she had the joy of bringing back to life this fine young strapper who, as luck would have it, had been very indifferently hanged.

" That's how my hangmen do my business ! " said
Louis with a laugh.

" Ha ! " said la Beaupertuys, " you won't have him
hanged again, he's too nice."

" The sentence does not say he is to be hanged twice.
But he shall marry the old maid."

And in fact, the worthy lady hurried off, as fast as her
legs could carry her, to fetch a first-rate leech, a good
barber-surgeon who lived in the Abbey, and brought
him back post haste. Straightway, he took his lancet
and bled the young man ; but alas ! the blood refused
to flow.

" Ah," said he, " 'tis too late ; the transfusion of
blood into the lungs has already taken place."

But, all on a sudden, the good young blood oozed a
few drops and then came in abundance, and the hempen
apoplexy, which had only begun to operate, was arrested
in its course. The young man made a slight movement
and looked more like a living being. Then nature had
its way, and he fell into a great faintness and profound
attrition and prostration of the flesh, and a notable
flaccidity of all his person. And the lady, who was all
eyes and noted all the great and conspicuous changes
which took place in the body of the half-hanged victim,
plucked the barber by the sleeve, and showing him the
drooping condition of the poor fellow, enquired with an
inquisitive and significant look :

" Will it always be thus with him now ? "

" Aye, very often," answered the veracious surgeon.

" Oh, he was much nicer hung ! " quoth she.

Hearing that, the King burst out laughing. Seeing
him through the window, the woman and the surgeon
were sore afraid, for that laugh sounded like a second
sentence of death for the unhappy victim.

But the King was as good as his word and caused
them to be married. Then, in order that justice might
be done, he bestowed the name and title of Sieur de

Mortsauf on the husband in lieu of that which he had lost on the scaffold. As la Godegrand had an ample supply of golden crowns, they founded a good Touraine family, which is held in great honour to this day ; and Monsieur de Mortsauf rendered King Louis the Eleventh right faithful service on many divers occasions. Only he never cared to encounter either gibbets or old women, and evermore refused to make assignations with a female after dark.

Whereupon we learn that we should carefully scrutinise and take stock of our women and never commit an error concerning the local differences which distinguish the old from the young, since though we be not hanged for our errors in matters pertaining to love, there are always big risks to be run.

THE HIGH CONSTABLE'S WIFE

STRAIGHTWAY HE TOOK HIS LANCET
AND BLED THE YOUNG MAN

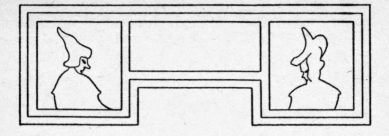

THE HIGH CONSTABLE'S WIFE

THE High Constable of Armignac, for the purpose of increasing his wealth, espoused the Countess Bonne, who was already very far gone in love with young Savoisy, son of the Chamberlain to King Charles the Sixth.

The Constable was a rough fighting man. His mien was grim, his skin tough and exceeding hairy. Dark and pitiless words were continually pouring from his lips. He had always someone or other to hang, was always dripping with the sweat of battles or dreaming of stratagems far other than the stratagems of love. So it came to pass that this doughty soldier, being little inclined to add his seasoning to the connubial stew, treated his gentle lady after the manner of a man whose heart was set on higher things, an attitude of mind which the ladies hold in pious horror, for the last thing in the world they wish for is that the joists of the bed should be the sole witness of their skill and prowess in the art of love.

Wherefore, the fair Countess, as soon as she had wedded the Constable, only grew the keener to indulge the love for the aforesaid Savoisy with which her heart was full to bursting.

Both of them being anxious to study the same music, they had soon got their instruments well in tune and quickly deciphered the score; and it was very evident to Queen Isabelle that Savoisy's horses were more frequently stabled at her cousin d'Armignac's than at the hostel of Saint-Pol, where the Chamberlain had been residing since the destruction of his own house, which, as everybody knows, had been demolished by order of the University.

This noble and wise princess, having a presentiment that some grievous mischance would overtake Bonne, since the Constable was as free with his sword-cuts as a priest is with his blessings, the said Queen, I say, who was about as sharp as a leaden dagger, said after church one day to her cousin, who was dipping her finger in the same Holy Water stoup as Savoisy:

" My sweet, don't you see blood in that water ? "

" Bah ! " said Savoisy to the Queen, " love loves blood, Madame."

The Queen thought that a very happy reply and put it in writing and later on into action, when her lord the King demolished a lover of hers, of whose affection this same story will relate the dawning.

You know, by manifold experience, that during the springtime of love, the two lovers are very chary about revealing the mystery of their hearts ; and not only out of prudence, but from the satisfaction they derive from elaborating the make-believe of love, they rival each other in their anxious endeavours to preserve the veil of secrecy. Then comes a single day of forgetfulness and all the fruits of their caution are thrown away. The poor woman pays the penalty of her rash delight like a wild creature taken in a net ; or her lover lets his presence be discovered by his scarf or his spurs, or some more intimate portion of his attire, which in a fatal moment of absent-mindedness he has left behind him ; and so behold, a slit of the dagger puts an end to the web so deftly woven by their golden joys. Yet when we are full of days there is little sense in repining at death, and the marital sword is a glorious end for a gallant lover, if any end be glorious. 'Twas thus that the secret amours of the Constable's wife were fated to be cut short.

One morning, when the flight of the Duke of Burgundy from Lagny had given Monsieur d'Armignac a little leisure, the Constable took it into his head to go and say good day to his wife, and thought he would wake her in a pleasant manner so as not to make her angry; but she being wrapt in the deep and heavy morning slumber, said, without opening her eyes, when she felt what he was about:

" Leave me in peace, Charles ! "

" Oh ho ! " cried the Constable, hearing the name of a saint who was not on his calendar, " so we've got a Charles in our head, have we ? "

Then, without touching the lady, he leapt from the bed and with flaming visage and naked sword, tore upstairs to the room where his wife's maid slept, thinking that she was doubtless in the plot.

" Ah, you hell-kite ! " he cried, giving full vent to his anger; "say your prayers, for I'm going to slay you here and now, because of this Charles who keeps coming here."

" Ah ! My Lord," answered the woman, " who told you that ? "

" Be assured that I will undo you beyond repair, if you confess not every little assignation and how they are arranged. If you speak not straight out or if you hesitate, I'll run you through with my poniard. Speak ! "

" Run me through, then ! " said the girl. " You'll learn nothing from me ! "

The Constable, interpreting amiss this most excellent reply, ran her right through the body, so mad was he with choler. Then he returned to his wife's bedroom and said to his squire, whom he encountered on the stairs, roused from his slumbers by the poor girl's yells:

" Go on up there; I've had to correct la Billette rather severely."

Before he returned to the presence of his wife, he went
and fetched his son who was wrapt in childish slumber
and rudely dragged him into the Countess's bedroom.
The mother opened her eyes pretty wide, as you may
imagine, when she heard the little one crying ; and she
was overwhelmed with terror when she saw him in the
clutches of her husband, whose right hand was all
covered with blood, and who was darting murderous
glances at mother and son.

" What ails you ? " she said.

" Madame," said the man of lightning execution, " is
this child the fruit of my loins or of Savoisy's, your
lover ? "

At these words, Bonne turned pale and pounced on her
son as a frightened frog will jump into the water.

" Oh, he is ours right enough ! " said she.

" If you would not see his head rolling at your feet,
answer me straight.   You've procured me a lieutenant ? "

" I have, indeed."

" Who is he ? "

" He isn't Savoisy, and I'll never pronounce the name
of a man I know not."

At that the Constable leapt to his feet and seized his
wife by the arm as though to silence her for ever with a
blow of his sword ; but she, casting a proud, imperious
glance upon him, said :

" Kill me if you will, but never touch me more."

" You shall live," retorted her husband, " for the
punishment I destine for you is more terrible than
death."

And full of misgivings as to the devices, traps, wiles,
and artifices familiar to women in these times of crisis, of
which, alone or with other members of the sex, they study
day and night, all the possible variations, he departed with
those grim and sombre words.   He went straightway
to cross-examine his servants, displaying a countenance
divinely terrible.   Wherefore they answered him as

they would have answered God Almighty on the Judgment Day, when every one of us will have to render his account.

Not one of them knew the seriousness of the trouble which was at the bottom of these swift and sharp interrogations; but, from all that they said, it was concluded by the Constable that no male inhabitant of the place had had a finger in the pie save one of his dogs which was dumb to his questionings and which he had set to keep watch upon the garden. So he took hold of him with both his hands and throttled him in his fury. This fact encouraged him peripatetically to infer that his *locum tenens* gained access to the house by way of the garden, which had a postern gate opening on to the river bank. To such as are ignorant thereof, we will explain the precise situation of the Hôtel d'Armignac, which occupied a conspicuous site near the royal residences of Saint-Paul. On this same site was afterwards built the Hôtel de Longueville. But at the time of which we are speaking, the house of the d'Armignacs had a fine stone porch looking on to the rue Saint-Antoine. It was fortified at every point, and the high walls along the river side, opposite the Île aux Vaches, where the Port de la Grève now is, were furnished with turrets. The plan thereof has been for a long time on view at the residence of Cardinal Duprat, the King's Chancellor. The Constable cudgelled his brains and in the depths thereof, among his choicest traps, selected the likeliest and adapted it so skilfully to the case in point that the gallant was bound to be caught like a hare in a gin.

" 'Sdeath! " said he; " but my horn-merchant is in the noose, and I have plenty of time to think what I shall do with him."

This is the plan of campaign which this worthy and hairy captain, who carried on such grievous warfare against Jean-sans-Peur, devised for the discomfiture of his secret enemy. He took a goodly number of his trustiest and most skilful archers, posted them in the towers overlooking the quay, commanding them, under the direst penalties, to shoot, without respect of persons, on anyone, save Madame, who should attempt to leave the gardens; and at any hour of the day or night, to admit the favoured gentleman.   Similar measures were taken on the side of the main entrance in the rue Saint-Antoine.

The servants, not excepting the Chaplain, had orders not to quit the house, on pain of death.   Then the task of guarding the two flanks of the house having been committed to members of his artillery company, who were enjoined to keep a good look-out on the side streets, it was absolutely necessary that the unknown lover, to whom the Constable was indebted for his pair of horns, should be taken piping hot, when, at the accustomed hour and all unsuspicious of traps, he should come insolently to plant his flag in the midst of the lawful appurtenances of the Lord High Constable.

It was a trap into which the alertest man was bound to fall unless he were as effectively protected by God as the good Saint Peter was by the Saviour when He preserved him from sinking beneath the waters on the day he took it into his head to essay whether the sea was as solid as *terra firma*.

The Constable, having business to see to at Poissy, was compelled to get into the saddle as soon as dinner was done.   Knowing this to be the case, the poor Countess had arranged the night before to invite her young adorer to that pleasant duel in which she always proved herself the stronger.

While, however, the Constable was encircling his house with a girdle of eyes and lethal weapons, and posting his men at the postern in order to wing the gallant as he went out, not knowing from what quarter of the sky he would fall, his wife was doing anything but shelling peas, or looking for black cows in the embers!

To begin with, the chambermaid unnailed herself, and dragging herself to her mistress, informed her that his cuckold lordship knew nothing; and being about to render up her soul, she comforted her beloved mistress, assuring her that she could put entire confidence in a sister of hers, a laundress in the house, who would willingly be cut up into mincemeat to please Madame. She added that she was the most adroit and cunning gossip in the neighbourhood, and renowned from the Tournelles to the Croix du Traboir, among the humble folk, for her resourcefulness in urgent cases of love.

Then, while weeping for the unhappy fate of her good chambermaid, the Countess sent for the laundress, bade her quit her wash-tub and, taking her into her confidence, fell to considering the problem in all its aspects, for she was ready to sacrifice all her future happiness, if only she could save Savoisy.

Their first task was to apprise him of the Constable's suspicions and to prevail on him to lie low.

So behold the good laundress loaded up like a mule with washing and proceeding to make her way out of the house. But on reaching the porch, she found her passage barred by a man-at-arms, who turned a deaf ear to all her most eloquent entreaties. In the circumstances she resolved, in a spirit of special devotion, to take the soldier in his weak spot, and so seductively did she cajole and caress him, that he played a most excellent duet with her albeit he was accoutred as if for the wars. But when the bout was over, he utterly refused to let her pass out into the street and, although she tried to get her passport sealed by some of the best-looking among the other guards, thinking they might be more gallant than their confrère, not one of them, archer, or man-at-arms, or any other person, would dare to open for her a single one of the narrowest passages in the house.

"You are an ungrateful set of wretches," she said, "not to do as much for me, as I did for you!"

One good thing, however, was that by this means she was able to reconnoitre the position, and she went back in great haste to her mistress to tell her about the strange machinations of the Count.

The two women resumed their deliberations, and it didn't take as long as singing a brace of Alleluias over all these warlike preparations, these sentries and defences, these equivocal, secret, specious and diabolical dispositions, to realise, through that sixth sense which is a special attribute of womenkind, that the Countess's poor lover was menaced by a very exceptional danger.

Madame, having quickly acquired the knowledge that she alone was permitted to leave the house, swiftly resolved to profit by the privilege; but she did not get a bow shot's distance by herself, for the Constable had given orders to four of her pages always to hold themselves in readiness to accompany their mistress, and to two of his own ensigns, never to quit her side.

When the poor lady returned to her chamber, shedding as many tears as the whole collection of Magdalens in all the Church pictures in creation, she cried aloud, saying:

"Alas! my lover will be undone, and I shall never see him more—he who was so soft of speech and so gracious in dalliance; and that lovely head, that has so often rested on my knees, will meet a bloody doom. And I powerless to toss my husband an empty, worthless head in place of my lover's so rich in grace and worth! A scurvy head for a perfumed one! A loathéd head for a belovéd one!"

"Oh! Madame," exclaimed the laundress, " suppose we arrayed in some nobleman's attire the cook's son here, who is in love with me and pesters me sorely with his importunities, and then, having thus accoutred him, thrust him out at the postern."

Whereupon the two women looked at each other with a murderous surmise.

" That spoil-sauce once slain, all the soldiers would take wing like a flock of cranes."

"Yes; but would not the Count recognise the scullion ?"

And the Countess, beating her breast, cried with a rueful shake of her head :

" No !   No ! my sweeting, 'tis noble blood that we must shed and never .count the cost."

She mused a while, then suddenly leapt for joy, and flinging her arms about the laundress's neck, she cried :

" Because your counsels have helped me save my lover's life, I will see that you want for nothing to the end of your days."

So saying, the Countess dried her tears, and looking radiant as a bride, picked up her bag and her book of hours, and set out for the Church of Saint-Paul, whose bells were ringing for the late Mass.   The Constable's wife never omitted to attend this beautiful service in her most sumptuous array like all the ladies of the Court. So it was that this particular Mass was called the Full Dress Mass, because the congregation consisted entirely of coxcombs, dandies, gentlemen and ladies drenched with perfume ; in a word, there were no dresses to be seen there save those adorned with coats-of-arms, no spurs save spurs of gold.

So thither the Countess Bonne departed, leaving behind her, much amazed, the laundress, whom she enjoined to keep on the alert.   The Countess proceeded, in great pomp, to the church, accompanied by her pages, the two ensigns and the men-at-arms.

It here behoves us to say that among the pretty knights that danced attendance on the ladies in that church, more than one looked on the Countess as the apple of his eye, and professed for her a heartfelt devotion after the fashion of the young who inscribe the names of full many ladies on their tablets in order to be sure of capturing at least one out of all the number.

Among these ornamental birds of prey, who were for

ever opening their beaks, and who gazed much more often about the church than at the priests and the altar, there was one whom the Countess sometimes deigned to honour with a glance, because he was less volatile and more deeply in love than the others. He always sat still and silent, continually glued to the same pillar and unfeignedly happy merely to look upon the lady to whom he had dedicated his heart. His face was pale and tinged with a gentle melancholy. His countenance bespoke a heart sincere and generous, a heart that feeds on ardent passions and sinks with ecstasy into the abyss of hopeless love. Of such folk there are few, for the reason that, as a rule, we love the thing you wot of better than those unknown blisses that merely trail their tendrils and blossom in the depths of the soul.

This same gentleman, albeit his clothes were of good fashion and clean and simple withal, nay even possessing a certain suggestion of refinement, seemed to the Constable's dame to exhibit the unmistakable characteristics of an impoverished knight obliged to seek his fortune far from his own home with nothing but his sword and cloak to call his own. And so, partly because she suspected that he was secretly in want; partly because he loved her dearly, and somewhat also because he had a handsome face, fine dark flowing hair, a good figure, and a gentle submissive air, the Constable's lady wished him all he longed for in the way of women and wealth. And in order to keep her full complement of admirers and because, being thrifty, she was careful to throw nothing away, she fanned his flame with little attentions, soft glances, which wound their way towards him like stinging aspics; making light of the young man's peace of mind, as is the way with princesses accustomed to playing with things more precious than a simple knight. Why, her husband, the Constable, would stake the kingdom and all that was in it, as coolly as you would put down a tester at a game of piquet!

Finally, it was only three days ago that, coming out of church, after Vespers, the Constable's lady, indicating with a glance this pursuivant of Cupid, had said :

" There's a man of parts ! "

The saying became all the fashion and very popular at Court.   It is to the Countess d'Armignac, and to no other, that the French language owes this charming expression.

As it happened, the Countess's conjecture regarding the gentleman in question was well founded.   He was a bannerless knight, Julien de Boys-Bourredon by name, whose estate, not having enough timber on it to make him a toothpick, and he himself having nothing more to his name than the goodly parts wherewith his deceased mother had most opportunely furnished him, he conceived the idea of deriving wealth and profit from these endowments at Court ; for well he knew what store the women set by such delights, and how highly and dearly they esteem them when they can be enjoyed in security between sunset and sunrise.   Many such as he have taken the narrow female path to push their way in the world.   But far from eking out his love in measured doses, he poured it all forth, principal and interest, when, having come to the stately Mass, he set eyes on the triumphant beauty of the Countess Bonne.   Then indeed he fell a victim to a deep and heartfelt passion highly beneficial to his exchequer, since he lost the desire to eat and drink.   This is the worst sort of love there is, since it incites you to love diet while you are enjoying your diet of love.   A dual malady, either one of which might readily kill a man.

Such was the young man whom the Constable's lady had thought of to fulfil her purpose, and to whom she hurried off to invite him to his death.

On entering the church, she beheld the poor knight who, to his desires most loyal, was longing for her arrival leaning against the pillar, as a sick man longs for the

sun, the spring-time, or the dawn. Seeing him, she
averted her gaze and made towards the Queen to solicit
her assistance in this critical juncture; for she was full
of pity for her lover; but one of the captains said with
a great show of respect:

"Madame, we are under orders not to suffer you to
speak to anyone, man or woman; even though it were
the Queen or your confessor. Upon the observance of
this command our lives depend."

"Is it not your duty, as a soldier, to lay down your
life?"

"Aye, Madame, but also to obey," answered the
man-at-arms.

Therefore the Countess knelt down in her customary
place; and, looking again at her faithful admirer, she
thought his face was thinner and more hollow-cheeked
than ever it had been before.

"Bah!" she said to herself, "his death will trouble
me not so much after all. He's half dead already."

Revolving such thoughts in her mind, she looked at
the gentleman with one of those warm seductive glances
only permitted to princesses and to strumpets; and the
false love, to which her lovely eyes bore witness, caused
a mighty pang to the devotee of the pillar.

Who does not love the warm onset of quickening life
when it flows about the heart and causes everything to
swell and bud? The Countess perceived, with a pleasure
whereof women never weary, the omnipotence of her
splendid eyes, from the mute response which the gallant
made thereto. Nay, the flush that overspread his cheeks
spoke with more telling eloquence than any words the
most gifted Greek or Roman orators could command.
Seeing him thus melting at her gaze, the Countess, in
order to be sure that she was not deceived, took pleasure
in essaying how far the magic of her gaze had power to
charm; and having thrice ten times set her loyal servitor
aglow with loving looks, she was fortified in the belief

that he would certainly lay down his life for love of her. So strongly did this thought take hold of her that, thrice amid her orisons she was tempted by the longing to cause him one single paroxysm of concentrated bliss and sum up her passion in one divine outpouring of love's essence, so that she might be free of the reproach of having dissipated not only the life, but also the happiness, of her devoted friend.   When, then, the celebrant turned towards the gilded throng of worshippers and gave them leave to depart, the Countess made her exit by way of the pillar where her admirer stood.   She passed in front of him and endeavoured by a glance deeply charged with meaning, to convey to him that she wished him to follow her.   Next, to confirm him in the understanding and interpretation of this fleeting appeal, she adroitly turned round a little after she had passed him, as though again to insinuate that she desired his company.   She perceived that he had left his place, but was prevented by his modesty from advancing further.   But when he saw this second signal, the knight, being now assured he was not indiscreet, mingled with the throng, and walked with little silent steps, like a bawcock that fears to betray his presence in one of those good houses of entertainment which are commonly denoted " bad."   And walked he behind or walked he in front, on her right or on her left, the lady gazed at him with fond alluring eyes so as the better to tempt him and draw him towards her, even as an angler gently lifts his rod in order to judge the weight of his catch.   In a word, the Countess gave such a lifelike performance of the strumpet trying to attract custom, that you would have vowed there was nothing so much like a whore as a high-born lady.   On arriving at the entrance to the house, the Countess hesitated to go in ; then turning her face once more towards the unhappy knight, so as to invite him to accompany her, she gave him a glance so devilishly alluring, that he bounded to the side of his heart's own queen with as much alacrity as if she had summoned him by word of mouth. Straightway, the Countess offered him her hand, and both of them, seething and shivering from contrary causes, found themselves inside the house. And now, alas, Madame d'Armignac was grieved that she had behaved herself so wantonly for the sake of Death, grieved that she had betrayed Savoisy the better to save him. But this minor remorse was as lame as the greater and came belatedly. Seeing that there was not a moment to lose, the Countess leaned heavily on her gallant's arm.

" Come quickly to my chamber," said she, " for I have urgent need to speak with you."

And he, never dreaming that his life was at stake, could find no voice to answer her, so breathless was he at the prospect of approaching bliss. When the laundress beheld this gentleman, who had been so promptly hooked, she exclaimed :

" Gramercy, there's nothing like a Court lady for despatching that sort of business ! "

Then she made him a profound reverence, eloquent of the mock respect due to those who possess the great courage to die for such a little thing.

" Picarde," said the Countess, pulling the laundress to her by the skirt, " I do not really feel as if I could tell him how I intend to requite his mute devotion and the beautiful trust he reposes in feminine loyalty."

" Bah ! Madame, wherefore tell him at all ? Dismiss him, richly content, by the postern gate. So many men die in the wars for nothing ; cannot this man die for something ? I will make another by him, if that will comfort you ! "

" Come, come ! " cried the Countess, " I will tell him all. It shall be the punishment for my sin."

Taking it for granted that his lady-love was concerting some secret plans with the maid so that she should not be interrupted in the pleasant occupation she had pro-

mised him, the unknown lover discreetly held himself at
a distance, gazing at the ceiling.   He thought to himself
that the Countess was very bold; but, as even a hunchback would have done, he discovered countless justifica-
tions for her actions, and was proud of himself for having
inspired such reckless conduct.   He was dwelling on
these pleasant thoughts when the Countess opened the
door of her bedchamber and invited her knight to follow
her.   There this great lady, laying aside all the appurtenances of her lofty rank, fell at his feet, a simple
unassuming woman.

"Alas, fair sir," said she, "I have committed a
grievous fault against you.   Hearken.   When you quit
this abode, you will be going to your death.   The mad
passion I entertain for another has put me beside myself;
and though here, you cannot take his place, you will take
it when you depart, for you will find yourself confronted
by his murderers.   This is the joy whereof I have invited
you to partake."

"Ah!" sighed Boys-Bourredon, hiding his dark
despair deep down within his breast, "thankful am I
that you have used me as your tool.   Yea, I love you so
that, every day, I longed, like a woman, to offer you
something which can be given only once!   Take, then,
my life!"

So saying, the unhappy knight looked at her with a
gaze that summed up within it all the bliss of the days
that might have been.

Hearing these brave and passionate words, the Countess started up.

"Ah, were it not for Savoisy, how wildly I should
love you!" said she.

"Alas, my doom is then accomplished," broke out
Boys-Bourredon.   "My horoscope foretold that I should
die for love of a noble lady.   'Sblood!" cried he, grasp-
ing his sword, "but I will sell my life dearly.   Yet I
shall die content, if my death assures the happiness of

the woman I love. I shall live dearer in her memory than in actual life ! "

When she saw how nobly he bore himself and how his face lit up with ecstasy, her heart bled for him. Natheless, she felt a pang that he should be willing to leave her without beseeching her to grant him just one single favour.

" Come and let me arm you," said she, making as if to fling her arms about him.

" Ah, dear lady," he replied, a teardrop veiling the fire within his eyes, " will you render death impossible, by making this life too precious ? "

" Come," she cried, overwhelmed by the ardour of his love, " come. I know not what will be the end on't ; but come. Afterwards we will die together at the postern ! "

The same passion inflamed their bosoms ; the same harmony united them both ; and so they fell to it in the time-honoured fashion, and in the delicious throes of that wild fever which you know of—at least, I hope you do—they became totally indifferent to Savoisy's peril and their own, totally oblivious of the Constable, of death, of life, of everything.

Meanwhile, the people on watch at the porch had gone to tell the Constable that the gallant had arrived, and to inform him that the gentleman in question was so blinded with passion that he had paid no heed to the significant glances which the Countess had sent in his direction, both in church and on the way home, doubtless in order to save him from his doom. They met their master coming in great haste to the postern, for, on their part, the archers on the quay-side had signalled to him from afar, saying :

" Behold the Sire de Savoisy is passing in."

And in sooth, Savoisy had come at the trysting hour and, as is the way with lovers, thinking of nought save his lady, he had not noticed the Count's spies, but had

THAT PLEASANT DUEL IN WHICH
SHE ALWAYS PROVED HERSELF THE
STRONGER

slipped in at the postern suspecting nothing. Thus it was
that the Constable cut short the words of the messengers
from the rue Saint-Antoine, saying to them with an air
of authority, to which they deemed it well to bow :

" I know that the quarry is taken."

Thereupon they all rushed with a great shouting
through the postern :

" Kill him !   Kill him ! " they cried.

And men-at-arms, archers, Constable, captains, all
flung themselves on Charles Savoisy, the King's godson,
whom they ran to earth just underneath the Countess's
window, and by a strange coincidence, the groans sighed
forth by the unhappy young man blended sadly with the
yells of the soldiers, what time the two lovers, who now
hurried away in fear, were breathing out their passionate
sighs and moanings of delight.

" Ah ! " exclaimed the Countess, white with terror,
" 'tis Savoisy dies for me."

" But, I will live for you," answered Boys-Bourredon.
" And for my happiness, I would willingly give the
price that he is paying for his."

" Hide yourself in this chest," cried the Countess.
" I hear the footsteps of the Constable."

It was not a moment too soon, for in the space of a
second or two the Sieur d'Armignac appeared carrying
a head in his hand, which he placed, all bleeding as it
was, upon the mantelshelf.

" There, Madame," said he, " is a picture which will
indoctrinate you with the duties of a wife towards her
husband."

" You have slain an innocent man," retorted the
Countess, without changing colour ; " Savoisy was not
my lover."

As she said these words, she glanced proudly at the
Constable with a countenance so masked by feminine
daring and dissimulation, that her husband looked as
big a fool as a girl who has inadvertently let a note escape

L

from her posterior in company, and he was sore afraid
he had done a grievous thing.

" Then of whom were you thinking this morning,
Madame ? " asked he.

" I was dreaming of the King," she replied.

" Then, my sweetheart, why did you not tell me so ? "

" Would you have believed me, seeing the brutal rage
you were in ? "

The Constable shook his ears and answered :

" But how came Savoisy to have the key of our postern
gate ? "

" That I cannot say," she answered briefly ; " if you
will do me the honour to believe what I tell you."

And the Constable's lady turned swiftly on her heel,
like a weathervane spun round by the wind, pretending
to hurry off to attend to some household duties. You
may imagine that Monsieur d'Armignac was greatly
embarrassed with poor Savoisy's head and that, for his
part, Boys-Bourredon took great care not to cough when
he heard the Count growling and grumbling all manner
of things to himself. At last the Constable banged his
fist twice on the table and said :

" I will go and drop on the people of Poissy ! "

Thereupon he departed ; and, when the night was
come, Boys-Bourredon put on some sort of disguise and
escaped from the house.

The ill-fated Savoisy was deeply mourned by his lady-
love, who had done everything a woman could do to
save her lover. Later on she did more than mourn for
him, she missed him ; for having told the whole story
to Queen Isabelle, the latter seduced Boys-Bourredon
from her cousin's service and took him into her own, so
touched was she by the parts and admirable firmness of
the gentleman in question.

Boys-Bourredon's defiance of death had made him the
cynosure of feminine eyes. Indeed, he stood up so erect
against everything in the exalted station to which the

Queen had called him, that having insulted King Charles, one day, when the poor fellow was in his right senses, the courtiers, jealous of the favour he enjoyed, informed the King of the true state of affairs. In a moment, Boys-Bourredon was stitched up in a sack and thrown into the Seine, hard by the Charenton ferry, as all the world doth know. It is not necessary for me to add that, ever since the day when the Constable took it into his head to make such a rash use of edged tools, his good wife made such good use of the two corpses he had made and threw them up so often in his face, that she made him as soft as a cat's fur and tamed him to the usages of the married state. And he proclaimed her a sage and well-conducted Constable's dame, as in truth she was.

As, in accordance with the practice of the great writers of antiquity, this book should contain not only amusement but moral edification, I beg leave to inform you that the quintessence of the tale is as follows : First, women should never lose their heads even in the gravest crises, for the God of Love deserts them not, especially when they are young, beautiful and well-born. Secondly, gallants, when proceeding to keep a love-tryst, should never act like heedless boys : they should comport themselves soberly and carefully explore the rabbit warrens, so as to keep clear of any ambushes that may have been prepared for them ; for next to a good woman, the thing most precious in the world is a pretty gentleman.

THE VIRGIN OF THILHOUSE

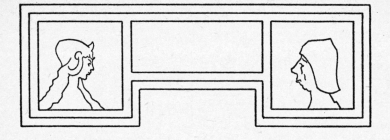

THE VIRGIN OF THILHOUSE

THE Lord of Valesnes, a pleasant place whereof the Castle is not far distant from the burg of Thilhouse, had taken to himself a delicate wife who, from taste or distaste, pleasure or displeasure, illness or health, suffered her worthy husband to go lacking those sweetmeats and sugared dainties which are provided for in every marriage contract. Justice, however, requires us to say that the aforesaid lord was a very foul and ill-favoured specimen of his sex, for ever hunting wild beasts and no more diverting than chimney smoke in a withdrawing-room. Then over and above all that, this sporting husband was a good sixty years of age; a fact whereof he made no manner of mention, no more than the widow of a gibbeted felon will talk to you of hemp. But Nature, who turns out all kinds of specimens, twisted, bandy, blind and ugly, by the basketful, with the same indifference as she manufactures the well-formed and comely (seeing that after the manner of one weaving tapestry, she knows not what she does), gives, to all alike, the same appetites, the same desire to taste of the stew. So, by some means or another, every beast finds a stable, whence the proverb: "There's never a pot so ugly but it finds a cover." Therefore did the Lord of Valesnes look about him for well-favoured pots to cover; and, besides the big beasts of the chase, often beat the coverts for smaller game. But the neighbourhood was very barren of such delectable game, and it was a costly

163

business to unearth a maidenhead.   Howbeit, by dint
of nosing here and nosing there, it came to pass that the
Lord of Valesnes was informed that there dwelt in
Thilhouse the widow of a certain weaver, who possessed a
very real treasure in the person of a little wench of sixteen,
whom she had always kept tied up to her apron-strings,
and whom, from lofty dictates of maternal prudence,
she even accompanied when she went to pee.   Likewise
did she put her to sleep in her own bed.   She watched
over her, told her when to get up in the morning and so
wearied her out with work that, betwixt the two of them,
they earned a full eight pennies a day.   On feast-days,
she kept her securely on the leash in church, giving her
but the scantiest opportunity of bandying a jest or two
with the lads of the village ; and even so 'twas forbidden
them to lay their hands over freely on the maiden.   But
those times were hard times, and the widow and her
daughter had only just enough bread to prevent them
dying of hunger, and as they lodged in the house of one
of their poor kinsmen, they often lacked wood in winter
and clothes in summer, owing rent enough to frighten a
sergeant of justice, a class who are not easily frightened
at the debts of other people.   To be brief, if the maiden
grew in beauty, the widow grew in poverty, and encumbered herself with heavy debts in thus preserving her
daughter's maidenhead, even as an alchemist screws and
pinches for the retort into which he pours anything and
everything.

When his enquiries were made and completed, it
chanced one rainy day that the Lord of Valesnes went to
seek shelter in the hovel of the two weavers ; and in order
to dry himself sent for some faggots to a neighbouring
plantation.   While he was waiting, he sat him down on a
form between the two poor women.   Notwithstanding
the dim and shadowy twilight that imperfectly illumined
the interior of the cottage, he noticed the well-favoured
countenance of the maiden of Thilhouse, her goodly

WHOM THEY RAN TO EARTH
JUST UNDERNEATH THE
COUNTESS'S WINDOW

THE VIRGIN OF
THILHOUZE

arms both red and firm ; her two advance guards hard as bastions, which kept the cold from her heart ; her waist as round as the bole of a young oak ; the whole as fresh and clean and spruce and trim as the year's first touch of frost ; green and tender as an April bud ; in a word, she was just like anything and everything that is beautiful in the world.   Her eyes were innocent and blue, and her expression even more demure than the Virgin's, she being less advanced in experience and never having had a child.

Had anyone accosted her and said, " Will you take your pleasure ? " she would have said, " Gramercy, but where ? " so prim seemed she and little given to taking the matter in.   So the worthy old lord turned and twisted on his form, sniffed and snuffed about the girl, and craned his neck like a monkey trying to pick up nuts.   The mother saw well enough what was going on, but dared not breathe a word for fear of the baron who owned all the land round about.   When the faggot was put on the hearth and began to blaze, the worthy sportsman said to the woman :

" Ah, ah ! That's nearly as warming as your daughter's eyes ! "

" Alas, my lord," said she, " her eyes be well enough, but 'tis a fire we cannot cook by."

" Of a surety, you can," he replied.

" And how ? " quoth she.

" Why, sweet dame, lend this child of yours to my wife.   She needs a maid, and we will give you two faggots a day in payment."

" Good my lord, and what would you have me cook at that excellent domestic fire ? "

" Why," answered the worthy, " plenty of good broth, for you shall have a minot of wheat with every harvest."

" And where would you have me store it ? "

" In your bin ! " exclaimed the collector of maidenheads.

" But I have no bin, no chest, no nothing."

" Well, then, I will give you chests, bins, stoves, and a goodly bed with a canopy."

" Ah ! " said the good widow, " but the rain will spoil them, for I have no house wherein to put them."

" See you not yonder," answered the noble lord, " the dwelling of la Tourbellière, where dwelt my poor huntsman Pillegrain, he who was gored to death by a boar ? "

" Aye," said the old woman.

" Well, then, you can go and burrow there till the end of your days."

" By my halidome ! " cried the mother as she let fall her distaff ; " are you speaking the truth ? "

" I am."

" Well, but what wages will you pay my daughter ? "

" Whatever she cares to earn when she is in my service," was the answer.

" Oh, my lord, but you must be joking ! "

" Not a whit," said he.

" Nay, but you must be," she replied.

" By Saint Gatien, Saint Eleuther, and the thousand million saints that swarm and pullulate in Paradise, I swear that . . ."

" Oh, well, then, if you are not joking, I should just like the notary to give a bit of an eye to those faggots."

" By heavens and your daughter's sweetest part, am I not a gentleman ?   My word's my bond ! "

" Nay, that I deny not, my lord ; but it is also true that I am but a poor weaver, and I love my daughter too well to part with her.   She is as yet too young and delicate ; and service would overtax her strength.   Why, 'twas yesterday the parson told us in his sermon that we were responsible to God for our children."

" Ah, well, well, go fetch the notary ! "

An old woodman hurried away to the notary, who came forthwith and drew up, then and there, a contract whereto the Lord of Valesnes affixed his mark, for he knew not how to write.   Then, when 'twas signed and sealed all in due form, he said :

" How now, Mother, and are you answerable to God for your daughter's maidenhead now ? "

" Ah, my lord, but the parson said, ' until she reaches the years of discretion,' and my daughter is already very discreet."

Then turning to her daughter the old woman continued :

" Marie Ficquet, the most precious of all your possessions is your honour.   Now in the place to which you are going, everyone—my lord apart—will endeavour to rob you of it.   But you perceive what a great value it possesses.   Therefore, never part with it, save when it shall profit you to do so, and in a seemly manner.   Now, so that your virtue may not be contaminated before God and man (save on a lawful occasion) take heed, beforehand, to season your treasure with a pinch of matrimonial salt, or it shall go hard with thee."

" Ay, Mother," said the maiden.

And thereupon she quitted her mother's house and came to the Château of Valesnes, in order that she might serve the lady thereof, who deemed her right comely and wholly to her liking.

When the poeple of Valesnes, Sacché, Villaines, and other places, came to know the high price given for the Maid of Thilhouse, the worthy peasant women, recognising that there was nought more profitable than virtue, endeavoured to rear and nourish all their daughters in a state of virginity ; but the task was no less precarious than the breeding of silk-worms which are so liable to accident ; for maidenheads are like medlars and ripen quickly on the straw.   Nevertheless, there were a few girls who had this reputation in Touraine and who passed for virgins in all the monasteries round about.   For this, however, I myself would not answer, never having examined them in the manner prescribed by Verville for testing the virtue of an alleged maiden. Finally, Marie Ficquet took her mother's sage advice and would listen to none of her master's sweet petitions, and honeyed speeches and pretty dalliance, without a little infusion of matrimony.

When the old lord made as if he would towsel her, she drew away in fear like a cat at the approach of a dog and cried :

" I shall tell Madame ! "

In short, six months went by and the old gentleman had not yet recovered so much as the price of a single faggot. Ever growing firmer and tougher in the discharge of her labours, the girl, on one occasion, replied to her master's importunities by asking :

" When you have taken it away, will you give it me back again, eh ? "

And on another occasion she said :

" If I had as many holes as a colander, I shouldn't have one for you, so ugly are you in my sight."

The old gentleman took this yokel badinage for the blossoms of virtue and never wearied of laying siege to her, making little signs, delivering himself of long harangues and vowing endless vows. For the sight of the girl's breasts, her rounded thighs, which certain movements brought out into strong relief through her petticoats, aye and by pondering with admiration on certain other things that would have turned the brain of a saint, the worthy gentleman had become enamoured of her with all an old man's passion, which increases by geometrical progression, unlike the passions of younger folk. For old men love with their weakness, and that increases ; and young ones with their strength, and that diminishes. And in order to deprive the young she-devil of all further pretext for rejecting his advances, the old fellow had recourse to one of the stewards of his household, whose age was seventy and something more, and informed him that he ought to take to himself a wife

in order to increase his bodily warmth, and that Marie
Ficquet was the very girl for him. The old steward,
who had put by some three hundred livres which he had
saved from the wages he had earned in divers capacities
in the house, only asked to live at peace for the rest of
his days without opening the front door any more. But
his worthy master, having asked him to marry as a special
favour to himself, assured him that no matrimonial
obligation should ever mar his peace of mind. On the
strength of this assurance, the old servitor drifted into
marriage. On the day of the betrothal, Marie Ficquet,
deprived of all her arguments, and having no further
objection to urge against her suitor, insisted on a fat
dowry and a generous marriage settlement as the price
of her virginity. These preliminaries being satisfactorily
settled, she gave full leave to the old cockbird to come
and sleep with her as often as he could, promising him
as many goodly bouts as he should give wheat to her
mother. But he was old and a single bushel was enough.

The marriage being completed, the old gentleman, as
soon as his wife was between the sheets, made straight
for the room, richly furnished with mirrors, carpets and
adornments, where he had lodged his canary, his shekels,
his faggots, his house and his steward.

To cut a long story short, he found the virgin of
Thilhouse the finest wench in all the world, pretty as
pretty could be by the soft light of the fire that glowed
and flickered in the fireplace, right cuddlesome between
the sheets, always ready for the fray, with a nice, fresh,
virgin smell about her ; and in short, he never had any
regrets about the heavy price he had paid for such a
jewel. Not being able to keep himself from dispatching
the first mouthfuls of this royal and delectable morsel,
the old lord treated her rather as a veteran than as a novice
in the matter of love. So it came about that the happy
man by being over-greedy, spoilt the game, slipped and
slithered and showed himself a poor performer in love's

sweet tourney. Seeing this, the good wench says innocently to her aged cavalier :

" Good Master, if it is well with you, as I think it is, give, I pray you, a little more swing to your bells."

This speech, which got abroad I know not how, made Marie Ficquet famous, and even now in our country they talk about " a pucelle de Thilhouse " when they want to make light of a married woman, and to imply that she is what they term a " fricquenelle."

Fricquenelle is a term applied to the sort of wench that I hope you won't find between your sheets the first night of your marriage, unless you are deeply imbued with the philosophy of the Stoics, and are of a nature to be dismayed at nothing. And indeed, there be many who are compelled to be Stoics at such a droll conjuncture, for they are still of pretty frequent occurrence. For the world spins round, but Nature changes not, and there will always be a goodly supply of virgins of Thilhouse in Touraine and elsewhere. Now, if you ask me to tell you wherein consists the moral of this tale, I should be well within my rights in saying to the ladies that my Droll Stories are designed rather to impart the morality of pleasure than to preach the pleasure of morality.

But if my interlocutor were a war-worn old veteran, I should say unto him, with the respect and deference due to his grey or yellow wig, that God wanted to punish the Lord of Valesnes for having tried to purchase a commodity that was made to be bestowed as a gift.

THE BROTHERS-IN-ARMS

THE ONE ALWAYS
SECONDED THE OTHER

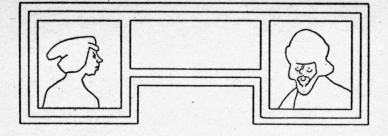

THE BROTHERS-IN-ARMS

IN the beginning of the reign of King Henry, the second of that name, he who so dearly loved the beautiful Diana of Poictiers, there still survived a ceremony which afterwards lapsed into desuetude and which has now fallen into complete neglect like countless other things of the good old days. This gracious and noble custom was the choosing of a brother-in-arms, a custom which no true knight ever failed to observe. When they had recognised each other for true and loyal souls, each one of the pair was wedded for life to the other; the two became brothers. The one would defend the other in battle against the foes that menaced him, and at the Court against the friends who slandered him. And, in the absence of his companion, the other was in duty bound to say to any who should accuse his good brother of any disloyal, mean or treacherous act, "You lie in your throat," and to go forthwith to the duelling-ground, so certain were they of each other's honour. It needeth not to say that the one always seconded the other in every affair, good or evil, and that they shared everything between them, good fortune or bad. They were nearer and dearer than the brothers who are merely united by the hazard of nature, since their fraternity was based upon feelings that were both mutual and involuntary. Thus this brotherhood of arms has produced some noble examples of character and conduct, as fine as any narrated of the Greeks or Romans,

M

or whom you will. But that is not my subject. The stories thereof are written in the chronicles of our land and they are known unto all.

In the days of which I speak, there were two young esquires of Touraine, one the Cadet de Maillé, the other the Sieur de Lavallière, who became brothers-in-arms on the day they won their spurs. They came from the household of M. de Montmorency and were imbued with the teaching of that great captain. Moreover, they had shown how contagious was valour in that noble company, seeing that, at the battle of Ravenna, they both earned the praises of the most experienced knights. 'Twas in the throng and press of that hard-fought day that Maillé, whose life was saved by the aforesaid Lavallière, with whom he had some slight misunderstandings, perceived that Lavallière had a noble heart. As they had each been smitten between the joints of their harness, they sealed their covenant with blood and were tended together in the same bed within the tent of M. de Montmorency their master. Now it must be put on record that, contrary to what was usual in his family, where good looks were ever the rule, the Cadet de Maillé was not well favoured, and such points as he possessed were rather calculated to win him favour with the Devil. He was as lithe as a greyhound, broad-shouldered and as strongly built as King Pepin, who was a terrible fighter. On the other hand, the Sieur de Château-Lavallière was a dainty youth for whom you would have thought fine lace, elegant hose, and latticed shoon had been specially invented. His long fair hair was lovely as a woman's tresses. In short, 'twas a lad with whom all the women would have liked to toy. Thus it chanced, one day, that the Dauphine, who was the Pope's niece, said with a laugh to the Queen of Navarre—for she had a taste for such badinage—"that that page was a plaster which would cure one of every ill." The little Tourainian blushed when he heard this, for being but sixteen years of age, he interpreted this piece of gallantry as a reproach.

On his return from Italy, the Cadet de Maillé found that his mother had arranged an advantageous match for him in the person of Mademoiselle d'Annebault, a charming maiden richly favoured in face and fortune, with a noble residence in the rue Barbette, plentifully stocked with furniture and Italian paintings, besides considerable estates to which she would succeed. Some days after the death of King Francis, an event which struck terror into every heart, seeing that the said monarch had died of the bad disorder and that henceforth there would be no such thing as safety for any man, not even with the highest princesses in the land, the aforesaid Maillé was obliged to quit the Court in order to go and settle some matters of grave importance in Piedmont. You may imagine how sad he was at leaving so young and fresh and dainty a bride in the midst of the dangers, lures, snares and surprises of that gallant company which included among its numbers so many fine lads, bold as eagles, proud of mien, and as hungry for women as folk are eager for ham at Eastertide. Being thus beset with jealous apprehensions, he considered the situation as highly disagreeable. But, after pondering long upon the matter, he decided to safeguard his wife in the manner here following. He requested his brother-in-arms to come to him at dawn, on the morning of his departure. When then he heard the clatter of Lavallière's horse in his courtyard, he leapt from his bed, leaving his lovely white-skinned bride still sleeping the downy slumber so dear to the indolent. Lavallière hurried to meet his friend, and the two comrades greeted each other with a loyal clasp of the hand ; then said Lavallière to Maillé :

" I had come last night in answer to your summons but that I had an amorous assignation with my lady, who had given me tryst. I could in no wise fail her. But I left her side this morning. Is it your wish that I

should come with you ? I have told her of your departure, and she has promised to remain pure and true to her
vows. And if she fail me, well, a friend is more important
than a mistress."

" Oh, dearest brother mine," said Maillé, deeply
touched at these words. " I am going to beg for yet a
nobler proof of thy true heart. Will you watch o'er my
wife when I'm away, guide her, hold her in check, and
answer to me for my love's integrity ? Here you will
stay, while I am far away, here in this chamber hung with
green, and you shall be my wife's true knight."

Knitting his brows, Lavallière made answer :

" 'Tis not of thee, nor of thy wife, nor of myself that
I'm afeared, but of the slanderous tongues of spiteful folk,
who will in this behold a means of sowing strife between
us."

" Mistrust me not," said Maillé, clasping Lavallière
to his breast. " If it were God's will that I should be a
cuckold, 'twould wound me less did I but know 'twas for
thy sake. . . . But, by my troth, I should die of grief,
for I madly dote upon my sweet and fresh and virtuous
spouse."

So saying, he turned away his head so that Lavallière
should not perceive the teardrop in his eye ; but the
comely youth saw the glistening pearl, and taking Maillé's
hand thus spake :

" Brother, I give thee my word as man to man that ere
anyone shall lay a hand upon thy wife, he shall feel my
dagger in his entrails. And unless I die, thou shalt
find her intact of body if not of heart. I say, if not of
heart, for another's thoughts it is not within the power
of any knight to control."

" Oh, then, 'tis writ in heaven that I shall ever be thy
servant and thy debtor."

Upon those words he turned and went, for he would
not give way to moans and tears and other luxuries in
which women, when they say farewell, indulge so freely.

Then Lavallière, having borne him company to the city gate, came to the house again, and waiting for Marie d'Annebault to come forth from her bed, told her of her husband's departure, placed himself at her command, all with such soft and winning grace, that the most virtuous wife would have felt the itchings of desire to keep such a knight for herself. But there was no need to ply the dame with these fair words, for she had over-heard all that had passed between the friends and sorely resented the doubts her husband entertained concerning her.

Alas, we may take it that God alone is perfect! Into all human ideas some base alloy will always enter. It is a fine accomplishment in the art of life, but one impossible of attainment, to take hold of things, even of a stick, by the right end. The reason that it is so difficult to please the women is that they include in their composition something even more feminine than they are themselves, to which, were it not for the respect I owe them, I should give a plainer name. Now it behoves us to take great heed not to awaken the fantasies of this plaguey organ. The proper management of women is a task to put a man beside himself; and the best thing is to yield submis-sively to all their fantasies : that, I fancy, is the best way to solve the agonising problem presented by the thorny state of matrimony. Marie d'Annebault deemed herself fortunate in having so willing and gentle a knight to serve her; but in her smile there was a twinkle of mis-chievous implication; in short, the intention of making her young look-after-my-what-you-may-call-it choose between duty and pleasure, so to importune him with love, so to foster him with tender attentions, so to pursue him with glowing eyes, that he should sacrifice friendship for the sake of love.

Everything favoured the execution of her plan, seeing the close relations which the Sieur de Lavallière was expected and required to have with her, as one dwelling under the same roof. And sith there is nought in the world that can deflect a woman from the aim she has in view, the minx lost no opportunity of spreading her snares for him.

Sometimes, she would beseech him to stay with her beside the fire, even until midnight, what time she would sing softly to him, losing no opportunity of displaying her lovely shoulders, the white and tempting breasts that filled her corsage, ogling him with countless amorous glances; and all without suffering her countenance to betray the thoughts and plans she harboured in her mind.

Sometimes, of a morning, she would take the air with him in the gardens of her house, and lean full heavily upon his arm, press it and sigh, and make him tie the latchet of her shoe which most conveniently would continually come undone. And then again, there were countless pretty speeches and all those numberless devices in which women are so skilled; little attentions a hostess might bestow upon her guests, such as coming to see if he was comfortable; if the bed was right; if he felt any draught at night, or if there was too much sun by day; enjoining him to make known to her his slightest wish.

" Are you accustomed to have something in bed in the morning ? Hydromel or milk, or a stimulant of some sort ? " " Have you a good appetite for your meals ? " " You shall have whatever you desire ; only say the word." " Why, I believe you are shy—— Come now ! "

And all this coddling she accompanied with all manner of pretty artless ways, saying, for example, as she went in to him :

" Now I am sure I am worrying you. Send me packing if I am ! Come, I see you want to be alone. Well, I will take myself off."

And every time she was graciously requested to remain. On every occasion too the cunning jade came very lightly clad, showing such samples of her beauty as would have brought a neigh of lasciviousness from a patriarch as time-worn as Methuselah at the age of a hundred and sixty.

The good brother-in-arms, who lacked not keenness of understanding, suffered the lady to do as she listed, mighty content to see her so busy in his behalf, for 'twas all to his advantage. But, like a loyal friend, he never failed to call up the vision of the absent husband to his hostess's eyes.

One evening, after a very hot day, Lavallière, apprehensive of the lady's advances, remarked how deeply Maillé loved her, how she had a man of honour for a husband, a gentleman full of ardour for her and very careful of his treasure.

" Wherefore then," said she, " if he be so careful, has he brought you here ? "

" Is that not a proof of his great caution ? " answered he. " Was it not well bethought to assign you some champion of your virtue, not, in sooth, that so far as you are concerned, it is necessary, but merely to protect you from evil-minded. . . ."

" So, then, you are my guardian ? " she asked.

" And right proud of my office ! " exclaimed Lavallière.

" In sooth," said she, " he has made an ill choice."

This remark was accompanied by a glance so openly lascivious that, by way of rebuking her, the good brother-in-arms assumed a look of lofty virtue and left the fair lady to herself ; and sore vexed was she at this tacit refusal to try a fall with her in the lists of love.

She lingered long in meditation and began to enquire into the real nature of the obstacle she had encountered ; for no woman could ever persuade herself that any worthy gentleman could really disdain that pastime which is held to be so precious and delectable.   Now so thoroughly did these ideas fit and match one another that, bit by bit, she completed the whole design and found herself head over ears in love. The which should teach the women never to play with men's arms; for if you handle the bird-lime some of it always sticks to your fingers.

Thus Marie d'Annebault finished where she ought to have begun, and she came to the conclusion that if the worthy knight was immune from her wiles, it was because he was entangled in someone else's. She looked about her to see where her young guest could have found a recipient of his affections, and she bethought her that the fair Limeuil, one of Queen Catherine's daughters, and Mesdames de Nevers, d'Estrées and de Giac were all well known as friends of Lavallière, and she concluded that, with one at least amongst them, he must be passionately in love.

Thus she added jealousy to all the other motives which urged her to compass the seduction of her Messire Argus, whose head she by no means wished to cut off, but only to cover it with perfume and kisses, and do no harm to any other part of him.

Certes, she was fairer, younger, more appetising and more dainty than her rivals; such, at all events, was the judgment which her own heart whispered to her. So, urged by every chord in her being, all those springs of conscience and physical causes which set women in motion, she returned to the charge, and renewed the assault on the heart of the doughty knight. For women dearly love to capture what is strongly fortified against them. Then she played the kitten, curled herself up so close to him, caressed him so lovingly, tamed him so gently, and petted and patted him so sweetly that, one night, when she had assumed a dejected air, though in her heart she was as merry as a cricket, she gave him no alternative but to say:

" What ails you, then ? "

Whereupon, with thoughtful mien she made answer in words that fell upon his ears like music, that she had married Maillé against the dictates of her heart and that

she was very unhappy on that account; that she had never
tasted the delights of love; that her husband had no skill
therein, and that the rest of her life would be full of
sorrow.   In short, she made herself out to be a virgin
at heart and indeed everywhere else, since all she had
experienced in the matter was pain and discomfort.
Then she added, that in spite of her experiences, the thing
must be full of every kind of sweetness and delight,
seeing that all the women rushed after it, insisted on
having it, were even jealous of those who sold it them, for
some had to pay dearly for their satisfaction.   She added
that she herself was so eager for the experience that for a
single good day or night of love, she would devote her
life without a murmur to her lover.   And then she went
on to say that the man, with whom it would delight her
most to taste of love, would not listen to her, and yet
their meetings might always remain a secret seeing the
trust her husband put in him.   Finally, she said that if he
persisted in his refusal, it would be her death.

And all these paraphrases of the little canticle, which
all women know as soon as they come into the world,
were gasped forth amid countless silences, broken by
sighs plucked from the heart, adorned with many writhings, appeals to heaven, upturned eyes, sudden little
blushings, and clutchings at the hair; in short, all the
herbs known to Saint John were put into the dish.   And
as at the bottom of all these words there was a gnawing
desire, which would make even a plain woman look
desirable, the good knight fell at the lady's feet, took them
in his hands, kissed them and bathed them with his tears.
You may easily imagine that the good lady was well
pleased to have her feet thus covered with kisses.   Aye,
and without looking too closely at what he might be
pleased to do with it, she suffered him to have a free hand
with her dress, well knowing that in order to raise it, he
would be obliged to take hold of it from below.   But it
was written that she should be virtuous that night, for

the handsome Lavallière said to her with despair in his voice :

"Ah, Madame, an unhappy and unworthy wight am I ! "

"Nay, nay, go to ! " quoth she.

"Alas, the joy of being yours is for ever denied me."

"How so ? " she asked.

"I dare not tell you how it is with me."

"Are you then in so ill a plight ? "

"Oh, I should make you blush if——"

"Say on ; I'll hide my face within my hands."

And the cunning jade so hid her face that she could see her well-beloved between her fingers.

"Alas ! " said he, "the other night when you spake such gracious words to me, I was heated with such a traitorous fire that knowing not my happiness was so near, and never daring to confess to you my passion, I hied me to the common stews. There, for love of you and to save my brother's honour, on whose escutcheon I would lay no stain, I was stung most grievously so that now I am in danger of dying of the bad disorder."

Seized with terror, the lady yelled like a woman in the pangs of labour and, quite overcome, very gently pushed him from her. Thereupon the hapless Lavallière, seeing himself in such a sorry plight, made as though to quit the chamber ; but no sooner had he reached the hangings of the doorway than Marie d'Annebault once more turned her eyes upon him and said to herself, "Oh, the pity of it ! " Then she fell into a deep melancholy, mourning over her gentleman's mischance and loving him the more passionately because he was thrice forbidden fruit.

"Were it not for Maillé," said she, one night, when he seemed to her more handsome than ever before, "I should love to catch your malady and share its tortures with you."

"I love you too dearly," answered the knight, "ever to take advantage of you."

And so he left her and sought his fair Limeuil. You may guess that since he could not receive the lady's warming glances, there burned, at meal-times and at eventide, a powerful fire which greatly heated them. Yet must she needs continue to live without touching the knight, save indeed with her glances. By this means, Marie d'Annebault found herself armed at every point against the gallants of the Court; for there is no more impassable barrier or surer guardian than love. Love is like the Devil. What it holds it encompasses with flame. One night, Lavallière, having escorted his friend's wife to a ballet of Queen Catherine, began to dance with the fair Limeuil, with whom he was madly in love. In those days knights would boldly flaunt it with two or even troops of ladies at a time. Now all the ladies were jealous of Limeuil, who, at that moment, was purposing to give herself to the handsome Lavallière. Before taking her place in the quadrille, she had given him the sweetest of assignations for the morrow during the hunt. Our great Queen Catherine, who, for reasons of high policy, fomented these loves and stirred them up as pastry-cooks make their ovens hot by poking, the Queen, I say, glanced at all the pretty couples enlaced in the quadrille, and said to her husband :

" As long as they do battle here, can they league themselves against you, eh ? "

" Aye, but what of the Huguenots ? "

" Why, we shall catch them too," said she with a laugh. " Look, here comes Lavallière who is suspected of being a Huguenot. See, he is a convert to my beloved Limeuil, who does not cut such a bad figure for a wench of sixteen. He will have her down on his list."

" Nay, Madame, never think it," said Marie d'Annebault, " for that same pox which made you Queen has ruined him."

At this delightfully naïve utterance, Catherine, the fair Diana and the King, who were standing there in a group, burst out laughing, and soon the speech was quickly passing from ear to ear. For Lavallière it meant shame and mocking banter without end. They pointed at the poor gentleman, and he soon began to wish he was in someone else's shoes, for La Limeuil, whom Lavallière's rivals lost no time in warning of her danger, looked utterly blank at her lover so great was her amazement and so heavy her dread of this terrible disease. Lavallière, therefore, was shunned and deserted as though he had been a leper. The King addressed him in a highly disagreeable manner, and the worthy knight left the ballroom followed by poor Marie, who was utterly crestfallen at the King's words. She had brought about the utter ruin of the man she loved ; she had robbed him of his good name and ruined his life since the physicians and master surgeons put it forward as an incontrovertible fact that such as were Italianised by this love-sickness, lost thereby their greatest advantages, ceased to possess any generative powers and turned black in all their bones.

Wherefore, no woman would suffer herself to be united in lawful wedlock, even with the greatest gentleman in the kingdom, if he were but suspected of belonging to that company whom Master Francis Rabelais named " his very precious scabs."

As the knight said but little and remained plunged in deep melancholy, his companion said to him, as they were returning from the Hôtel d'Hercules, where the ball was being held :

" My dear lord, I have wrought you a grievous ill."

" Madame," replied Lavallière, " my malady is curable ; but to what a pretty pass you have brought yourself. Ought you to have been aware of the danger of my love ? "

" Ah ! " said she, " henceforth I am sure always to be able to keep you for myself. In exchange for the grievous dishonour I have brought upon you, I will for ever be your friend, your hostess, and your lady, aye,

and more than that, your servant. Thus I am resolved
to give myself to you and obliterate the traces of this
shame, to tend you and to nurse you back to health; and
if the folk, who are learned in these matters, declare that
the evil is too deeply rooted, that it will be the death of
you, even as it was of our late King, still must I abide
with you in order that in dying of your malady, I may die
a glorious death! But alack-a-day!" she cried, bursting
into tears, "there is no torment so dire as would atone
for the wrong that I have done you."

Great tears fell from her eyes as she uttered these words.
'Twas more than her right virtuous heart could endure,
and she fell back unconscious.

Beside himself with terror, Lavallière caught her and
placed his hand upon her heart above a breast of matchless
beauty. The lady revived at the warm touch of this
beloved hand, experiencing such exquisite delight that
she nearly fainted a second time.

"Alas!" she sighed, "such teasing and superficial
titillations will henceforth be our passion's only satisfaction. Even so they are whole worlds above the joys
which poor Maillé endeavoured to procure me. Leave
your hand where it is!" said she. "Of a truth it rests
upon my soul and touches it."

Hearing her say these words, the knight, his features
still o'erspread with melancholy, innocently avowed to
his lady that it filled him with such bliss to touch her
that the pains of his malady were much increased thereby
and that death itself were preferable to such a martyrdom.

"Then let us die together," she exclaimed.

But the litter was in the courtyard and, as the means
of death were lacking at the moment, they slept each
apart from the other sorely incommoded with love, for
Lavallière had lost his fair Limeuil and Marie d'Annebault
had found joys incomparable.

From this mischance, which was entirely unforeseen,
Lavallière found himself cut off alike from love and

marriage. He dared not show his face anywhere, and it was borne in upon him that the guardianship and safe-keeping of a woman's virtue was a costly business; but the more he recognised that it was a question of honour, the more pleasure he derived from the great sacrifices made to his brother-in-arms. Nevertheless, he found the path of duty very arduous, very thorny, and impossible to negotiate towards the end of his trust.

This is how it befell:

The confession of her love, which she believed was requited, the wrong which she had wrought her knight and the experience which she had never dreamt, imparted great boldness to the conduct of the fair Marie, who lapsed into platonic love slightly tempered by those pleasing little indulgences which involve no risk.

From this cause proceeded the devilishly attractive pleasures known as "the little goose trimmings" invented by the ladies, who, since the death of King Francis were afraid of infection, but at the same time wished to give gratification to their lovers. To play his part in these delights, Lavallière could not refuse, thus every evening the love-lorn Marie would strain her lover to her, hold his hands, cover him with kisses and glue her cheek to his, and as this virtuous embrace in which the knight was caught and held like a devil in a holy-water stoup, she told him of her great love, her love which had no bounds, for it plumbed the infinite depths of unsatisfied desire. All the fire which women bring to their incarnate passions when the shadows of night are illumined only by their eyes, she conveyed with mystical movements of her head, the exaltations of her soul and the ecstasies of her heart; then, naturally, and with the delicious joy of two angels united solely by the understanding, they breathed out together the sweet litanies which lovers were wont to recite in those days in honour of love, anthems which the Abbot of Theleme paragraphically rescued from oblivion by engraving them on the walls of his abbey, situated, according to Master Alcofribas, in our land of Chinon, where I have seen them in Latin and have here set them down for the benefit of my Christian brethren.

" Ah me ! " sighed Marie d'Annebault ; " you are my strength and my life, my joy and my treasure."

" And you," answered he, " are a pearl, an angel ! "

" Thou art my seraph ! "

" You are my soul ! "

" Thou art my god ! "

" You are my evening and morning star, my honour, my beauty and my universe ! "

" Thou art my great, my divine master ! "

" You are my glory, my faith, my religion ! "

" Thou art my gentle, handsome, courageous, noble loved one, my knight, my defender, my king, my darling ! "

" You are my fairy, the flower of my days, the flower of my nights ! "

" Thou art my thought at every moment ! "

" You are the delight of my eyes ! "

" Thou art the voice of my soul ! "

" You are my light in the daytime ! "

" Thou illuminest the darkness of my nights ! "

" Thou art the most adored of men ! "

" You are my life's blood, more really *I* than I myself ! "

" Thou art my heart, my light ! "

" You are my saint, my only joy ! "

" I yield thee the palm of love, and great as is my love, I hope thou lovest me still more, for thou art my lord and master ! "

" Nay, the palm is yours, my goddess, my Virgin Mary ! "

" Nay, I am thy servant, thy handmaiden, thy nothing that thou canst crush to dust ! "

" Nay, nay, 'tis I who am your slave, your faithful page, yours to use as you would a breath of air, yours on whom you may tread as on a carpet ; my heart is your throne ! "

" No, my friend, my loved one, for thy voice pierces me through ! "

" Your eyes set me on fire ! "

" I only behold things through thine eyes ! "

" I only feel through you ! "

" Ah well, lay thy hand upon my heart, thy hand alone, and thou shalt see how pale I grow when my blood has grown warm from the contact of thine own."

During these antiphons of love, their eyes, already so bright, gleamed still more rapturously, and the knight, for all his virtue, could not but share some of the bliss which Marie tasted when she felt his hand upon her heart.

Thus in this gentle dalliance, he put forth all his strength ; all his desires were awakened, and so vividly was the picture brought to his mind that he melted wholly and completely. Hot were the tears they shed as they clasped one another, even as the fire seizes hold of houses— but that was all.

Lavallière had promised to return her inviolate in body—but not in soul—to his brother-in-arms.

When Maillé made known his return, it was not a moment too soon ; for no virtue could have held out any longer against the heat of such a fire, and the less freedom the lovers had to indulge their passion, the more delicious were the dreams that visited them.

Leaving Marie d'Annebault, the worthy brother-in-arms journeyed even to Bondy to meet his friend and to help him pass through the forest without mischance ; and the two brothers laid them down together according to ancient custom in one bed in the town of Bondy.

There in that bed, they exchanged all manner of tidings ; the one telling what had befallen him upon his journey, the other all the scandal and gossip of the Court. But Maillé's first question concerned Marie d'Annebault, and Lavallière swore that she was intact in that precious

THERE IN THAT BED THEY EXCHANGED
ALL MANNER OF TIDINGS

spot where dwells a husband's honour. Whereat the amorous Maillé was well content.

On the morrow they were all three united again to the great regret of Marie, who, with lofty jurisprudence which characterises the attitude of the female, made a great fuss of her husband; but with her finger she pointed out her heart to Lavallière, making pretty gestures as though to say to him, " All this is thine." At supper, Lavallière gave out that he was leaving for the wars. Maillé was deeply grieved at this weighty resolution and wished to accompany his brother, but Lavallière would have none of it.

" Madame," said he to Marie d'Annebault, " I love you more than life but not more than my honour."

He grew pale as he said this, and Madame de Maillé grew pale as she heard his words; for never into all their dalliance had there entered so much of love as into that single speech.

Maillé insisted on travelling with his friend as far as Meaux. When he came back he fell to talking with his wife what mysterious and hidden reasons could have brought about this departure, but Marie, who knew the sorrows and troubles of poor Lavallière, said :

" I know the reason well enough : 'tis because he is ashamed to remain here, for everyone knows that he has the evil malady."

" What ! " said Maillé thoroughly amazed. " I saw him when we were sleeping at Bondy the other night and again yesterday at Meaux; there's nothing the matter with him, he's as healthy as your eye."

The lady dissolved into tears, wondering at such great loyalty, this sublime resignation to his vow, and to the terrible sufferings he must have endured within him. But, as she cherished her love within the depths of her heart, she died when Lavallière met his death before Metz, as has been elsewhere set down by Messire Bourdeilles de Brantosme in his gossip's tales.

N

THE CURE OF AZAY-LE-RIDEAU

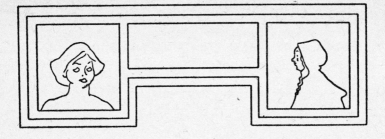

THE CURÉ OF AZAY-LE-RIDEAU

IN those days priests no longer took to themselves women in lawful wedlock, but concubines, kind of heart and pretty if so it were possible. But this has been forbidden by the council, as everybody knows, because it was not pleasant that people's particular secrets should be related to a wench who would laugh at them—to say nothing of the abstruse doctrines, ecclesiastical arrangements and speculations which abound in the policy of the Holy Roman Church. The last priest of our countryside, who theologically kept a woman in his parsonage, regaling her with his scholastic love, was a certain vicar of Azay-le-Rideau, a right pleasant spot which was afterwards called Azay-le-Bruslé, whereof the castle is one of the marvels of Touraine.

Now, this time, when women were not averse to the smell of a priest, is not so far away as some might think, for the see of Paris was occupied by Monsieur d'Orgemont, son of the preceding bishop, and the grievous quarrels of the Armignacs had not come to an end.

To say the truth, it was well for this curé that he parsoned it at this period, for he was an upstanding, full-blooded, sturdy man, stoutly built, tall and strong, who ate and drank like a convalescent; and indeed he was always rising from a pleasant malady that overtook him from time to time. If he had lived later on he would have been his own executioner had he attempted to observe the rules of canonical chastity. Besides all that, he was a son of Touraine, that is, swarthy, with fire in his eyes to illumine, and water to extinguish, any domestic fires that wanted lighting or putting out. Never has there since been seen at Azay another such curé: square-shouldered, fresh-complexioned, always blessing and bussing, very much fonder of weddings and baptisms than of funerals, a jocular fellow, religious in church and a real man everywhere. There have been other curés who could eat and drink well, others who blessed well, and others who did other things well, but all of them together could hardly make up the single and separate worth of the aforesaid curé; and he liberally distributed his blessings about his parish, he kept it merry and consoled the afflicted, and so thoroughly, that no one saw him coming from his house without wishing to be taken to his bosom so greatly was he beloved. He was the first priest to say in the course of a sermon that the Devil was not as black as he was painted, and who, for Madame de Cande, turned partridges into fish, saying that the perch of the Indre were the partridges of the river, and similarly partridges were the perch of the air. He never did anything under the cloak of morality, and oftentimes used jestingly to say that he would rather sleep on a good bed than on a testament, that God had furnished all needs and that he lacked for nothing.

With regard to the poor folk and those in need, no one whoever came to his parsonage in search of wool ever went away unsatisfied, for he always had his hand in his pocket and softened, albeit he was so firm, at the sight of so much misery and weakness, and stiffened himself for the task of stanching every wound; and so it came to pass that manifold stories were told concerning this king of curés. It was he who provoked such laughter at the wedding of the Lord of Valennes near Sacché. Whether it was that the mother of this lord had a good deal to do with the victuals, roast meats and other delicacies which would have fed, at least, a town, it is certainly true that people came to the wedding from Montbazon, Tours, Chinon, Langeais, and from everywhere and stayed there a whole week.

Now the good curé, as he was going into the room where the guests were making merry, met a little scullion who came to tell Madame that all the primary substances and the rudimentary fats, syrups and sauces were in readiness for a pudding of very excellent quality, the secret mixing of which she wished personally to superintend, intending it for a great treat for the girl's relatives. The curé patted the little scullion on the cheek telling him that he was too foul and filthy to be seen by people of high degree and, that he himself would convey to Madame the message.

The jovial curé pushes open the door and makes the fingers of his left hand into the form of a sheath and into this aperture he inserts several times very gently the middle finger of his right hand; thereupon he looked very cunningly at the lady of Valennes and said to her, " Come, all is ready ! " Those who were not in the secret burst out laughing when they saw Madame rise and go to the curé, for she knew that it was the pudding to which he referred and not what the others thought.

But a true story is told of how our good curé lost his mistress, to whom the ecclesiastical authorities permitted no successor; but the curé did not lack for domestic utensils. In the parish, everyone deemed it an honour to lend him theirs, because the worthy man would never spoil anything and was always careful to rinse them out thoroughly. But here is the truth. One evening, the good curé came home to supper with a melancholy expression on his face, because he had just buried a good farmer, whose death occurred in a strange fashion, which is still a subject of conversation in Azay.

Seeing that he only toyed with his food and turned up his nose at a dish of good tripe which had been cooked in his favourite manner, his good woman said to him :

" Have you passed in front of the Lombard (*vide*
Master Cornelius *passim*), seen two black crows or
beheld the dead man turn in his grave, that you are so
disturbed ? "

" Ho ! Ho ! "

" Have you had some disappointment ? "

" Ha ! Ha ! "

" What *is* the matter then ? "

" My sweetheart, I was still quite upset about poor
Cochegrue's death, and for twenty leagues around there
isn't so much as the tongue of a good housewife or the
lips of a virtuous cuckold that are not talking about it."

" And what was the manner of it ? "

" Listen. The worthy Cochegrue was coming home
from market, where he had sold his wheat and two fat
pigs. He was mounted on his pretty mare which, ever
since they had passed Azay, had been growing lovesick,
though he, poor man, had not the slightest wind of it.
And so poor Cochegrue trotted and trotted along, counting over his gains. Now behold, at a turn in the road,
a master stallion which the Sieur de la Carte was keeping
apart in a paddock in order to have a good breed of
horses, because the said animal was swift on the course,
handsome as an abbot, tall and strong, so that the admiral,
who came to see it, pronounced it a beast of the first
rank ; well now, this devil of a horse scented the pretty
mare, winked his eye, but neither neighed nor delivered
himself of any manner of equine ejaculation, but, waiting
till the mare was just passing by, he jumped forty rows
of vines, came snorting and thundering along on his
four iron hoofs, lets forth the fanfaronnade of the lover
bursting to get to close quarters, gives forth noises so
prodigious as to make the boldest pass their water, and
so loud that the people of Champy heard them and were
sore afraid. Cochegrue, by this time alive to the danger,
rides like mad across the plain, digs the spurs into his
lascivious mare, and trusts to her speed to bring them

PICKING HER UP IN A RAGE,
HE THREW HER ON THE BED

SHE THRUSTS THE HUNCH-
BACK INTO THE PRESS

both to safety. And in truth, the good mare gives heed,
obeys and flies, flies like a bird. But a bowshot off, comes
gallopading on the mighty stallion, beating the ground
with his hoofs like blacksmiths hammering at the anvil.
In full panoply, with all his weapons displayed, his mane
flying in the wind, he answered the mare's dainty gallop
with the frightful ' patapan, patapan ' of his inexorable
hoofs. Then the good farmer, feeling that death was
following hard upon him, dug the spurs again into his
poor mare's side, and she galloped harder and harder
till at last, pale and half dead with terror, he comes to the
great courtyard of his farmhouse. But finding the door
of the stables shut, he falls to shouting, ' Help, ho!
Help, wife, help! ' Then he turned about the mare's
neck, thinking to avoid the cursed stallion, whose love
was at white heat, who was mad with lust and growing
madder every minute, to the great danger of the mare.
None of his folk, who were terrified at the danger, dared
open the stable door, for they dreaded the fierce onset
and savage kicks of the iron-shod lover. So Cochegrue
had to do the job himself; but just as the mare was
passing in through the open door, the cursed stallion
was upon her, clasping her, gripping her, and with his
two forelegs round her, pinches, squeezes, pounds and
crushes her, and, in the process, so pounds and kneads
the unhappy Cochegrue, that when they went to pick
up what was left of him after the fray, they only found a
shapeless mass, crushed together like a heap of nuts
with the oil squeezed out of them. 'Twas a piteous
sight to behold him thus crushed alive, mingling his
wails with the great love-sighs of the stallion."

" Oh, happy mare! " exclaimed the parson's wench.

" What! " cried the good priest in amazement.

" Yes, happy mare! Why, you men wouldn't have
done enough to split a plum."

" There," replied the priest, " you do me an injustice! "
Picking her up in a rage, he threw her on the bed and

gave her such a gruelling with his paint-brush that she split asunder on the spot and gave up the ghost; and neither surgeons nor physicians could tell how the solution of her continuity was brought about, so violently were the hinges and median partitions rent asunder. For you see he was a fine figure of a man, a handsome vicar, as we have already remarked.

The good folk of the countryside, even the women, agreed that he was not to blame and that he was within his rights. This, perhaps, is the origin of the proverb so popular in those days, " *Que l'aze le saille!* " which proverb I will refrain from explaining, out of respect for the ladies.

But it was not only in this way that the vicar displayed his prowess, and before this misfortune he performed such a feat that no robbers dared ask him how many angels he had in his pocket, even had there been twenty or more to fall upon him. One night—his good woman was still alive—when he had had his supper, during which he had highly enjoyed his goose, his wench, his wine and everything, and was lying back in his chair thinking where he could build a new barn for the tithes, behold there comes to him a message from the lord of Sacché, who, being about to render up his soul, was fain to make his peace with God, receive the sacrament and perform all the other things you wot of. " 'Tis a good man and a true-hearted lord, and I will go," said he. Thereupon he crossed over to the church, took up the silver box containing the sacred bread, rang his little bell himself in order not to disturb his clerk, and started, light of foot and full of zeal, along the road. Hard by the Gué-droit, which is a stream that finds its way into the Indre across the meadows, our good vicar was aware of a highwayman. Of a what? Of a clerk of Saint Nicholas. And what is that, pray? Why, one who can see in the dark and who gains instruction by tapping and turning over purses and takes his degrees by the roadside. Now do you know

what I mean ? The highwayman, then, was on the
look-out for the box which he well knew to be of great
price.

" Ah, ha ! " said the priest, as he deposited the ciborium
by the bridge of stone. " Stay you there a while and
budge not."

Then he walked up to the robber, tripped him up,
seized his loaded stick, and when the rascal got up to
give battle, planted him a well-directed blow right in the
middle of his stomach-part.

Then he went back and picked up the viaticum, saying,
" Well now, if I had put my trust in you, we should
have been done for ! " Now to utter such words as
these upon the high road to Sacché was speaking to the
point, seeing that he was saying them not to God but to
the Archbishop of Tours, who had called him over the
coals, severely admonished him and threatened him with
excommunication, because he had told certain poor-
spirited folk from the pulpit that good harvests came not
from the grace of God, but by dint of hard work and
skilful toil ; a doctrine which smelt strongly of heresy.
And indeed, he was in error, for the fruits of the earth
have need of both. Nevertheless, he died in that heresy,
for he could never bring himself to believe that harvests
could come without the mattock, and if it pleased God
to send them—a doctrine which learned men have
proved to be true, for they have shown that in times long
past, wheat grew of its own accord without the aid of
man.

But I cannot leave the subject of this model shepherd
without including here one story of his life which shows
with what zeal he copied the saints in their habit of sharing their worldly goods and their cloaks, which of old
they were wont to give to poor folk and chance way-
farers. Riding home, on his mule, one day from Tours,
whither he had been to pay his respects to the Bishop's
Chancellor, he was drawing near to Azay. When he had

arrived within a stone's throw of Ballan, he fell in with a
pretty girl who was faring her way on foot, and it grieved
him sore to see a woman travelling along just as a dog
might travel, more especially as she was visibly weary and
could scarcely drag herself along. Wherefore he hailed
her gently, and the comely damsel stayed her steps and
looked at him. The good priest, who knew how to
avoid scaring little birds, especially the crested variety,
invited her so winningly to mount behind him on the
saddle, and with such a gracious address, that the girl got
up, not without a little mincing and coquetry, such as all
women indulge in when they are invited to take a little
food or something else they like. The lamb now safely
stowed behind the shepherd, the mule jogs on in right
mulish fashion, and the girl goes slipping from this side
to that, sitting her saddle so badly that the curé told her,
as soon as they were out of Ballan, that she had better
hold on to him. So, the girl clasped her plump arms
about her cavalier's waist, but not without a touch of
squeamishness.

"There! Can you sit tight now? Is all well with
you?" asked the vicar.

"Yes," she answered, "quite well. How fares it
with you?"

"I," said the priest, "am even better."

And in very truth, he was most comfortable, and soon
began to be conscious of a grateful warmth behind,
imparted by a pair of protuberances which rubbed against
him and seemed desirous of imprinting themselves
between his shoulders, which would have been a pity
seeing that it is not the right place for that beautiful white
merchandise. Little by little, the motion of the mule
brought about a simultaneous calorification in the
internal economy of the two worthy equestrians and
stimulated the activity of their circulatory systems, till
at length the girl and the parson, if they did not know
what the mule wanted, were quite clear and unanimous

as to what they wanted themselves. Then when they had become thoroughly acclimatised to each other, the parson to the wench and the wench to the parson, they felt something stirring within them that in the end made them conscious of no uncertain desires.

" Beshrew me ! " exclaimed the parson, turning round in his saddle. " Yonder's a bit of wood where the trees have grown nice and close together."

" It's too near the road," answered the girl. " Bad boys will cut the branches, or the cows will eat the young chicken."

" And are you not married ? " asked the vicar, trotting on again.

" No," she answered.

" Not at all ? "

" No, i' faith ! "

" But 'tis disgraceful at your age."

" Faith, you're right, your reverence. But then, you see, a poor girl that has had a child is not a very marketable piece of goods."

Thereupon the good parson, having compassion on her ignorance, and remembering that the canon saith among other things, that it behoveth the shepherds to indoctrinate their flock and to show them and explain their various tasks and duties in this life, deemed he would be doing well if he taught her about the burden she would one day have to bear. Then he implored her sweetly to have no fear, saying that if she would but have faith in his loyalty no one should ever know of the experiment with the matrimonial shoehorn which he proposed to carry out with her then and there. And as this was precisely what the girl had been thinking about ever since they had left Ballan, and as her desires had been fostered and fomented by the bringle-brangle motion of the beast on which she was riding, she said roundly to the priest :

" If you talk like that, I shall get down."

Then the good parson continued his gentle importunities, until they came to the woods of Azay, where the girl insisted on alighting. There indeed, the good priest put her down, for need was to be elsewhere than on horseback to finish the discussion. And the virtuous maiden sped away into the wood, where the trees were thickest, to escape the parson, crying, as she ran:

"Oh, you wicked man, you will never find out where I am!"

The mule having come to a glade where the grass was smooth and soft, the girl stumbled over a mound and began to blush. The parson dropped down beside her; and then, as he had rung the bell for Mass, he proceeded to say it, and both of them enjoyed a generous instalment of the joys of paradise. The good priest felt it his duty to drive his lessons home and found his catechumen very docile, her heart as soft as her skin, a proper jewel. Then was he sore afflicted that he had abridged the lesson so much by giving it so close to Azay, seeing that it would have pleased him much to impart it again and again, as do the learned doctors who repeat the same thing many times to their pupils.

"Ah, sweetheart!" cried he; "wherefore were you so wayward that we did not come to an understanding till we were nearly at Azay?"

"Ah," she said, "because I come from Ballan!"

To cut a long story short, I will only add that when the good man died in his cure, many were the folk—children and adults—who came, mournful, grief-stricken, weeping and sorrowful, and all said with one voice, "Alas, we have lost our father!" And the wenches, widows, wives, and little girls, all looked at one another sorrowing for him more than for a friend, and all said, "He was far more than a priest, he was a man!" Of parsons like him the seed is scattered to the winds, and we shall not look upon his like again, despite the seminaries.

Even the poor folk, to whom he left his savings, found

they were losers still. And an old cripple, of whom he had taken care, wailed aloud in the courtyard, crying, " I shall not die, I shall not ! " meaning to say, " Why did not death take me instead of him." And some of the people laughed, whereat the shade of the good parson would not have felt aggrieved.

THE REBUKE

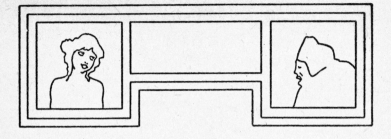

THE REBUKE

THE fair laundry-maid of Portillon-lez-Tours, one of whose quaint sayings has already been recorded in this book, was a wench gifted with such a wealth of cunning that she must have stolen the share of at least three women and half a dozen priests. And so she had plenty of followers, so many indeed, that when you saw them swarming about her, you would have taken them for bees trying to get into the hive at eventide. A certain old silk-dyer, who lived in the rue Montfumier, and kept up a most scandalously luxurious establishment, coming home one day from his vineyard at la Grenadière near the lovely slopes of Saint Cyr, happened to ride past Portillon on his way to Tours. The evening was a warm one, and he was suddenly seized with the most libidinous longings when he caught sight of the fair laundry-woman seated on her doorstep. Now his thoughts had long been dwelling on this mettlesome wench, and he suddenly made up his mind that he would take her to wife. So it came to pass, soon afterwards, that she cast off her laundry-woman's estate and became a silk-dyer's wife, a highly respected citizeness of Tours, with plenty of fine lace to call her own and a profusion of furniture. Moreover, she was very happy, notwithstanding the dyer, for she knew exactly how to bamboozle him. The good dyer numbered among his friends a manufacturer of silk-weaving machines. He was a little humpbacked fellow, full of guile. So, on the night of the marriage, he said to the dyer, " You did well to get married, gossip; we shall have a pretty wife." Then he delivered himself of endless remarks of the broad description commonly applied to blushing bridegrooms.

It was, however, a fact that the hunchback did try to make love to the dyer's wife. But she, being naturally little attracted to ill-built specimens of humanity, laughed at his attentions and twitted him effectively on the springs, engines and bobbins of which he had more than enough in his shop. However, so great was the love of the hunchback for her that he was never discouraged, and his attentions became so trying that the lady resolved that she would cure him by hook or by crook. One night after a further experience of his endless importunities, she told her lover to come to the back door about midnight and she would let him in. Now I would have you note that it was a beautiful winter's night; the rue Montfumier abuts on the Loire, and down its draughty passage, even in summer time, blew winds as sharp as needles. The worthy hunchback, well muffled up in his cloak, did not fail to put in an appearance and began to walk about to keep himself warm till the hour of his tryst should arrive. Towards midnight, being half-frozen, he fell to cursing and swearing like two-and-thirty devils caught in a stole, and was just about to throw up the sponge when a feeble light filtered through the cracks of the blind and lit up the back door with its fitful ray.

" Ah, 'tis she ! " he said.

The hope of seeing her warmed him up again: he put his ear to the keyhole and heard a small voice.

" Are you there ? " said the lady.

" Yes."

" Cough for me to hear."

The hunchback began to cough.

" It is not you ! "

Then the hunchback said in a loud voice :

"What do you mean 'it's not me!' Don't you recognise my voice? Open the door!"

"Who's there?" asked the dyer, looking out of the window.

"Good lord, you've awakened my husband, who came back to-night unexpectedly from Amboise."

Thereupon the dyer, seeing, by the light of the moon, a man at his door, empties a jugful of cold water on him and calls out, "Stop thief!" So that the poor hunchback had nothing for it but to cut and run, and in his panic he caught his foot in the chain stretched across the street and fell into the evil-smelling sewer, which the authorities had not yet replaced by the sluice-gates for carrying away the mud into the Loire. The poor fellow thought this bath would be the death of him, and he roundly cursed the lady whom the people of Tours called Tascherette, because her husband was called Taschereau. Carandas—for such was the name of the manufacturer of machines for spinning, weaving and winding silk—could not help thinking that the dyer's wife had arranged this little accident, and swore that he would hate her like the devil; but a few days afterwards, when he had quite got over his sousing in the dyer's vat, he came to supper with his friend. The lady put forward such a good story on that occasion, spoke such honeyed words and beguiled him with such fair promises, that all his suspicions were put to flight; so he begged her for another assignation, and the fair lady, looking as if there were nothing she would like better, said, "Come to-morrow night, my husband will be at Chenonceaux for three days. The Queen desires to have some old tapestry dyed and wishes to discuss the matter of colours with him: that will, of course, take a long time."

Carandas put on his best clothes and appeared on the stroke of the appointed hour to find a splendid supper all prepared. There were lampreys, wine of Vouvray, snowy napery, for it would never have done for the dyer's wife to be called to account about the colour of her linen ; and all was so beautifully ordered that it was a pleasure to behold the metal dishes so highly polished, and to smell the savoury odour of the viands, to contemplate the countless elegances of the room, the lady herself eager, arrayed in her very best, appetising as an apple on a very hot day.   Now our manufacturer, his blood heated by the agreeable spectacle, was about without more ado to take the lady by storm, when Master Taschereau was heard thundering at the street door.

" Ah ! " said the lady ; " here he is back again ; into the chest with you ! People have been coupling your name with mine, and if my husband found you here, he might be the death of you, for he is a devil when he is roused."

Quick as lightning, she thrusts the hunchback into the press, takes out the key and hurries to meet her husband, who, she knew, would be back from Chenonceaux in time for supper.   Then the dyer was duly kissed on his two eyes and two ears ; and he, on his side, administered two explosive osculations on his wife's chaste cheeks ; then husband and wife sat down to table, bandied jests awhile, and at length got into bed ; and the hunchback overheard it all.   The poor fellow was compelled to stand upright and stock-still and dared not even cough ; there he was all among the linen like a sardine in a tin, and got about as much air as barbels get sunlight at the bottom of the stream ; but he had the music of love to divert him, the sighs of the dyer and Tascherette's pretty prattle.   At length, when he thought that his gossip was asleep, the hunchback tried to make his way out of the press.

" Who's there ? " said the husband.

" What's the matter, darling ? " asked his wife, putting her nose above the counterpane.

" I can hear something scratching," said the good man.

" That's the cat," answered his wife ; " we shall have rain to-morrow."

The worthy husband, after being softly patted and coddled by his wife, reclined his head again upon the pillow.

" There, then, sonny," said she, " you're a light sleeper. Clearly it would not do at all to try to put a pair of antlers on you. There, then, be a good boy and go to sleep. Oh, but, Papa dear, your nightcap's all awry. Come, put it on again, my little corker, for you must look nice, even when you're asleep. There, are you all right now ? "

" Yes."

" Do you feel like sleep ? " said she, giving him a kiss.

" Yes."

In the morning, the fair dame went on tip-toe to let the mechanic out of the press. He was paler than a corpse.

" Air," he gasped. " Give me air."

Away he rushed, quite cured of his love ; with as much hatred in his heart as you can cram black oats into a pouch. The hunchback left Tours and went to live at Bruges, whither some merchants had invited him to come and put up some machinery for making hauberks. In the course of his long absence, Carandas, who had Moorish blood in his veins, for he was descended from a Saracen who had been left for dead in the great battle between the Moors and the French in the Commune of Ballan (whereof mention is made in the preceding story), in which district are situate the plains of Charlemagne as they are called, where nothing ever grows because accursed unbelievers lie buried there and the grass is poisonous even to cows—well then, this Carandas, I say, never rose up or laid him down in the foreign country, where he was tarrying, without thinking how he might give nourishment to his desire for vengeance, for he was always thinking about, and would be satisfied with nothing less than, the death of the good laundry-woman of Portillon. And many a time and oft he would say to himself, " I will eat of her flesh. Yea, I will have one of her nipples grilled and crunch it without any sauce." He hated her with a ruddy hatred, a deep-dyed hatred, a cardinal hatred, a waspish or old-maidish hatred— nay, with all the hatreds that were ever known poured into one single hatred which boiled and seethed and stewed and simmered and resolved itself into an elixir of wormwood, of wicked and devilish designs heated over a fire of the fiercest embers of hell : it was indeed a monumental hatred.

Now, it befell that one fine day, Carandas came back to Touraine with a goodly stock of shekels amassed in Flanders, where he had trafficked successfully in his mechanical secrets. He bought him a fine house in the rue Montfumier, which may still be seen there and which excites the amazement of the wayfarer, for it has some highly jocular bas-reliefs carved in the stonework of the walls. Carandas, with his heart full of hatred, found that some very notable changes had taken place in respect to his friend the dyer, for the good fellow now had two fine children which, as chance would have it, presented no likeness either to the mother or the father. But as children have of necessity to be like someone or another, some cunning gossips will find resemblances to the grandparents, when they are pretty, the little flatterers. Then, on the other hand, it was discovered by the worthy husband that his two youngsters took after an uncle of his who had formerly been a priest at Notre-Dame de l'Esgrignolles. But there were other wights who would have it that the two brats were the living images of a certain tonsured gentleman who belonged to the church of Notre-Dame la Riche, a well-known parish between Tours and Plessis. Now there is one thing you may believe and take as gospel, and even if out of the whole

of this book, you never hit off, caught hold of, extracted
or pulled forth anything save this one basic principle of all
truth, you may yet regard yourself as right lucky ; to wit,
that never will a man be able to do without a nose, that
is to say, he will always be running at the nasal organ ;
in other words, man will always be man, and in all future
ages, he will go on laughing and quaffing, and be the same
sort of being in his shirt—neither better nor worse—that
he always has been.   But these prolegomenous remarks
are intended the better to prepare your understanding
for absorbing the truth that the soul on two legs called
Man will always believe as true the things which flatter
his passions, foment his animosities and further his love
affairs.   That's what logic springs from.   Thus, the
very first day that Carandas clapped eyes on his crony's
children, on the gentle priest, on the fair lady and the old
dyer himself, all seated at table, and saw the best portion
of lamprey bestowed by the hostess on her friend the
priest, the mechanic said to himself, " My old friend
is a cuckold, his wife sleeps with the little confessor,
these children were made with his holy water, and I will
show them all that hunchbacks possess something over
and above other folk."

And that was true, just as true as that Tours has
always had and will always continue to have its feet in the
Loire, like a pretty girl that bathes and plays with the
water ; making it go " flick-flack " hither and thither
with her white hands.   For 'tis a smiling, laughing,
loving, fresh, beflowered and perfumed city, fairer than all
other cities in the world, which are not even worthy to
comb her hair or fasten her girdle.   And if you go thither,
you will always find, about the middle of her, a pretty
alley-way, where there is always plenty of breeze and
shade and sun and rain and love.   Ha! Ha! Laugh
your fill, and into it you go!   'Tis a street that is ever
new, ever royal, ever imperial, a patriotic street, a street
with two side-walks, a street open at both ends, well

pierced, a street so broad that no one ever shouts " Get out of the way, there ! " a street which never gets worn out, a street which leads straight to the Abbey of High Mountain ; 'tis a thoroughfare which fits in very perfectly with the bridge, and at the bottom of it there's a fine piece of ground for a fair. 'Tis well paven, well laid and well washen, clean as a mirror, well patronised, yet sometimes quiet, neat and tidy with its blue tiled roofs. In a word, 'tis the street where I was born ; 'tis the queen of streets, ever 'twixt earth and heaven, a street with a fountain, a street which lacks nothing to be called famous among all the other streets that are. And, in sooth, 'tis the true, the only street in Tours. If there be others, they are dark, winding, narrow and damp, and all of them come to pay their respects to this noble street that commands them all. Now where am I ? For once I get into this street I never want to come out of it, so pleasant it is to abide there. But it was my duty to pay this act of filial piety, to chant this descriptive hymn that came from my heart, to the street of my birth, whose corners only lack the brave countenances of my worthy Master Rabelais and the Sieur Descartes, who are unknown to the natives of the place.

Now upon his return from Flanders, Carandas was feasted and entertained by his gossip, the dyer, and by all who took delight in his facetious and entertaining conversation. The good hunchback seemed to have quite recovered from his former love-sickness, and shewed himself very agreeable to the lady, the priest, and also to the children ; and afterwards, when he was alone with the dyer's wife, he reminded her of the night he spent in the chest, and the night he fell into the drain, saying :

" 'Zounds, what a fool you made of me ! "

" But you deserved it," she answered with a laugh.

Thereupon Carandas laughed a savage laugh. Seeing the press in which he had nearly given up the ghost, his wrath grew all the greater because the lady was lovelier than she had ever been, as is the way with those who renew their youth at the fount of love. The mechanic studied the symptoms of cuckoldom displayed by his friend, in order to have his revenge. For in this kind of matter there are as many variants as there are houses in a city. And although all loves resemble one another just as do all men, it has been proven to the satisfaction of the abstractors of good things that, for the happiness of women, each love has its own particular physiognomy, and that if there be nought so much like a man as a man, there is also nought so unlike a man as a man. This it is which confounds everything, and explains the unnumbered fantasies of women, who seek the best among men with countless pains and countless pleasures, and perhaps more pains than pleasures. But how shall we blame them for their experiments, changes and tergiversations? What, Nature is for ever jigging and turning and twisting about, and would you have a woman always fixed in the same place? Know you if ice be really cold? No. Then neither do you know whether cuckoldry be not a fortunate hazard, a producer of well-stocked brains, aye, and better made ones than any others. Look then for other things besides windiness under the heavens. That will increase the philosophic reputation of this concentrifical treatise. Aye! Aye! To it, my hearties. He who shouts out " Rats' bane! " is further advanced than the man who would humour Nature; for she is a proud bitch, full of whims, and won't show herself save when it suits her. Dost hear? So it comes about that in every language she belongs to the feminine gender as being a thing essentially mobile, fruitful and fertile in trickeries.

So in no long time Carandas came to perceive that among the divers manners of cuckoldry the best reputed and the most discreet is the ecclesiastical. And in truth, this is the manner in which the dyer's wife had ordered

her procedure.   She always betook herself to her country
retreat at Grenadière-lez-Saint-Cyr of a Saturday night,
leaving her worthy spouse to finish his work, complete
his accounts and calculations and pay his workpeople.
Then he would proceed to join her next morning, finding
a good lunch all ready for him, his wife in happy mood.
And he always brought the priest along with him.   As a
matter of fact, the confounded priest used to cross the
Loire in a boat the night before in order to go and keep
the dyer's wife warm and calm her fantasies so that she
might sleep the better during the night—a task which
young men are specially well able to perform.   Then
this fine young tamer of fantasies would be back in his
house next morning by the time the dyer called to take
him to spend the day at La Grenadière.   And the
cuckold always found the priest in bed.   The boatman
was well paid for his services, and no one ever got wind
of the affair, for the lover always went overnight under
cover of darkness, and the next day, in broad daylight.
When Carandas had thoroughly and satisfactorily verified
the constant and punctual enactment of these gallant
devices, he waited for a day when the two lovers should
meet, right hungry for one another after a period of
accidental continence.   Such an occasion soon arrived
and the inquisitive hunchback perceived the boatman,
just off shore, close to the canal Sainte Anne, waiting
about for the priest, who was a young, slim, fairheaded
fellow, as shapely as the caitiff lover whom Messire
Ariosto has so wisely celebrated.   Then the hunchback
went for to seek the old dyer, who still dearly loved his
wife and believed that he was the only one to dip a finger
in her holy water stoup.   " Good-day, gossip," said he.
And the dyer doffed his bonnet.

Then did the hunchback pour forth a full account of all
these secret devices of the lovers, unburdened himself of
all manner of speeches and drave thorns into the dyer
on every side.

At length, seeing that he had made up his mind to kill his wife and the priest, Carandas said:

" Good my neighbour, I brought back with me from Flanders a poisoned dagger which brings death to whomsoever is but scratched withal. As soon therefore as you have merely touched your wench and her lover therewith, they both shall die."

" Come, let us seek them out," cried the dyer.

Then came the two merchants with great speed to the hunchback's dwelling to fetch the sword and get to work.

" Shall we find them a-bed ? " asked the dyer.

" Wait and see ! " said the hunchback with a cunning leer.

And in truth, the cuckold was not obliged to undergo the heavy trial of waiting long to behold the lovers' blisses. The fair lady and her well-beloved were busy seeking to snare, within that pretty lake you wot of, that lovely bird which ever manages to escape therefrom. They laughed and went on trying ; they tried and went on laughing.

" Ah, sweetheart mine," said the dyer's wife, clasping him to her as though she were fain to imprint his form upon her stomach, " I love you so that I would I could eat you. Nay, better still, have you all within my skin, so thou shouldst never leave me."

" Would that thou couldst," replied the priest ; " but since I cannot all be there, needs must thou be content to take me piecemeal."

'Twas at this blissful moment that the husband entered, brandishing his naked sword. The fair lady, who read her husband's face full well, saw it was all over with her darling priest. But, suddenly, she sprang towards the worthy merchant, half-naked, with dishevelled hair, beautiful with shame, and still more beautiful with love, crying:

" Stay, unhappy man, wouldst thou slay the father of thy children ? "

Hearing these words, the worthy dyer, amazed at the paternal majesty of cuckoldom, and peradventure by the fire within her eyes, let fall the sword on the hunchback's foot, for he was just behind, and slew him.

Whereby we are taught never to be spiteful.

EPILOGUE

HERE endeth the first volume of these tales, a knavish sample of the works of the frolicsome Muse born long since in this our land of Touraine. She is a kindly wench and knoweth by heart this fine saying of her friend Verville writ in his "How to hit the Mark." *A man needs but courage to obtain the prize.*

Ah, little madcap, get thee to bed again and sleep; thou art out of breath with running. Peradventure, thou hast been farther afield than this. Wipe thy pretty naked feet; stop up thine ears and betake thyself again to love. If thou dream of other laughter-woven poesies to bring these merry inventions to an end, heed not the vain clamour and jeers of those who, hearing the song of a merry jesting lark, shall cry, "Out on the shameless bird!"

THE END